LIGHT IN THE CHAOS

BRIDGET SHEPPARD

LIGHT IN THE CHAOS

ISBN: 978-0-578-72260-3

Editing: Caroline Tolley

Cover Design & Interior Formatting: Lindsay Heider Diamond

LIGHT
IN THE
CHAOS

PROLOGUE

August
Sacramento, California

Drawing out the details of a death was like planning the intricate choreography of a beautiful ballet. Those details, those plans, took weeks and sometimes months to formulate, put to the test, and carry out. Everything had to be perfect, as the clients paid for the best.

Of course, there were many other projects to plan as well, but in that office, high above the streets of downtown Sacramento, death was the typical order of the day. Many people were unable to reconcile their fears, anger, or inadequacies, so they needed someone to do it for them.

It was in this office, which didn't look all that different from the many other offices crowding those busy streets, that hours were spent researching, devising, and painstakingly planning those scenarios of death – those intricate stories of life-ending events.

To most, it would have emulated a space of horrible darkness, but to those who worked there, it was a place of business – a place where suits, laptops, and reports were commonplace. To those engineers of death, darkness held a different definition, and they didn't have an inclination of creating evil. They saw themselves as employees doing a job.

This car crash was no different. It took place outside the city of Davis, but the plan was created, and all possibilities considered many times over, in that

Sacramento building. Those involved had tight schedules, with understudy drivers available should they be needed. Operatives followed the subject for weeks beforehand, in order to study her exact driving habits.

The subject left her home early, as she always did on her trips to Northernmost California, and the sun had not yet come up. The wrong-way driver hadn't put his lights on, and she hadn't had time to react. It was over right away, and while reported as a tragedy, wasn't found to involve any foul play.

Two of their own players were killed in that collision, which had been a known risk, as it was difficult to measure how hard the vehicles would hit or in what precise directions they would spin. Those lost were young operatives who did their best to impress but were still expendable, so their deaths didn't result in any real grief.

Life moved forward.

CHAPTER 1

September
A world away in the same city

Kassidy flew down the stairs from her apartment, which was one unit in a Midtown Victorian home that had been converted into a multi-family building. She despised running late.

The feeling of Sacramento summer engulfed her, and she swore to herself.

She'd had two phone interviews that morning. She should have scheduled at least one for another day, but she'd been trying to talk to these sources for a few days, and her deadlines were looming.

She got in her car, which was parked on the street right in front of her building. It was a choice spot, and she hated to give it up, but these appointments were important.

She made a retching sound as she rolled down her car window. The inside of the vehicle felt like a giant, claustrophobic bubble of heat that was happy to swallow her whole.

At that moment a jogger ran by, giving her a funny look. Her eyes hit the ceiling of her car, and she had to keep herself from sticking out her tongue at the man. Why would anyone in his right mind be jogging in this heat?

As she pulled away from the sidewalk, she noticed the jogger had stopped on the corner and was taking a drink from his water bottle. She felt his eyes on her, and to her, his face looked cold. She shook her head. It was all in her mind. She'd wondered if Kurt would come after her again, but he had to be satisfied with how deep he had already buried her. There was no reason for anyone to be following her.

A little over an hour later, Kassidy wished the sun had melted her in her car. She respected her therapist, but she was exhausted and tension coursed through her veins. Her heart was slamming in her chest. Her brain held the fog of anxiety. As she left the office, she closed the door with a clunk, wishing she could slam it.

"I want you to journal again." Her therapist, Lina, had held up her hand before Kassidy could protest. It was right before the end of their appointment. "It might be difficult to take time out of your day to purposefully think about your pain in order to trap thoughts and feelings of Kurt on paper. But because you have no real closure, and you're so often a prisoner of what he did to you, getting things out of your head and forcing them to sit elsewhere will be a good thing."

"It's the panic I have while getting them out of my head that I'm worried about." Kassidy hadn't tried to hide her frown.

"I've given you the tools to deal with that. You haven't journaled in years. This is something I want you to try, Kassidy," Lina responded with a take-no-crap expression.

Lina never pulled any punches. She challenged Kassidy and played devil's advocate more often than not. She told Kassidy after their first few meetings that she needed to open her mind to new ideas and try to be more flexible with change. This wasn't long after Kassidy moved back to Sacramento, when her life was one big change. Lina wanted to help her overcome and adjust. Kassidy had resented her words at first, but her advice had proved helpful when Kassidy followed it, so she stuck with Lina.

Why do I still feel like this when Kurt comes up? Kassidy thought as she marched to her car. *I'll never have closure with him, so why can't he fade away and get the hell out of my life? I can't journal. I haven't journaled since I moved here. I don't want to write these feelings down. I want them to leave me alone. I want to move on. Why do I need to keep dealing with the past?*

***

A swing shift in a Sacramento September meant heat. The kind of heat that soaked through his uniform, his skin, and into the part of his soul that felt called to a bright Pacific Ocean beach. The kind of heat that Brett could have enjoyed in the hammock in his backyard, his Dodgers baseball cap placed squarely over his face to provide necessary shade. He might live in Northern California now, but the southern part of the state would always have his loyalty. One of his only tattoos was the blended "LA" made famous by his favorite team.

He rolled down his window after getting in his patrol car, and the sun warmed his left arm. He didn't bother to turn his air conditioning on. He didn't need it. This heat was what he needed. He wished he could have it every day.

Sleeping in a hammock would have been great, but working was just as good. Any extra shifts that came his way, any requests from friends and colleagues to fill in for them while they spent time in other parts of their lives, he happily accepted. Work was his life. It was what he enjoyed about every day. It was his stress, it was his comfort, it was his plan for the future. To be honest, falling asleep in his hammock would have probably resulted in dreams about his job. His colleagues called him obsessed. He shrugged, grinned, and reminded them without that obsession, they wouldn't have someone to fill their shifts next time their kids had a science fair or their spouses wanted to go on vacation a day early.

As he drove through a residential Midtown street, the sun beating off the asphalt beneath his cruiser, he ran the odds of what kind of call would come in next. His eyes wandered to a man walking at a quick pace down the sidewalk on the right, approaching the intersection. As Brett rolled to a stop, the three cars in front of him waited at the stop sign for oncoming traffic to cease. He kept his eye on the guy on the sidewalk. Something about that guy was off. His movement was a little jerky, and as he approached the stop sign, he was running.

The first car moved on. Brett felt his heart speeding up in each second, adrenaline making it pound in his ears, as the next car, a small silver sedan, stopped at the sign and then made to go. Brett went to open his door, to run for the man. But instead, the man rushed into the street. With some kind of strangled cry, he jumped onto the windshield of the sedan. With his window rolled all the way down and his door now open, Brett could hear the scream from the driver of the car reverberate off the homes around them. The car slammed to a stop, tires giving a piercing squeal. The man was flung from the car and into the intersection. He staggered to a standing position, swaying as if to fall again. A sickening thump followed as a pickup truck trying to stop crashed into him.

Chaos ensued. Brett threw on his lights and jumped from his car, calling in the incident, requesting assistance and an ambulance as he raced toward the man, who was still lying in the intersection.

"Officer, I…I don't know…" the driver of the truck stammered, standing outside his vehicle, staring at the man on the ground.

"I know. Hold on!" Brett felt for the man's pulse. It was there. He was alive somehow. He was breathing. Brett felt a flood of relief. No one deserved to die like that.

He began moving the man carefully into the recovery position, noting obvious injuries as he went. The ambulance siren was closer. Grabbing the first aid kit he'd thrown on the ground beside him, he began addressing some of the man's bleeding. Feet pounded pavement behind him, and two paramedics edged their way in front of Brett.

"He jumped onto the windshield of that car," he pointed toward the sedan, "was thrown into the intersection. Truck tried to stop, couldn't, hit him. He's had a pulse and been breathing since then." The words flew from Brett's mouth. The paramedics nodded and continued their work, a stretcher already waiting to get the man into the ambulance and to the hospital.

Brett stood, peeling off the bloody gloves he'd thrown on. Quick realization set in that two of his colleagues had arrived. One was already talking to the truck driver, who looked like he was going to pass out. One was approaching the silver sedan's driver. Drivers in both directions had stepped out of their vehicles to survey the scene.

The paramedics lifted the man onto the stretcher. Two other officers had blocked off the area so no other cars could get through.

"Green!" His colleague talking to the sedan driver called him over. "You saw what happened?"

"Yeah." Brett strolled over. He recounted the incident. While the other officer called in some information, Brett turned to face the sedan driver.

"She's pretty agitated. Doesn't want to talk to me anymore," his coworker mumbled in his direction before turning away to hear information coming back from dispatch.

Momentary distraction stopped Brett in his tracks. The young woman had been crying based on the puffiness of her eyes, but she was beautiful. Her nearly-black hair was pulled back in a ponytail. Her eyes reminded him of midnight in the country, where no city lights could break through. She was wearing ripped jeans, a tank top, and Converse. There was a dusting of freckles across her cheeks. She was pale as she stared at the man being loaded into the ambulance.

"Is he alive?" Brett barely heard her question, as he was still admiring her face.

What the hell? Do your job, Brett.

"He is. I'm Officer Green. I was a couple cars behind you. Is he someone you know?"

"No. I already told the other officer that. I don't know anyone who jumps on cars!" She turned to look at her sedan, assessing the damage. Her hood was a little dented, but it didn't look that bad.

"Ma'am, I know this was scary and upsetting, but we have to find out whatever basic information we can at this point. Then a detective can talk to you again later."

"Talk to me again later? Why? I don't know the guy! I can't give you any other information!"

Agitated was an understatement. "He didn't look familiar at all? The only reason I ask is it looked like he was trying to keep up with your car as you got close to the stop sign, like he picked your car out of the line."

She closed her eyes and sighed. "I just want to go home. I have work to do."

"We do, too," he said firmly, getting a little tired of her evasiveness.

She scowled. Those eyes were a storm.

A sudden flash of guilt crossed her face, and he waited. She looked like she was going to cry again, but she steeled herself against it.

"Look, I don't know him. I've never seen him before today. I feel horrible, even though I have no clue why he'd do what he did." She motioned toward her car. "This morning, he jogged past my car. I was already in it, trying to cool it down before driving away. I made some stupid noise because of the heat, and maybe he thought I was making it at him. I must have pissed him off. I don't know how he saw me again, but he did. There must be something wrong with him, to make him do something like that! He could have tried to talk to me."

Brett nodded, jotting down notes in a small pad he carried. Then a voice came over his radio and he stopped to listen. When he met her eyes again, that storm had become a hurricane.

"Our detective is on her way."

"A detective? Now? I thought I would get a call later. I really need to go. You have to understand, this has been a really crappy day. I don't have any other information to give you guys."

"The detective is going to talk to everyone, including me. She'll decide what else she needs to know before you go." He paused for a moment and said, "I'm sorry about your crappy day, but this guy just threw himself into traffic." He ended on this, thinking maybe she needed to be reminded that it wasn't only a bad day for her.

She stuttered. He turned and walked away, surprised he didn't get a response.

CHAPTER 2

The next morning, Kassidy's three best friends informed her that to get her mind off the freak incident, she needed to go to a new club in downtown Sacramento with them. She hadn't gone to a club since her early twenties, when she was living in San Francisco, at the beginning of her journalism career.

I NEED to go? she texted on their group chat.

Yes, had been the response of all three.

She'd grown up in the Sacramento suburb city of Folsom, and when she moved back to Sacramento from San Francisco two years ago, she had gotten back in touch with some of her high school friends, many of whom were moms now. They used to go to eighteen-and-over clubs right after graduation, before any of these women had to worry about toddlers wandering into their rooms at six o'clock in the morning. But it was a Friday night and they had babysitters or husbands watching their kids, and they seemed determined not to care about their potential early-morning wake-up calls.

Kassidy didn't have any children. After college, when she had secured a job as a reporter with the *San Francisco Chronicle*, she hadn't allowed herself time for anything else. Her job was too important. She couldn't let anything take away from that. That was, until she had met Kurt Leonard while working on a story about a tech conference.

Stop thinking about that. I've already done my uncomfortable journal reflection for the day.

That night, Kassidy's borrowed heels were way too tall. She was five-foot-eight and now felt far too close to six feet. The black dress on loan from Melissa was too tight. She preferred her frayed Levi's and beaten-up Chucks.

"Do you have to bring that?" Melissa sighed, pointing at Kassidy's *Doctor Who* purse. It hung from a chain and looked like the TARDIS. It was the only small purse Kassidy had, and she loved it. If she was going to be forced to go to a club, she had every right to have a little something that expressed who she really was.

"Yep." She grinned at Melissa, who looked like a blond-haired, green-eyed model and knew it. Melissa shook her head and sent her eyes straight to the ceiling in one of the longest eye rolls Kassidy had ever seen. She loved Melissa, but sometimes the woman still cared too much about what other people thought. A little TARDIS never hurt anyone.

The temperature had peaked at over one hundred that day, so even though they were only weeks from autumn, the heat of the evening made it feel like mid-afternoon. It was also somewhat overcast, so the humidity was high, and it felt like she was walking into a sauna when they stepped out for pre-club dinner.

The city of Sacramento was alive that night. The trendy Mexican restaurant was loud with conversation and music, and it was packed to the brim. Residents and visitors strolled the city's streets, stepping in and out of restaurants, bars, and clubs. It wasn't all beautiful of course. As with any city, darkness came with the light.

They had only been inside the club for about fifteen minutes, scoping out the dance floor, the House music vibrating the ground beneath them when she happened to look to her left and saw him looking back at her.

He was tall, dark, and handsome – like one of those guys in high school she would have been too intimidated to talk to. Anger and mortification immediately swept through her.

He sent her a forced smile.

"He's cute. You should go talk to him," Jennifer, who was far too enthusiastic for her own good, gushed, looking as if she was going to raise her hand to wave him over.

Kassidy yanked her arm. "No. That's the jerk cop from yesterday. The one I told you guys about. Why is he here?" She quickly grabbed the margarita Melissa offered.

"Seems like he wants to talk to you." Stephanie shrugged and gave her an empathetic smile. "He keeps looking over here."

Kassidy groaned and looked around until she found the exit to the back patio. "I'm going to get some air."

"Do you want us to come with you?" Stephanie asked.

"We just got here," Melissa said at the same time.

"No, you guys go have fun. I'll be right back in." Kassidy waved away her friends with a smile she hoped looked genuine.

She opened the door to the patio, greeted by the evening's warmth and the hum of conversation and laughter. The beat of the music mingled with the other sounds around her, and Kassidy felt like disappearing in the crowd. She found a cushioned chair underneath a small overhang wrapped in a string of twinkling lights. All around her, people flirted, drank, and continued to dance wherever there was room.

She loved people watching – probably a side effect of her chosen profession. She imagined people's lives and how they knew each other. She could effortlessly write fictional profile pieces about each of them.

"Hi. Mind if I sit down?" The deep voice broke her from her daydream.

She blushed and wanted to kick herself. She recognized that voice. She'd been thinking about it since the previous afternoon. The cop. The guy had to think she was a horrible person.

His dark brown hair had a small wave to it and was brushed to the side, and his eyes were a green-brown. He smiled at her, but it looked forced. Or maybe nervous?

"No problem." She waved her hand in the general direction of the chair facing hers. She picked up her phone, trying to look too busy to talk.

He cleared his throat, but she continued to scroll through her Instagram feed.

"We got off on the wrong foot, and I was hoping to redeem myself," he said in a confident voice. There was something else in his tone – something he was attempting to mask. Amusement?

She looked up at him in surprise.

"Yes, I am capable of acting like a regular human." He grinned at her expression.

This man was completely disarming. Not at all like the man she remembered. Was it an act?

She thought about trying to pretend he wasn't there, but then he stuck out his hand.

"I'm Brett Green."

She looked at his extended hand for half a second. *Don't be ridiculous, Kassidy.*

She put her hand in his, liking the feel of his firm grip. A weak handshake was a pet peeve of hers.

"Kassidy Turner." She tried to say her last name as quietly as possible, but he heard it. For a second, she saw it, a flash of partial recognition – knowing a name but not knowing why. But the look was gone quickly, and he didn't say anything about it.

No one had recognized her name in quite a while. The story of her former life hadn't been such a big one in Sacramento.

"I'm sorry about yesterday. It was a crazy situation, and I was trying to do my job. But I know I wasn't being very empathetic."

I was there for hours, she wanted to respond, but she didn't want to be that kind of person while he was trying to make amends.

"I'm sorry, too," she said instead. "I know you probably think I'm horrible, but it was a really rough day, and it felt like there was enough chaos around me without another crazy curveball. Is the guy going to be okay?"

"He's in critical condition, but showing some improvement, so they expect him to pull through."

"That's good," she sighed. "I hope he gets the help he needs." She'd called her therapist right after, even though she was still holding a grudge about the journaling.

He studied the throng of people around them. She took those moments to study *him*. He was in shape, which she could notice more now that he was in a button-up shirt instead of his uniform. He didn't appear to be older than his mid-thirties. There were noticeable laugh lines around his eyes when he smiled, which she typically found to be a good sign. He appeared distracted by the boisterous crowd. She noticed he was tapping one of his feet. Was that nerves?

"Not your usual haunt?" She tried to joke as he turned to look at her again.

His smile grew. "You could say that. A few of my coworkers dragged me here. They're in their twenties, but for a thirty-two-year-old…" He shrugged. "I guess I should have asked for an old-man-appropriate activity."

She couldn't help but laugh. "I feel the same way. This is something I would've done seven or eight years ago, but it's not my go-to for fun now. I have a bunch of mom friends who felt like partying tonight, so here I am."

"Are you from around here?" His eyes were focused on hers, and she started feeling the very beginning of her anxiety building. She'd done her best to steer clear of guys in the two years that she'd been back in Sacramento. The trauma she'd experienced with Kurt was not something she needed to repeat.

But he's not interested in me, right? He's making small talk.

"I grew up in Folsom and moved to San Francisco for college. I lived there for a while after that. I moved back to Sacramento a couple years ago."

Best to keep it simple.

"San Francisco must've been a cool place to live. Why'd you move back?"

She wanted to shut this line of conversation down, so giving a hint at the awkward truth might not be a bad idea. "I went through a bad break-up. And some other journalism opportunities opened up here."

Freelance opportunities where I run myself ragged rather than having a stable job.

"How about you? Did you grow up here?" she continued.

"I grew up in Orange County, but I moved up here five years ago for the job with Sac PD. My family still lives down there. Being a journalist has to be an exciting job."

"I love it. It's what I was meant to do. I'm freelance writing for quite a few different Northern California newspapers and magazines at the moment."

Yeah, adding the "quite a few" didn't make it sound like a regular day job. Ridiculous.

"You light up when you talk about it," he said, which really threw her off.

"I do?"

He nodded. "And you're a fellow nerd, I see."

She was confused at first, but realized he was looking at her purse and laughed out loud. "There is no way you're a nerd! You like *Doctor Who*?"

The laugh lines at the corners of his eyes expanded as he grinned. "Don't judge a man by his uniform. And what self-respecting nerd wouldn't? David Tennant was the best."

She shook her head in disbelief. "That's probably an argument for another time. I'm pretty serious about Matt Smith."

He feigned shock and shook his head slowly, yet again causing her to laugh. The knots that had been tightening in her stomach loosened a little.

The crowd around them ebbed and flowed as they talked on about their favorite shows, movies and music. Families came up, and they both commiserated about having younger siblings. His two years with the Orange County Sheriff's Department had cemented his love of law enforcement. He briefly mentioned a previous marriage, but, like her, didn't slow for further conversation there. Her love of journalism had started in her high school newspaper class. The rush of a hard news story and emotions of a profile piece kept her in love.

Gonna get going, so we're coming to get u! Her phone buzzed with a text from Melissa. She was shocked to see it was one o'clock in the morning.

"I didn't realize how late, or early, it is, and it sounds like they want to get going." She motioned toward the patio door.

"Sorry about that. I usually work graveyard, so I don't notice when it's getting regular-person late." His smile was still there, but it had lost a little something now.

She stood up and he followed suit. "Thanks for the talk. It was really nice." She had to admit, he was an interesting, funny guy, but she wasn't looking for anything.

He nodded in agreement, his eyes studying hers.

Her three friends waved from right outside the patio door, annoying grins on their faces.

"Would it be okay for me to get your number?" he asked, pulling her away from the scowl she was sending her friends.

"Um, sure." Her stomach churned, but she heard herself saying the digits anyway.

"Talk to you soon, Kassidy," he said as he moved over slightly so she could make her way to the door. He sounded certain it would happen.

She gave him a smile and a little wave.

Later, after her friends had dropped her off, she leaned against her kitchen counter. Glancing at her TARDIS purse, she smiled and switched off the light. It'd been fun, but he wouldn't call.

CHAPTER 3

"What the hell, Mary? What the hell happened? Is it normal for one of your operatives to do something so fucking stupid? To completely give himself away?" Kurt had all but stormed into the mostly-dark downtown Sacramento office building.

It was a disgustingly hot night and Mary was nearly ready to abandon the city that had been so good to her, because the unrelenting heat and her stormy mood were a dangerous mix. She and Christopher, another Northern California project manager, were working late that night on a number of projects she deemed far more important than Kurt's wasted ego.

"There's no indication she knew who he was. She probably thinks he was some homeless nut job. It's not ideal, but sometimes things happen." She shrugged.

Christopher was watching Kurt from his desk with eager eyes, but he said nothing.

"Things happen? It shouldn't fucking happen! He could have spoken to her! Why the hell did he do it?" Kurt hovered over Mary at her desk, looking ready to strangle her at any moment.

"I don't know. I haven't exactly gone for visiting hours at the hospital. But when he gets out, he'll be terminated. I already assigned a new operative to

Kassidy." Mary barely looked up from her computer screen.

"Try not to be so cavalier about the jobs I give your organization. I'm fairly sure your boss doesn't want to lose my donations." Kurt had grown quieter now, and Mary felt a chill go through her bones.

"It's not going to happen again." She tried to sound annoyed rather than afraid.

She heard a slam, and when she looked up, Kurt was gone.

"Asshole!" she called after him when she was pretty sure he wouldn't hear her.

"I know the operative you put on that case, Mary. He's subpar at his best. I realize you're locked in some kind of perverted power struggle with Kurt, but with how much money he gives the organization, the boss expects you to provide him the best operatives. He may not have requested Ms. Turner to be terminated yet, but that doesn't make the case less important."

"I understand that." Mary glared across the room at Christopher, who spoke with his usual monotone voice. He couldn't bring himself to make eye contact with the person he was speaking to. Mary had worked with him for years, but he still managed to piss her off when she was in the right mood.

"Do you?" Christopher's eyebrow raised the smallest bit, but he continued to stare at his laptop screen.

"The operative had passed all his monthly tests. There was no reason to think he'd lose his shit for no reason." She slammed her laptop closed. She'd never get any work done here.

"He barely passed anything. He should have been terminated long ago. It's your head. You can do what you want with Kurt's cases, but it'd be such a pain in the ass to have to be assigned another partner, especially in this incredibly boring part of the state. It'd be so much easier for me if you'd stay alive." He shrugged.

Mary's jaw dropped. She wasn't sure how she could still be surprised by anything Christopher said, but her sociopathic colleague never failed to take it to the next level.

He clicked away on his computer keys, his expression completely blank, as if Mary had already ceased to exist.

***

Brett's heart was slamming in his chest when he called Kassidy on Tuesday afternoon. He rarely got nervous, but he hadn't asked anyone out for a long time. Her face had floated through his mind since the weekend, but he was picking up as much overtime as he could and hadn't had the opportunity to call her sooner.

That's a joke. You're nervous as hell and have no idea if she's interested in you. Freaking get over yourself.

"Hello?" she answered after a few rings, sounding rushed and distracted.

"Hi. Kassidy? It's Brett…Brett Green, from the other night."

Silence, as if she'd pulled the phone away to look at it.

"Oh, Brett." Complete surprise. She'd clearly thought he'd never call her. Was she hoping he wouldn't? "Sorry. I was waiting for a source to call me back, and I didn't look at the screen. I also dropped my phone pretty hard, so I'm surprised it still works." She abruptly cut herself off, and he swore he heard a light smack sound. Had she just done a facepalm?

He chuckled. His nerves eased a little bit. "Glad it does. Sorry I didn't call sooner. I had a lot of overtime the last couple days."

"That's okay. I can't imagine how busy your job keeps you. I've been hanging out with some millennials myself."

He laughed. "I'm sure that's connected to an article. Aren't we both lumped into that category?"

"Exactly. The range of ages and the vastly different lives this group of people experienced growing up, and the vastly different lives they lead now, are big pieces of the story. The main focus is how living in Sacramento has come into play in all of it. The magazine I'm writing for wanted a super-local take on the truths and myths of millennials, since it's such a popular topic at the moment."

"Sounds interesting. You'll have to tell me when it's published. I'd love to read it." He looked down to see his foot tapping and forced it to stop. It was an annoying tell he'd had since childhood.

She paused again. "I will."

He could tell she wasn't sure about him. Did she wonder about his interest in her, or was she not interested? She'd dazzled him during their first meeting, even though she'd been pissed at him. Their conversation at the club had only made him want more time with her, so he had no plan to bow out.

"I know this is last minute, but I don't work again until tomorrow night, and I'd really like to see you if you have time." He threw the request out there, hoping it wouldn't boomerang right back at him.

"Sure, that'd be nice." She didn't sound sure at all, but there was a definite note of intrigue, which had to be a step in the right direction. "Maybe dinner tonight?"

"Sounds great. Do you like sushi? There's that new place by the Golden 1 Center." The words came tumbling out of him, and he felt like a fool.

"I do. Oh, yeah, I read a good review on it yesterday. Is six-thirty okay? I can meet you there."

"That works great. See you tonight, Kassidy."

"See you tonight."

Relief washed over him as he ended the call, and he rolled his eyes.

Not sure if my job's ever even scared me that much.

***

The man outside Kassidy's apartment returned after an hour-long break. He was exhausted. This freaking woman spent most of her day running around the city. Mary had said she was some kind of journalist, but that she worked from home. She sure as hell didn't spend much time at her home.

He'd left his car across the street from her place and walked to a restaurant for dinner. But when the GPS on her phone showed she was leaving again, he'd had to leave without finishing his food.

"Fuck," he muttered as he made his way back to her apartment. He despised following people who never stayed still.

She'd already driven away, but there was no way for him to lose her. He lit a cigarette in his car and took a long drag before trailing after her. She parked in a garage near the arena but stayed in her car. He parked on the floor above her and took the stairs down two at a time to try to get ahead of her. Sometimes it was more fun to guess where people were going.

When he got to the bottom of the stairs and left the garage, he almost ran into her hurrying in the opposite direction.

"I'm sorry!" she said distractedly, heading back into the garage. He could have touched her in that moment. Grabbed a fistful of hair and pulled. He could smell the lingering hints of her perfume as she retreated back into the structure. How good her skin must feel to touch. He had to calm himself down. He wasn't going to fuck this job up like the last guy. He'd been working for this organization for far too long.

He'd been pretty surprised when Mary chose him for this job because of his recent probation for a termination he'd nearly botched. But Mary had said this was an easy task and a good way for him to redeem himself with the boss before he was out of chances.

His target's phone still showed it was in the car. He took a chance that she was only going back to get it and walked down the block and around the corner to wait. She was back in a few minutes, heading toward the many restaurants in Downtown Commons.

She stepped into a sushi place, where she greeted a guy standing by the window. Interesting. A date? If the date went well, maybe he'd finally have the time to finish a meal. He liked sushi.

CHAPTER 4

Kassidy couldn't deny how attractive Brett was. Laughter, music, and countless conversations flowed around her, but she spotted him easily, gazing out the window in the opposite direction from where she'd come. He was wearing dark gray slacks and a short-sleeve button-down shirt, which displayed his muscled arms. She silently chastised herself when she started wondering what it would be like to run a hand through that wavy hair. She shook off the romantic day dream. Those were a thing of her past.

"Brett?" She was directly behind him now, but had to raise her voice to be sure he heard her over the background noise. She could have touched his arm to get his attention, but with the direction her mind had been wandering, she decided against that.

"Hey, Kassidy," he said, a smile lighting his face. Her heart skipped a beat. She couldn't remember when a man had last looked that excited to see her.

His face spoke of great confidence, but she was fairly good at reading people, and she could see the nervousness in his eyes. Nerves were good. They meant he was a normal person.

"It's great to see you again." That smile stayed, and boy, was it intoxicating.

"You, too." She returned the expression and took a moment to tuck her hair behind her ears to break eye contact. "How have you been?" She wasn't sure what else to say as the hostess ushered them to their table.

"I've been good," he answered, pulling her chair out. "Work's been crazy. It's like the end of summer freaks people out. My regular patrol rounds take me twice as long, because people are doing weird stuff."

"I'm sure. That happens when the seasons change, and when there's a full moon."

"Ugh, yeah. That's always bad." He shook his head. "'Don't blink' status." His eyes flicked up from his menu to meet hers.

Her eyes got wide and she covered her mouth to stop herself from spitting out her soda. She managed not to choke as she started to laugh. "Did you just compare regular people to the Weeping Angels from *Doctor Who*?"

"That full moon is a powerful thing." He shrugged, his eyes full of mischief.

"You really are a nerd."

"Could I be considered a reliable protector of this city if I lied about something like that?" A shocked expression filled his face, and she nearly spit her soda out again.

"I'm pretty sure those are two very unrelated things."

He shrugged, but this time with a silly grin. As she tried to regain her composure, she noticed he was studying her face, and her discomfort returned.

"Are you glad you moved up here?" Was all she could think to ask. She needed the attention to be off her.

He nodded. "There was that culture shock at the beginning, but I needed the change, and the community hasn't disappointed. Even when there are dark times, there's a lot of pride here, and it's nice to see new development and efforts to keep the city competitive and interesting."

He motioned toward the arena, which had been completed several years earlier. "And it's amazing the variety of people you can meet walking around downtown. It's a dichotomy for sure, and it never gets old."

She smiled in response. "It's why I like reporting here. It has its flaws, like anywhere you'd go, but there are so many passionate people here. It's their stories I like to write best."

He was quiet for a moment after she said that, his eyes holding hers whether she liked it or not. Her heart picked up speed.

"How many articles do you usually write at a time?" His question broke her from the fog.

"I'm working on three at the moment, and I'm hoping to pick up a couple more tomorrow since I'm almost done with the millennial story. I try to keep myself as busy as I was when I was a full-time reporter, but it depends on who needs what stories when. I have six local publications I regularly write for."

"Wow, that's impressive." His green-brown eyes were so intriguing, and Kassidy found herself thinking it would be fun to learn to read them better. "So, you were a full-time reporter before this?" He continued. "For the *Sac Bee*?"

She looked down at her plate as shame ran through her. "I freelance for the *Bee* now, but I was actually a reporter in San Francisco. I interned at the *Chronicle* and managed to get a staff writing position after graduating from San Francisco State. I reported there for a little over three years."

He nodded, but didn't push any further. He must remember what she'd told him the night they met, and she was thankful for his respect.

"Okay, here's the important question," he said, looking serious enough to ask her how to dismantle a bomb in sixty seconds. She braced herself. "*Star Trek* or *Star Wars*?"

This time she had to try so hard not to spit out her drink that she started choking on it instead. He reached toward her with a guilty look, but she waved away his hand with a laugh when she was able to breathe again.

"You must love a good spit take." She sent him a teasing smile.

He shrugged with a chuckle. "I'm a sucker for classic comedy techniques. And my question still stands." His eyes danced.

"But that's like discussing politics or religion. It can be so dangerous to get into." She put her hand to her heart. She regarded him, trying to make it look as if she was gauging his true character. "*Star Wars*."

He sat back with an exaggerated sigh of relief. "You had me worried."

Stories of families and jobs floated through the air between them as they ate. Kassidy had a younger brother, and Brett had two younger sisters. Brett had started to follow in his father's insurance sales footsteps. Then one day he saw an Orange County deputy talk a man who planned to jump off a building, safely back down to the ground. He realized he wanted to make a difference by doing the same kind of work. He quit his job, went through the academy and began working for the sheriff's department.

Kassidy loved telling a story, no matter what kind. Learning what made people tick and seeing the world how they saw it were eye-opening experiences. Sure, journalism could be very stressful when there were tight deadlines and she had no idea how to get a story started, but somehow it worked out. Her favorite stories to write were those of people overcoming extreme odds or bringing something beautiful to the world after tragic heartbreak. While she knew she'd never be the next Katie Couric, she hoped she could make even the smallest difference with her reporting.

"Oh!" She looked down and realized the server had left their check and all their plates were gone. She checked her watch. How was it already almost ten? She got all daydreamy when she spoke about her writing.

He quickly grabbed the check before she could even think to reach for it, and handed his card to the server as she walked by. He chuckled at Kassidy's apparent frustration.

"You don't have to do that," she protested, reaching after the retreating server as if she could will her back.

"I don't think you have control over the Force..." He shook his head with a smirk, and she glared at him.

"Well, thank you. That was very nice of you." She politely admitted defeat, but had to have the last word. "But next time I'll get it."

"A next time sounds great." A warm smile filled his face. "But I have no comment about you paying future checks. I wouldn't want to perjure myself."

"Hmm, yes, better to consult your legal counsel first." She nodded and managed to keep a straight face.

They cut through the warm, sleepy air as they made their way to her parking garage. Various topics of conversation swirled around them. *To Kill a Mockingbird* had all but changed her life in high school. *The Lord of the Rings* trilogy was where he found solace during those years. He'd been trying to read it again, but only had time to read before going to bed, so he fell asleep after reading about a page.

"Who knew old age would set in so soon?" He laughed, and she shook her head.

"Do you live downtown?" she asked.

"I live in Natomas. I bought a house there a couple years after I moved here. How about you?"

"I live in Midtown. I've been renting there for about a year." She decided against telling him that she had lived with her parents for the first year after moving back, because she hadn't had enough money to rent without running her savings dry.

They made it to her car as he was explaining the detective interview process he'd be starting in early October. It was something he'd been thinking about for the last couple years.

"I'll still take patrol shifts as overtime every now and then, because patrol never gets old. But figuring out the reasons and story behind a crime is so interesting, so I think it'll be a good move."

"Sounds cool." She smiled as she unlocked her car. When she turned back to him, she was surprised at how close he was. Her heart sped up and she wondered if he was going to try to kiss her. It was a scary, yet exciting thought.

He smiled slowly as he looked down at her. "I'd like to see you again. I've signed up for a lot of overtime in the next few days, and then I offered to cover my buddy's shift at 2nd Saturday this weekend…"

She brightened when she heard he would be working during the city's art walk, when Sacramento galleries and businesses opened their doors to the perusing public during the evening of the second Saturday of the month.

"I was actually planning to go to 2nd Saturday with a couple friends, so maybe I'll see you there. And we can make a plan for next week."

His smile was steady as he nodded. They stood awkwardly for a few moments, and she found herself hoping he would do something, because she was too chicken to. As if he could read her thoughts, he opened his arms and put them around her for a hug. She was surprised how comforting the embrace felt, and she was happy to be there for the ten seconds it lasted.

Was leaving her trauma behind and starting something new going to be this easy?

CHAPTER 5

"I don't know why you're so worried lately. Has something new happened that I don't know about?" Mary looked across the room at Kurt.

He was pacing in front of the large windows of his San Francisco office, looking down at the city streets fifty stories below.

"I don't think you understand the seriousness of my situation. I don't know how many more times I'm going to have to ask you to arrange things like the last termination. When I talked to Christopher, he said you were rather… hesitant about it." His eyes were burning as they met hers.

Mary scowled back at him. "Look, you can act holier than thou with everyone else, but I've known you way too long and well for you to pull that shit with me. You should be working with one of our more junior project managers. Your needs are low-level compared to most of my clients."

When she met his gaze again, the darkest leer covered his face. It startled her. What was really going on with him? Had someone threatened him? She was sure she would have heard something.

"I'm trying to say anyone could have arranged that termination for you if you had made the call. I'm trying to get much larger projects done at the moment, and I don't have a ton of free time." She wanted to make sure he understood his place - he needed to be brought down a peg or two. But when

he continued to stare at her with hatred, she decided maybe it was best to backtrack a bit. For now. "Look, I did it, didn't I? She's dead, isn't she? Isn't that what matters? And you should stop listening to Christopher. The guy's a sociopath. He enjoys seeing people squirm because he doesn't feel empathy. It's like he's constantly testing the limits to make sure his soul is still dead."

He never took his eyes from hers, and her stomach twisted.

"Did your operative tell you Kassidy is dating a cop? Do you not see that as a problem?"

"He said they've been on one date since meeting at that club. And there's no evidence that she even thinks about you, Kurt. And Sac PD knows nothing."

"So, you didn't know he was the first cop on the scene of your last operative's little breakdown? It looks like that's where he and Kassidy really met. Your idiotic operatives need to be careful, Mary. Someone is going to start piecing these things together. I could simply request to have them terminated now, I suppose."

How had Mary not known Kassidy's cop was on that scene? The information must have gotten lost in the transition to a new operative. But how had Kurt known? "Of course I knew! That was completely random. And there's a detective assigned to that case now, so he's not involved. We're not going to start killing cops. Too much attention follows."

"Your organization has killed them before."

"Yes, but we have to create complete scenarios of them falling apart for whatever reason or getting into horrible accidents. Even then, cop deaths are crawling with investigation and media coverage. Those have to be serious situations, Kurt. We're monitoring Kassidy and the cop. We'll keep you apprised. There is no reason to go to that extreme right now."

He nodded, looking only somewhat satisfied. When he turned back to his office window, his hands clasped behind his back, Mary took a gulp of air.

***

Brett and Officer Rodriguez were in the heart of the 2nd Saturday festivities. They chatted about light topics as they walked, keeping an open eye and ear on the spectators milling around them. This was typically a peaceful event, but last month a group of four drunk men had wandered around, spouting off disgusting things to women, so his department was making it a point to have a stronger presence this month. Brett had taken the shift as a favor to his friend whose daughter had a choir performance. He'd worked with Rodriguez only once before, when he'd picked up another shift for the same friend. She was level-headed and calm, even though she'd only been an officer for a year. It was his favorite personality type to work with.

It was a warm evening, and there hadn't been a cloud in the sky that day. It reminded him so much of Southern California weather that for a few moments he had an unexpected bout of homesickness.

"Excuse me, officers." Two women who appeared to be in their sixties or seventies approached them. "How do we get back to Old Sacramento from here? We're visiting, and we've gotten a little turned around."

"No problem." Brett smiled and gave the women directions toward the river-front district.

"Thank you so much," one of the women gushed. "We're from upstate New York and we're visiting our niece. We hardly ever make trips to Manhattan, which is so much crazier than this, even though we live in the same state. It's so difficult to make your way through a city like that. It's an amazing place, don't get me wrong, but it's so overwhelming. A city like this seems more manageable."

Brett did his best to stay attentive as the woman talked on and her companion smiled shyly, but at that moment he spotted Kassidy and her friends across the street. Damn, she was beautiful. He wished he could be next to her. Man, he hadn't felt like this in a long time.

The women were chatting more with Rodriguez now, but Brett was still trying to stay focused. Kassidy spotted him and a small smile lighted on her face as she gave him a little wave. Her two friends noticed him, too, and were clearly giving Kassidy crap. She shook her head and turned to them. Her black hair was down, and it twirled around her shoulders. Was she into him? Yeah, she hadn't shoved him away when he hugged her the other night, and he'd made her smile and laugh often enough during their dinner, but something about her was a little off, a little unclear. Her name had sounded familiar when they'd met, but he didn't know why. He felt weird looking into her, but maybe he should.

The women thanked them again and went on their way. Kassidy cast him another glance, her smile closer to a grin this time. He felt like an idiot, but he couldn't help return the gesture. Dammit, it was too late for him. He gave her a little wave as he and Rodriguez continued their walk.

"Who's that?" Rodriguez had seen more than he wanted her to, and she was ready.

"Don't worry about it." Brett rolled his eyes and she laughed.

A man across the street caught his eye. He was probably at least twenty feet behind Kassidy, but was he watching her? He glanced into the shops and galleries like everyone else around him, but there was something weird about the way he kept looking in front of him. And Kassidy was in his direct line of sight. There were people all around, though. Maybe he was looking for someone.

Calm the hell down. Brett shook his head.

But the guy was familiar, too. Where had Brett seen him before? He tried to place him, but the man ducked into a gallery, giving a wave to someone inside.

See? He was looking for someone. So why don't I feel satisfied with that thought?

Just then their radios came alive. Three patrons on the next block were fighting, and the responding officer had called for backup. Rodriguez responded on her radio, and they took off toward the scene. Brett told himself to try to remember later why he recognized that guy.

***

Too late, he'd noticed the cop watching him from across the street, but he'd ducked into the next shop and tried to make it look like he was meeting someone. He needed to be careful, but following this lady and not getting any closer was difficult, especially after she bumped into him outside the garage. Her body was intoxicating, and she had to know it. He was jealous of the cop.

But he could handle it. He needed to remember this was a job, and he needed to keep it. Mary'd told him this Kassidy woman was a pretty big concern to their client, so she'd be more trouble than she was worth anyway.

Did the cop recognize him from the restaurant? He'd come in behind Kassidy, but his table had been close to theirs. He needed to be more careful in the future. The guy was a cop, so he was gonna see things most people wouldn't notice. And he really didn't need to be following her so closely. She seemed to live a pretty cautious life, even if she never stayed still, so she couldn't realistically be much of a risk. But then again, this was his only assignment right now, so he didn't have anything else to do.

He watched as the two cops retreated down the street, then he ducked out of the shop and picked up the tail again.

***

Sunday morning, Kassidy was in the middle of writing two articles, editing another, and trying to reach three different sources (who'd been incognito for the last few days) for yet another. Stress was the name of the game.

Her phone began to ring, and she grabbed at it desperately, knocking it off the table. It clattered to the floor and continued to ring a few more seconds before the call ended.

"Noooo!" She let out an aggravated sound that might have alarmed listeners if anyone had been there to hear it. "They won't call me back and then finally…Gaaahh!" She fished her phone off the ground and checked the screen.

To her surprise, it was Brett's number on the screen. Not that she hadn't been thinking about him, because whether she liked it or not, he'd been one of her prominent thoughts. But work was so demanding, her social life felt like a luxury she couldn't afford. She also didn't trust this. Was getting into something new the best thing for her right now? She wasn't in a stable place in life. And could she open herself up to someone again? Her therapist had told her to knock it off and enjoy herself. Take it as slow as she wanted and be careful, but move forward, even though it was scary.

She clicked the missed call in her phone log to call Brett back.

"Hey." He sounded exhausted, and she wondered how much sleep he'd gotten. "Sorry, was just leaving you a message."

"It's okay. Are you doing all right?" She heard the concern in her own voice as she hit save on the article on her computer and tried to rearrange some notebook pages for another.

He was quiet for a moment, as if analyzing something she couldn't see. "Yeah, I'm okay. Didn't get a lot of sleep last night. How are you?"

"Okay. Stressed about some articles. It's a little nerve wracking when sources don't get back to you. I need their quotes for these stories to even be passable." She sighed, pinching the bridge of her nose.

Anxiety bubbled below the surface, but usually things like this didn't send her into a full panic attack anymore.

"Sorry to hear that." He was quiet again for a moment. "It's a really nice day. Come for a walk with me this afternoon."

"A walk? I don't…" She looked around at the mess of papers on her dining table, and something in her was done. "A walk would be really nice. Where?"

"Land Park? Around one?" His voice was brighter as he responded.

"Yeah, that sounds great."

"Want to meet by the amphitheater? I'll bring coffee. I need a lot today."

She chuckled. "Sounds perfect. The stronger the better."

"Looking forward to it, Kassie." He tried to suppress a yawn and barely failed.

This made her pause. She felt heat go to her cheeks, and a smile tugged at her lips. "Kassie, huh?"

"I thought I'd try it out, if you don't mind." His tone was sheepish.

She put her cold hand to her warm cheek. "I don't mind." To be truthful, it was what most people called her, but something about him saying it insinuated a familiarity she couldn't help but be excited for.

"Great. See you then, Kassie." There was a slight tease in his voice as he ended the call.

This man's gonna keep me on my toes, she thought as she sat back in her chair and closed her eyes.

CHAPTER 6

When Kassidy arrived at the park's amphitheater just after one, Brett was already waiting, holding a coffee cup out to her.

"Bless you." She breathed in the aroma, closing her eyes for a second. When she opened them, his eyes were studying her with more than a little interest. She looked away across the park to hide the stupid blush she felt rising in her cheeks.

As they started walking, she glanced over at him. He looked the most casual she had ever seen him in jeans and a green t-shirt that brought out the green in his eyes. She realized she was staring and quickly took a drink of her coffee, burning her tongue.

"Thanks for joining me." His eyes met hers. They still looked tired, but he sounded much more awake.

"It was a great idea. Sometimes I have to let articles go for a while. They'll work out. They always do somehow, even if I have to change them enough to make them work without the quotes I was hoping for."

"A constant lesson in flexibility." He nodded with a knowing smile, taking a sip of his coffee and clearly relishing it.

"Your job is, too, I'm guessing." A slight breeze passed over her face. Fall was coming whether Sacramento liked it or not.

"You could say that." He laughed. "The other day I had to tell a guy he couldn't leave the mall with a shirt he hadn't purchased so he could drive across the street to show it to his girlfriend at their apartment, because she was pissed at him and wouldn't meet him at the mall. I mean, he'd already left, so he had to turn around."

She had barely swallowed her coffee this time, so she only had to cough a few times to breathe. "You have to start paying attention to when I'm taking a drink." She gave him a playful shove, which made him grin.

"Sorry, but it really happened. And he was sober. Not one drink that day."

"Well, I think the patience award goes to you today." She shook her head, and as she smirked up at him, she was surprised to feel his free hand slipping into hers. Her heart skipped, but she didn't want to pull away.

He had confidence, and she liked that.

They walked in silence until they came to an unoccupied bench in the shade.

As they sat, he turned to her, still holding her hand. "I really like spending time with you."

"I like it, too." She managed a smile, but guilt crept in. She felt somehow she was dragging him into a situation in which he didn't have all the information, unless he'd looked her up since they first met. "I'm having a really good time, but I feel like I need to tell you something about myself because I don't know if it would change anything."

"Okay." His eyes grew visibly darker, and he couldn't hide the concern that appeared there. He continued to hold her hand, and she appreciated his faith, but wondered if it would stay.

She took a few deep breaths. She had to do this to try to squelch down the anxiety that threatened her breaths.

"Have you heard of Kurt Leonard?"

His brow furrowed for a moment as he thought. "Oh, yeah. Isn't he that tech guy? He owns that company in San Francisco…Reliable? Wasn't there some issue with him and a girlfriend a couple years ago? She said he sexually assaulted some of his employees, but there was no proof, and none of the women came forward. Then the story disappeared."

"Yes. The company is Reliant. That...was me. I was the girlfriend."

"Oh." Recognition flashed across his face. "Kassidy Turner. I thought your name sounded familiar..."

She could feel red, hot shame written across her face. She made to pull her hand from his, but he held onto it.

"Wait. Tell me what happened."

She stared at him, but he just waited.

She took another breath. "I was working for the *Chronicle* at the time. I met Kurt Leonard at a technology conference in San Jose. He was a keynote speaker. Reliant was booming, and he was a self-made millionaire. My editor sent me to interview several of the bigger names there so we could do a series of profiles, and we managed to set up an interview with Kurt."

He sat quietly, his eyes studying her face. His fingers were still intertwined with hers.

"To say he's charming is an understatement. He's also very commanding in a way you never quite see coming. I thought I felt an instant connection with him, and he acted...well, he acted like he wanted me. We started dating right after that. He was busy a lot, but I spent any of his free time with him. I managed to keep up with my deadlines at work, but it wasn't easy.

"Maybe six months later, my editor informed me the paper was writing an investigative piece on Kurt. Someone had tipped the paper off to allegations of tax fraud and embezzlement. My editor wanted me to help with the piece. She had heard rumors I was dating Kurt. Kurt was very possessive of his privacy, so we hadn't been spreading it around. I confirmed we were dating, and that I didn't see how those allegations could be true. I refused to write the piece or provide any assistance.

"Work was horrible after that. Most of my coworkers lost respect for me. They didn't like Kurt. Journalists are usually fairly good judges of character, but I guess I wasn't in that case. The stress ate away at me, and it was hard to come up with any story ideas to pitch. I got bottom of the barrel stories, because I was barely participating, but somehow I managed to complete them. It got harder to go to work, and sometimes I didn't.

"After a while, the paper terminated my employment. My editor said I had lost my motivation to be there. She wasn't wrong. I was so ashamed of myself, but I still loved Kurt."

She met his eyes at this point. They were dark, but he didn't say anything, waiting for her to continue.

"The investigation for the story went forward, but Kurt's attorneys had a field day with the fact that while there were rumors, there wasn't any actual evidence. So, the story was squashed.

"I was living with Kurt after I was fired. Two women who used to work for Reliant approached me. I'd never met them before. They told me their stories and stories of a number of other women. They had a list of names. They told me Kurt had been sexually assaulting women for many years - but only his employees. This was done so that if they ever threatened to come forward, he would fire them and make it very difficult for them to find jobs again. Several of these incidents happened while he and I were dating.

"It disgusted me. I didn't want to believe them, but Kurt was gone a lot, and I realized I didn't know what was going on in his life most of the time. They told me details and locations, and some of it added up. They told me Kurt had been having a couple of consensual affairs as well, and they mentioned they heard one woman sometimes came over when I visited my parents. At this point I became physically sick." She stopped to take a breath, pushing the panic down. She was almost done. She had to finish. When he knew her story he could decide if it was too much.

"They told me they were trying to save me from total embarrassment and possible infections. They didn't expect me to write a story about it or be some kind of savior for them, but I felt like I had to be. The women wouldn't come to the police with me. They were afraid of what he could do with all his power and influence. I asked them to reach out to others they knew, and I waited for weeks, trying to have as little to do with Kurt as possible while living in his house. None of the women would come forward. I understood, but I was frustrated and angry. I couldn't let it go. I really thought I could stop it.

"I went to the police. I could tell they wanted to believe me. I think they had suspected Kurt of various things for many years, but there was no proof of any of it. Kurt was far too good at cleaning up after himself and keeping people scared. They told me they would investigate. They wanted me to continue to ask some of the women to speak with them. I tried, but no one was willing to say anything, even though I knew they wanted to. I felt for them. They were clearly terrified for their livelihoods, but I couldn't do much more without them." She looked into his dark eyes again. His face was like stone.

"Somehow it got back to Kurt that I went to the police. I confronted him, and he called me crazy. He said some…horrible, hateful things about me and then kicked me out of his house. Not that I wanted to stay there. He didn't even try to convince me it wasn't true. He told me to leave San Francisco.

"I did try to stay in the city for a while after that. I tried to freelance, but I wasn't finding much work. I hadn't had much time to build up contacts from different publications. I lived in an apartment with three other people in an attempt to stay in the city, but I couldn't make enough money even for that. I was also getting a lot of unwanted attention – most of it was outright nasty. The police investigation wasn't getting anywhere.

"Kurt spread a story filled with lies. The media played it that I went to the police with ridiculous accusations. They painted me a jilted woman who'd been dumped. Kurt was enjoying being some kind of victim. Maybe he started believing he was. With the news reports, and horrible stuff said on social media, I honestly started getting frightened.

"So, I had to leave. I moved home a little over two years ago. I tried to erase my San Francisco life. I stepped away from a lot of the friendships I developed there. It was really hard, because I love that city." Her voice caught on her emotions. "I lived with my parents for a while. Then my landlord, who is a friend of my parents, offered to help me out with my apartment. My freelancing is going great, but it's not quite enough."

Understatement of all time.

"Are they still investigating Kurt in San Francisco?" His voice was dark, and she wasn't sure what he was thinking.

"I don't know. I haven't heard from them in a long time. I don't see what new developments there would be, unless someone came forward. I can't blame his victims for staying silent. With what it did to my life, I can't imagine what it would have done to theirs."

It was clear he wasn't sure what to say, and when he spoke, it felt like he wanted to say more. "I'm sorry you had to go through that. It's crazy."

She nodded and sighed. "It sounds like something from a movie, but now we know countless women have been in this same situation with a lot of powerful men. My experience was obviously nothing like his victims'. They must be suffering, and I wish I could help them. I'm waiting for even one of them to feel comfortable enough to come forward. I hope they know they'll have support from a large community of people."

"Hopefully. I wish there was some other evidence." He leaned forward, clearly in his law enforcement frame of mind.

"And maybe there is somewhere. But Kurt must have worked hard to cover it all up." She sighed and leaned back against the bench. She noticed then that their hands had come unclasped. She wanted to gauge his reaction, but he appeared lost in thought.

"I should probably go. I can only escape for so long." She tried to smile, but it was next to impossible.

He broke from his thoughts as she stood up. "Okay, I'll walk you back to your car."

They walked in silence as they crossed the street. She had parked in an overflow parking lot, and it felt like it took forever to get there.

She stopped outside her car, messing with her keys, not sure what to say.

"Sorry. That wasn't the relaxing walk I wanted you to have." His chuckle sounded forced.

"No, it was my decision. I thought you should know about it before…" She sighed, sure there'd be nothing else between them now. She had such an awkward and heavy past.

"I'll call you soon," he murmured as she went to unlock her car.

"Okay," she said, but even she could hear the doubt in her voice.

She turned the engine over, hot tears stinging the corners of her eyes. She'd been so, so stupid, that naïve twenty-five-year-old girl.

She started backing up, willing the tears to stay where they were until she got home, or at least out of the parking lot. A tapping on her window made her jump. She slammed on the brake. Brett stood there motioning for her to open her door. She slowly put the car in park, looking up at him in confusion.

"Come out for a sec."

Unbuckling, she stepped out to stand right in front of him.

He put a warm hand to the side of her face and into her hair, pulling her gently to him. His other arm went around her waist. He bent down and kissed her for several slow minutes. Her heart threatened to explode from her chest. She gripped his upper arm, like she couldn't afford to let him go.

When they broke apart, he put his forehead to hers. "I really like you, Kassie, and when I say I'm going to call you, I mean it."

"Okay, you convinced me." She grinned up at him, and he shook his head with a laugh.

He kissed her again, and she gave him another little shove. "Now let me go home and get some work done."

As she drove away, her heart flew. She watched him again in her mirror. Thoughts of being cautious drifted away in the breeze. She was done for. He'd never really said what he felt about her story, but that was her past, and she was allowed to move on from it. Wasn't she?

CHAPTER 7

A few days after their walk, Brett was on his way to Kassidy's apartment for a very late lunch before he had to go to work. He hadn't felt this way about anyone or anything besides work in a long time.

Yeah, that's pretty sad.

Not that Kassidy's story hadn't thrown him off. It was a lot to digest, but he couldn't fault her for being young and falling for a jackass who was also a closeted misogynist and rapist. Then she'd tried to do her best with a crappy situation. The officer in him wished there was a way to find some evidence on the guy so he'd be sent to prison, but he was sure the San Francisco police had done their best.

They hadn't talked about it since their conversation in the park, and he'd purposefully kept their texts and calls as light as possible. He knew it'd taken a lot for her to tell him, and he didn't want her to feel like she had to offer up anything else right now.

He had to park a couple blocks from her place in order to get a spot, but he didn't mind the walk. She lived in a pretty bustling part of the city, and he liked seeing the life all around him. He could never have worked outside a city. Sure, you were bound to meet some interesting people doing some interesting things in the country or suburban towns, but cities were light and dark, peaceful and chaotic. They were filled with the ideas, actions, and art of so many different people. It was thrilling to spend almost every day working among it all.

When she opened her door, a smile lit her face, but there was something troubling in her eyes. He pulled her close and kissed her long and slow. One of his favorite things now. Her smile had widened considerably when they separated, and her cheeks were flushed, which made her freckles stand out even more.

"You're beautiful," he couldn't help but say. The smile was still there, but something in her eyes bothered him. "What's up?"

She handed him a glass of water and ushered him toward her small oak dining table, where she'd set some sandwiches and fruit.

He took a sip as she answered. "I got tested, you know, after Kurt."

This time it was him who coughed for several minutes as he tried to breathe through the water choking him.

"Umm, I mean, I assumed," he managed to say.

"Not that I'm saying I think we'll…I just thought you should know…" Her cheeks were beet red now.

"I appreciate that." He sat back, studying her eyes. "Trying to think of reasons why this won't work?"

She laughed nervously. "You're good at reading people."

"Have to be," he answered, keeping his voice quiet. He didn't want to say it hadn't been that hard to figure out. "Do you want to see where this goes? Because I do. I'm not worried about that other stuff, Kassie."

Her eyes became thoughtful as she made contact with his. He suddenly felt like he was the one being studied. She was a journalist. She was good at reading people, too. She was making it clear she was judging his character in that moment, because she wasn't going to waste her time on anyone again.

What am I getting myself into? he mused as excitement coursed through him.

"Yes, I want to. I have a habit of over-analyzing." She kept the eye contact going.

"Not always a bad trait, but in this case, you don't need to." He felt like they were having a staring contest now, reading each other's thoughts.

She sighed as she took her eyes from his and took his hand. Her smile was warm, and that was it. She was trusting him, and he knew he better not take that for granted.

A knock interrupted their lunch, and he automatically turned toward the door as she got up. He wasn't comfortable with his back to doors in general, let alone when they were opened.

She answered on the second knock without asking who it was first, which he didn't love.

The male voice was very deep and quiet. Brett heard something about an alarm service and a deal for the month of October. He wasn't good at sitting while there was activity of some kind going on around him, so he went to stand behind Kassidy.

"Sorry, I don't own the place, so I can't sign up for anything," she was saying as Brett reached her.

The man didn't move. Was he going to argue that point? The moment his face came into view, Brett's adrenaline began pumping.

"Hey. It's you." Brett heard his tone drop into what his sisters called his "cop voice." Kassidy turned to him in confusion. It was the guy Brett had seen at 2nd Saturday.

"I understand, miss. Thanks for your time." The man was talking to Kassidy, but he was having trouble not looking at Brett. His expression had been surprised at first, but then turned hard. He made to leave.

"Hey! Sir, I want to see your solicitor's license." Brett followed him, taking the stairs down two at a time.

"Brett?" Kassidy called after him.

"No problem." The man whirled on Brett, pulling the document from the clipboard he was carrying.

Brett reviewed it. It looked legitimate. He studied the guy. He was wearing a shirt with the security company's logo. The materials on his clipboard appeared real in the quick glance Brett took at them.

"Thanks." Brett handed the license back. The man nodded; his eyes fierce. He quickly got in his car and pulled away. He'd been in a spot right outside Kassidy's apartment. How was that possible? Just lucky? And why didn't he walk on to someone else's place? Brett made a point of memorizing the car's license plate. He'd check into it at the station.

Kassidy was standing at the top of the stairs. "What happened? Did you know him?"

"No, I don't know him." He took her hand and led her back inside. "I saw him at 2nd Saturday, right after we saw each other. And he looked familiar to me then, but I still don't know why." He didn't mention his thought that the man had been watching her. "It's weird to see him again."

"He probably lives down here. It can be like a small community when everyone lives and works in the city." She shrugged.

"Yeah," he nodded, trying to sound appeased. But his spidey senses were still tingling.

***

Mary hated to fly. If she never had to fly again, that would suit her fine. She was currently thousands of feet in the air, heading for Los Angeles. Southern California was never her thing. She'd been there enough times to get used to it, but it was too much. Too much traffic, too much sun, too many people. She couldn't stand an excessive amount of any of those.

The only good things that ever happened in Southern California were related to her boss. He was in charge of the California chapter of their organization. He called himself John. It wasn't his name. It was the latest in a long line of different identities. His employees called him either John or "the boss." Mary often wondered if he remembered his birth name. It had been discarded long ago.

John held Mary in high esteem. Most of his employees were terrified of him, and even Mary sometimes felt a small tinge of fear when she looked at his face, but she idolized him more than anyone else she had ever known.

Her life had been one of darkness the night she first met John in a downtown San Diego bar. She'd been visiting a friend who'd moved there after college. With her friend at work, she'd been there by herself, nursing a beer, trying not to panic about her future. She was done with college. She wanted to get into real estate, to own property, but she had no money and plenty of debt. John sensed her distress easily. She knew now how very good he was at taking advantage of someone in distress.

He agreed to front her the money to buy her first two buildings. However, his giving her money depended on her doing some work for his organization. She'd been so naïve and so hungry for a chance, that she'd said yes before much thought. His charm and easy demeanor didn't hurt. He was at least ten years older than her, but they had been lovers for a time. She knew this was a common relationship between him and his new recruits, but she'd felt a strong connection with him. Now they were simply business associates, but he took her opinion seriously.

Real estate was her true love now, and she spent as much time working that part of her life as she could. What with that and spending so much time on Kurt's many requests, the quality of her work on other organization projects wasn't what it should be. She was sure she could make the boss understand this, and maybe he would assign Kurt to another project manager.

John greeted her with a smile when she strolled into his Los Angeles office, and she plunked her work bag down next to his desk, pulling a chair up to sit across from him. His office was very modern, all whites and metals. It was cold and stark. The only fabrics were those of the chair cushions and the white curtains hanging at the windows. Employees often murmured that everything in John's office had to be easy to clean and bleach because of all the blood that was spilled there. Mary had never seen him terminate anyone in that office, but she had no doubt it happened. John enjoyed having remnants of death surrounding him.

She looked up and his smile was still there, but she took pause as she noticed it didn't look right. Was it more like a tightly-controlled leer? It made her think of being in the eye of a storm, where the weather was deceptively calm, but you were surrounded by complete chaos.

"I'm glad you made it safely down," he said, but his voice was too quiet. He never used that tone with her. What had she done?

"Umm, yeah. I brought the reports you wanted. I know we're not as far along on some of the projects as you wanted, but I'm working on getting the priorities completed. I've made a schedule for everything else." She handed him several folders of information.

The organization used hard copy documents as often as possible. It was too easy to track digital data and impossible to fully destroy it. In a split second, actual paper could be shredded or destroyed a number of other ways. Any documentation that had to be digital was heavily encrypted. The organization employed hundreds of professional hackers to test the encryption on a daily basis.

He reached for the papers from across his imposing metal desk and briefly glanced through them. He then put them to the side and glanced up at her. "Could you give me a synopsis of where the priorities stand?"

She frowned, glancing at the documents she had taken great pains to prepare for him. "We led the feds to information that makes it appear Cranston was committing tax fraud, so he's been arrested. Only a couple loose ends to tie up with that one."

"Excellent. I did tell him to take my advice on the sale of those passports. I don't care to be ignored."

She nodded. "The La Shay termination is scheduled for Sunday. He'll have just gotten back to California from visiting his kids in Manhattan, so suicide should seem realistic. You know how depressed he gets after leaving his kids."

"That should have been handled the last time he came back," he said, his voice monotone.

"I know, but the last guy we assigned to do the job blew his cover and La Shay took him out before he could take La Shay out." She sighed. Some things were beyond her control.

"Blown covers are a common occurrence lately. Go on."

She stared at him for a moment. What was he talking about? The only other person she could think of who'd blown his cover lately was the operative who threw himself at that Kassidy woman's car.

John's eyes were hard, but he motioned for her to continue.

"Next month we've scheduled the final steps for the destruction of that highway patrol officer in Mendocino County. He'll be found to have drugs in his patrol car, and a search of his personal computer will reveal those pictures you suggested. We've been slowly pulling his life apart, so he's nearing emotional breakdown. At this point, the drugs and photos won't come as a surprise to those who know him."

"That should have already been done. I feel like you've let him go on too long. His curiosity has been a nuisance."

She gave a slight nod, growing tired of his commentary on the cases. "I'm sorry. I've been doing the best I can with the workload you're giving me."

"Have you, Mary?"

"What do you mean? Of course, I have. I've been keeping up with Kurt's special needs, covering all these priority projects, and trying to build my real estate business."

"I funded your first buildings so you could have some kind of income – not so you would make real estate your top priority. This organization should be your focus. You should be putting all of your energy into every project you're given." His tone was still even, but she could tell by his murderous eyes that he was pretty pissed.

"The organization is *my focus," she lied. "Where is this coming from?"*

"You have no idea what happened, do you? Are you even monitoring your

projects, Mary?"

"What are you talking about?" She was trying to sound brave, but her heart was racing. What had happened?

Another door to the side of the office opened, and Kurt walked in – the most satisfied sneer on his face. He wore a perfectly-tailored slim-fit suit that showed off the muscles in his arms. His shoes were shiny black. He looked like he was on top of the world.

She knew she looked shocked. She tried to clear her expression as quickly as she could. Vulnerability was never a good thing in this office. "What is he doing here?"

"Thank you for the warm greeting," Kurt said with a giddy smile, but evil lived in his eyes.

"Mary, do you recognize that Kurt is one of this organization's top-funders? His generous gifts are currently supporting thirty-seven different projects throughout the state. His requests should be treated with the utmost respect and diligence. You've been given the esteemed position of project manager for his cases, but you aren't taking that position seriously." John had turned to look out his floor-to-ceiling windows.

"I've arranged everything he's asked for." She stood up from her chair, rage flowing through her.

"In the sloppiest way possible." Kurt growled.

Mary's jaw dropped, and she stared at John's back.

"Kassidy Turner is a threat, Mary. And now that she's involved with a cop, she has the potential of being even more of a threat." John sounded sincere, but Mary wanted to laugh. That stupid woman wasn't a threat. She was too traumatized by what Kurt had done to her in San Francisco, and she wasn't in contact with any of Kurt's victims. "Yet, you're not using reliable operatives to track her."

She couldn't deny that she didn't give a crap about who followed Kassidy. It was a waste of the organization's time and money. The first time she hadn't even tried, but she'd put a bit more thought into the second operative.

"It was one bad operative, and I thought he was ready for the job. He did fine on his testing. I don't know why he snapped. But I had him terminated the day after they took him to the skilled nursing facility. It was a pretty believable overdose." She shrugged.

"Mary!" John slammed his fist down on his desk, and she jumped. "Your second operative went to her apartment! He approached her and spoke to her! He posed as a salesman! He told us he'd been having some sexual thoughts and believed if he could get into her apartment, he could do what he wanted with her – whatever the hell that disgusting thing would have been. He didn't know the cop was there, and the cop followed him out of the apartment. He got away, but the cop tried to look into him and his car later. We had to terminate the operative immediately and completely strip the car and get it out of state. Why do we know all of this, Mary, but you don't? What am I supposed to think about that?"

She felt her face go white. It was difficult to keep standing. It must have just happened. No one had updated her. How had they found out so quickly?

"He went to Christopher, and Christopher called me." Kurt answered her silent question.

"Christopher? He wasn't managing the project. And I'd just checked in with the operative," she lied again. She hadn't checked in with the man since he'd started following Kassidy.

Kurt shrugged. "Your operatives don't respect you."

"That's not true!" Mary growled back. She had never wanted to wring someone's neck as much as she wanted to in that moment.

She looked to her boss. "John. I don't know what happened. That operative was with us for years. I swear he was reliable."

She could see John was controlling his anger again, but it still filled his eyes and threatened to overflow into the rest of his body. "We've assigned a female operative to Ms. Turner. She's been working in the Los Angeles area with us for twenty years, and she's performed countless terminations. If it becomes necessary, she will be the one to terminate Ms. Turner. We hope it won't come to terminating the cop, as you know what kind of issues that can cause, but she's prepared for that possibility."

"John, I don't think..." Mary wanted to tell him what a waste it was to focus so much attention on that woman, but for probably the first time in their relationship, he cut her off.

"Mary, you've been working for this organization for a long time. I want to know that you're still serious. I want to assign you high-level projects, but I can only give you one more chance." Mary guessed by the tone in his voice that he didn't mean one more chance to keep working priority projects. He meant one more chance to keep her job. "And I've enlisted Kurt's assistance with this."

"What? How?" she responded, trying not to stutter.

"He's going to be taking a larger role in our organization." Her boss turned to once again stare out at the late-September sky. "He'll be providing checks and balances for your and Christopher's projects. He'll be signing off at various parts of the process. If he has concerns, he'll bring them to me."

"That makes no sense! He's a client! He has no idea how this all works!"

"He created his own technology company from the ground up. I'm sure he can figure it out. This is the way it has to be, Mary, until I can trust you again." Her boss stared at her with eyes like stone. The message he was sending with those eyes was clear: he could discipline her now, but he had decided not to. She needed to take that and feel grateful. "I'd like you to get back to Sacramento tonight and get started."

"Tonight? I..."

"Tonight." He pushed a button, and his secretary opened the door to his office. Both John and Kurt turned away from her, talking quietly as if she no longer existed. She shoved her documents in her bag and dragged herself out of the office, waves of guilt, shame, and deep anger flooding through her.

CHAPTER 8

Hey. So, I may have been attacked by a vicious pack of squirrels yesterday afternoon.

Kassidy had to stop herself from spitting out the sip she had taken from her second cup of coffee when Brett texted her Friday afternoon. Would she ever be able to drink without worry again?

Hey yourself! Please stop talking to me when I'm drinking things. I had no idea your job was that dangerous!

Haha, oops, sorry. It's a gift. Yeah, these are the hazards they don't tell you about. It would probably scare away too many recruits.

And what did you do to provoke said carnivorous squirrels?

I didn't do anything! I was working some overtime yesterday. I pulled this guy over, and when I asked him to get out of his car, he was eating a sandwich. And he kept eating it. I had to ask him to drop the sandwich.

Hahaha! What??

She officially put her coffee cup down. There was no point in trying.

You can't make this stuff up. He pulled over by the edge of a park, so he finally threw the sandwich in the grass when he went to stand in front of my car. I was going around to talk to the passenger, and these squirrels came out of nowhere and started mauling the sandwich. I think they thought I was going to take it away from them, and they started jumping at me! They were ruthless!

Started jumping at you, Brett? Hmmm...

Not making it up!! Another officer came to assist me, and he was laughing when he walked back to his patrol car to run the guy's information. I had to go around the back of the car so they'd leave me alone!

Well, I'm very proud of you. It's truly admirable that you'd fight off savage squirrels to keep the public safe.

For some reason I don't think you're taking this seriously...

As her phone dinged with this message, he called her.

"Hello, Officer Green, Defender of the People, Champion Over the Squirrels," she answered in as normal a voice as she could.

He laughed out loud. "Definitely a nice ring to that. I'll have to shorten it somehow, or people will get tired of saying it every time they see me. Hey, so, I was wondering if you'd like to take a trip with me tomorrow. Take a break from work?"

I couldn't want anything more, she thought, looking at the disheveled state of her writing space.

"Where are you going?"

"Our department is developing new training for active-shooter situations, and we're trying to get input from other local departments. I'll be presenting it twice, back to back, at the Auburn Police Department tomorrow at two o'clock. It's easier on a Saturday, because their public desk is closed and both presentations are for a different set of officers and staff. I thought you'd like to tag along. We could drive around after, get some dinner."

"Sounds like fun. Do you want me to meet you there?" She glanced out the window by her couch, thinking how nice it would be to spend an afternoon in the Foothills. There were finally hints that Fall weather was on its way, and it'd be great to get outside.

"I can pick you up. The whole thing will probably take a few hours. Do you mind hanging out by yourself for a while? I didn't think this through, did I?"

"No, that's no problem," she responded without pause. "I love Auburn. There's a book store I've been wanting to get back to. And walking around that city is relaxing."

"Great. I'll pick you up around one. You'd be okay if I bring coffee, right?"

"Uh, yes, please," she laughed. "I'm sure I'll need a cup by then. Please be safe at work tonight, Squirrel Conqueror."

This again caused him to laugh out loud. "I will. My lieutenant said he was going to look into recommending me for some kind of medal, but for some reason he sounded like he was joking…"

***

Brett had to drag himself out of bed just after noon on Saturday. It wasn't enough sleep, but it would have to be. His adrenaline had been rushing after work, so he'd tossed for a couple hours before he could calm down, the sounds of the guns still ringing in his ears. It'd been a while since he'd responded to an active shooting.

The smell of brewing coffee gave him a little more life as he made his way to the bathroom. As he brushed his teeth, he looked at his face in the medicine cabinet mirror. He'd be thirty-three tomorrow. He looked half dead, and sometimes he felt so tired he might as well be. He had to cut back on the overtime, especially if he got the detective position. He loved patrol, and he'd miss it, but he had to get more sleep. And now that he'd found Kassidy, he really wanted to spend more time with her.

He said good morning to his cat, Isla, as he made his way into the kitchen. She was the most anti-social cat in the world, except with him. She bugged him for some of his eggs, and as he chugged his coffee, he left some in her dish. He was wearing khaki pants and a collared shirt with the Sac PD logo, but he grabbed his Dodgers cap on his way out. He'd take it off before the presentation, but he needed a little Southern California right now. As he looked up at the sun, his eyes closed, he thought about his family. He felt the ache he sometimes did when he thought about them, and he shook his head. He'd known it'd be hard to see them when he moved up here. He'd made the choice.

He stopped by Temple Coffee on his way to Kassidy's place. He knew she liked strong coffee. She needed it like he did. He put ten dollars in the tip jar. He had to show his thanks to any establishment that kept him thriving with this magical drink.

He was never late. He couldn't stand to be. He took the stairs quickly at her apartment. He knocked on her door, one coffee cup balanced on top of the other. She opened it with a huge smile on her face, taking the top cup. She knew they were both the same.

She looked effortlessly beautiful. Her long hair was up in a ponytail, and she didn't look like she was wearing much make-up. He never wanted her to hide those freckles. He waited to see her eyes as they opened again after that first sip of coffee. But when her eyes met his, she frowned.

"Are you okay?" She put her free hand up to his face, and he was the happiest he'd been since the last time he saw her.

He pulled her into a kiss. "I'm fine. Just tired. It's great to see you." He tried to make his voice sound more upbeat, less exhausted.

He could tell by her eyes that she wasn't satisfied, and she wanted to say something, but she didn't. Would she have if they'd been seeing each other longer? Then some kind of realization dawned on her face.

"Were you at that shooting this morning by Cal Expo? That's your regular beat, isn't it?"

He nodded, studying how she processed this information. How would she handle the danger factor of his job? He needed someone who could try to handle it, but he didn't expect that right away.

"Was everyone okay?" Those dark eyes showed genuine concern as she grabbed her purse from inside her door and they made their way back down the stairs.

He nodded again. "None of us were hit. One of the guys involved had to go to the hospital, but his injuries weren't life-threatening. Luckily, they were both pretty bad shots."

She stared at him for several moments as he started his car. "How can you experience something like that and then get up the next day and give a presentation?"

He chuckled. "I don't know. It's not something I do a lot. But I'm talking to a group of people who can relate to what I go through on a daily basis, so it should be fine."

"Do you have counselors, therapists you can see if you need to? Other police friends you can talk to?"

He gave her a quick, small smile. "Yeah, the department arranges that for us if we need it. And we're a pretty tight community, so I have a lot of people I can talk to."

Not that you're great at that.

"Okay, good. You can talk to me, too…if you want." Her voice sounded a little nervous as she looked forward, taking a long sip of coffee. "Thanks for getting Temple. I love them."

"You're welcome." He was quiet for a moment, but as they approached the freeway, he felt the sudden urge to be very open with her. He hadn't had anyone he'd really wanted to talk to in a long time. And she'd trusted him enough to share her story.

He took a breath, feeling his foot wanting to tap on the floorboard "I'd like to tell you about my marriage."

She looked at him with surprise. "You don't have to do that now."

"I know, but I want to." True, he wanted to be open with her. He didn't want to tell this story, though. It didn't paint him in the best light.

She turned toward him in her seat and was silent.

"I met my ex-wife, Leann, at Cal State Fullerton, in one of our classes. She already had her future planned out. She had an internship at an advertising agency in Fullerton. She already knew how she was going to work her way up to a top management position. I thought it was pretty admirable. I was all set to work for my dad's company after graduation. We dated for a couple years, graduated, and then I proposed. I started working for my dad that same week. A month later she got a permanent position at her agency.

"We got married almost a year after I proposed. We'd been married less than a year when I saw a deputy talk a jumper down from a building. It was the most life-changing thing I'd experienced. I went home that day and told Leann I wanted to be a deputy. She didn't take me seriously at first.

"I tried to talk to her about it a couple more times, and she finally started believing me. She had a good job, and we had some savings, so I quit my job. I talked to her about doing this, but she wasn't sure. We weren't on the same page, but I didn't get that at the time. I felt a call to be a deputy, and I couldn't consider anything else. I was an idiot.

"I went through the academy, and we had to supplement our income heavily with our savings. When I graduated, I was working graveyard shifts. It wasn't an easy adjustment. Graveyard shifts are my thing now, but it was hard for me to get used to, and I know I took it out on her. She got angrier, and I resented her.

"We didn't try to make it work. We were young and stubborn. We separated for a couple months and then she filed for divorce. It was pretty ugly, because there was only anger by then. We didn't have much, but we split what we could. She didn't ask me for anything else, because she wanted to be done.

"My parents were pretty upset. They loved Leann, and they said I'd screwed up. How could a dangerous job be more important than my marriage? Talking to them about it didn't help.

"I stayed with that department for two years, but I needed some space from everyone. So, I moved up here."

"You said you're glad you moved here, but being away from your family has to be hard," Kassidy commented with an empathetic smile.

"I'm glad to be here. Sacramento wasn't a mistake, but yeah, I miss my family. But the police community around here is close, and I love my job. The overtime is great. Of course, that's why, before I met you, my closest relationship was with my cat."

She snorted as she laughed, and he grinned at her. "Your cat. You haven't told me much about her yet."

"Isla, my statue cat."

"Isla is a pretty name. Your statue cat?" He glanced over to find her raising an eyebrow at him.

"She's the most anti-social creature on this planet. She likes me, because I've had her for four years. She hates other people, but when they're around, instead of running away and hiding, she freezes and stares. Wherever she is, she stops and stares. When you stop looking at her, she inches out of the room. Every time you look at her again, she stops and looks at you. It's the funniest thing I've ever seen."

"I feel like you *should* have a cat like that." She twirled her now-empty cup in her hands and gave him a small smile. "I can't wait to meet her."

Excitement went through him. It was thrilling to think of her in his house. He didn't like playing games. He wanted Kassidy in his life, and he would never hesitate to make that known. He knew she had some reservations based on her experience with Kurt Leonard, so he was trying to let her set the pace. But it was hard to stay calm when he thought about kissing her – and more – in a place where he could make sure they weren't disturbed by anyone else.

"And your parents?" Her words broke into his thoughts. "How do they feel about your career now?"

The question caught him off guard, and he couldn't answer for a moment. "Um, they accept it, but I wouldn't say they're happy. They don't like the possibility of danger, and they don't like that I chose it over

Leann."

She nodded, looking straight ahead again. "I'm sure they're still proud of you."

He didn't know how to respond, so he was silent until they got to Auburn.

CHAPTER 9

Kassidy wondered if she had pushed him too far, asking him about his parents. He clearly had some unresolved stuff there, and maybe it wasn't her business. But it was hard to pretend she wasn't curious.

She decided to test the water. "So, my millennials article is coming out next month if you'd like to read it."

"I'd really like to." He flashed her a quick smile as he pulled off the freeway and stopped at a red light.

Okay, he's fine. At least I didn't cross a line. Or maybe this is what being with a mature adult is like? Who knew?

"I happened to see your byline in the *Bee* the other day. I didn't know you write political articles." He pulled her from her thoughts.

She cringed a bit. Politics weren't her specialty. She'd felt the article was pretty strong, but it could have been better.

"Thank you. I don't often, but one of their regular Capitol reporters is back east visiting his daughter, and the rest of the staff is pretty swamped at the moment. They knew I had some political writing experience from my time in San Francisco, and they asked, so I took a stab at it. It wasn't front page news, but I was pretty happy with it..."

"You should be. Politics can be confusing, but your article wasn't."

"Thank you." Confidence wasn't her strong suit, but it was different with her writing. She'd been told she was a good journalist, and she worked hard every day to maintain that status. But words and stories came to her fairly effortlessly. If anything in her life could be called destiny, it was her writing.

"Do you think you'll freelance for the foreseeable future?" he asked as he turned into the shared parking lot of the Auburn city hall and police station.

"Yeah, I think so." She nodded, gazing out her window as he parked. She couldn't help but bristle whenever someone brought up the temporary nature of her work. "Someday I'd like to get a staff writer job, and I did try when I first left San Francisco. But after being fired from a fairly influential publication, I wasn't seriously considered. I think an extensive freelancing portfolio will change that when I interview again."

"I'm sure it will. You've been doing it for a couple years now, and you do the work of a full-time employee. No one could doubt your dedication." He turned the car off and motioned for her to stay put so he could open her door.

When his door closed behind him, she breathed a sigh of relief. She'd talk about writing all day every day, but she felt the opposite about her career path.

She lingered in front of him as she got out of the car and she enjoyed seeing the hungry look in his eyes as they met hers. She was starting to remember that the flirty beginning part of a relationship was a lot of fun. She knew he would never try to kiss her in front of a building of his colleagues with how serious he was about his job, and she found herself enjoying the ability to tease. "So, encounter any more vicious rodents since Thursday?"

She saw the sudden surprise on his face, and she couldn't help but laugh. His eyes danced, but he feigned frustration. "No. I'm sure those squirrels sent a loud, clear message to their friends."

He went around to get his laptop out of his trunk as an Auburn officer left the building and headed their way with a wave.

"Do you think there's pretty good dash cam footage of those squirrels attacking you? I've been trying to picture it in my head, but the actual video would be so much better," she murmured, smiling at the man approaching them.

"I'll never live that down." He smirked at her. "I was trying to bring a little comedy, a little light, to your day, but I guess I had no idea how you would use it against me."

"Hey, Brett! We're all set up for you." The officer stopped in front of them. He was in full uniform.

"Great. Thanks, Mike." Brett shook the man's hand heartily, a big smile lighting his face. "Kassidy Turner, this is Lieutenant Mike Semenya. He was with Sacramento when I first came up north. He's been an important mentor for me as a police officer."

Lieutenant Semenya turned to her with a welcoming smile, and she was thankful to see no recognition of her name on his face.

"Nice to meet you, Ms. Turner. Brett tells me you're one of the best reporters in the Sacramento area."

She chuckled lightly and shook the man's hand. "Nice to meet you, too, Lieutenant. I think Brett is a little over-zealous with his praise."

"I don't know. I've found him to be a pretty good judge of character," the lieutenant responded, but also laughed as he turned to look at Brett, who was smiling sheepishly at them.

"Okay." He took her hand lightly. "I'll call you when I'm done, and we can have dinner?"

"Sounds good." Her heart floated as he held eye contact for a moment longer than he probably should have in front of his colleague. "Nice to meet you, Lieutenant."

"You, too, Ms. Turner."

She waved as she walked away from them toward the crosswalk that would take her across the street and into the heart of downtown.

As she'd stepped into the town square, she heard a voice calling from her left. It was a voice she hadn't heard for years.

"Abigail?" She turned to face the woman, who sprinted up and gave her an immediate hug. She stiffened. She hadn't seen Abigail since San Francisco. They'd gone to school together and kept in touch after both had started working in the city. Abigail had gone the public relations route, and she'd been working in a successful firm when Kassidy left the city.

What is she doing here? She swore she'd never leave the Bay Area.

Not that Abigail was a bad person. She'd been one of Kassidy's only friends to visit at Kurt's house after the fiasco with the *Chronicle*. She'd called to check on Kassidy every other day, but Abigail was a naturally flirty person. She'd paid close attention to Kurt when he was around. Kassidy had tried to ignore the fact that Kurt enjoyed the woman's attention.

Did she ever sleep with him?

She hadn't spoken to Abigail since moving to Sacramento. She had never been able to confront her friend about Kurt, fearing she was paranoid.

"It's so great to see you," Abigail gushed, releasing Kassidy from the embrace, but holding her arms, as if she couldn't quite let go.

"You, too. I'm surprised to see you here." Kassidy tried to keep her voice light, to not sound suspicious. She hated that her mind went there. She needed to see her therapist again. And write in that damn journal.

"I work in Sacramento now. I started my own firm a little less than a year ago. I kept some of the clients from the firm I worked for in San Francisco, but I've been lucky to drum up a ton of local business. You look great."

"Congratulations." Kassidy tried to sound overjoyed. "I thought you'd be the last one to leave the Bay."

Something passed over Abigail's face then. It was a quick shadow, and then it was replaced by her previous peppy expression. "Yeah, I know, but things got a little heavy in San Francisco. A relationship I was in started to go sour, and I wanted a fresh start. Things are a little less demanding around here." She looked around the Auburn intersection, as if feeling a deep connection with the city. "I'm enjoying exploring all these foothill communities."

A relationship. Was she dating Kurt? There's no way I can ask her.

"I forgot you moved to Sacramento. Why haven't we kept in touch?" Abigail's tone sounded sincere.

"I don't..."

"You know what's weird?" Abigail cut her off, her voice sounding too casual. "I was grabbing lunch downtown in Sac the other day, and I swear I saw Kurt."

Kassidy felt herself go white. "What? In Sacramento?"

"Yeah, he came out of that weird-looking black high rise and got into a car. It was pretty quick, but I swear it was him."

Why would he be in Sacramento? What the hell would he be doing in Sacramento? She has to be wrong. Kassidy tried to calm herself as her heart started slamming in her chest.

"Are you seeing him again?" Abigail sounded way too interested. "Hey, are you okay? All your color is gone." Abigail gripped her left arm tightly and motioned for her to sit down in a nearby chair.

Kassidy stayed where she was, hugging her purse tightly. She concentrated on its smooth fabric. She concentrated on the slight chill in the air. She watched a leaf blow past them on the ground. She grabbed at the sound of children laughing nearby.

Stay here. Feel what's real. Don't give in to it. Pay attention to what's real around you. The panic attack had been coming on fast, but she wouldn't let it drown her. Not here, in the middle of this city, with no one around she felt comfortable with.

She made her way to a chair sitting next to a wrought iron table and Abigail followed – her eyes wide. "Are you okay?"

"I'm fine. You know what happened with me and Kurt. It's hard to hear he might be close by." She took gulps of breath. It was starting to pass. She was proud of herself. She was getting better at fighting them off. "I'm sure it wasn't him. There'd be no reason for him to be in Sacramento." She was trying to comfort herself and happened to be speaking out loud.

"I'm sorry, Kassie." Abigail looked truly distraught. She really wasn't a horrible person. Maybe she'd made some of the same mistakes with Kurt that Kassidy had, and maybe she was still a little obsessed with Kurt, but she'd have no reason to want to hurt Kassidy.

"It's okay." Kassidy tried to smile at her. Her heart was starting to slow, and she didn't feel so faint.

"I'm glad I got to warn you though, because I'm almost one hundred percent sure it was Kurt. I wouldn't want you to be surprised if you run into him." Abigail's voice had picked up its pep again, and Kassidy wondered if she should lie and say she had to get to an appointment.

Then, as if it was the most well-timed exit strategy, Abigail's phone started to ring. She checked it with a guilty look. "I'm sorry, I have to take this. You'll be okay?"

Kassidy nodded.

"Let's get together soon?"

Kassidy nodded again, and Abigail walked away, her phone to her ear.

Feeling the iron table under her fingers was soothing. It was strong and felt like an anchor to the earth. She took a few more deep breaths and stood up. Thankfully, she didn't feel woozy. She didn't want to let the strange encounter ruin her afternoon in a city she rarely got to visit.

***

Brett felt invigorated after the presentations. Spending time with colleagues he didn't get to see much and bouncing ideas off each other for the training, had been the inspiration he needed after last night's shooting.

It was right before five o'clock when he left the building and hit her number in his phone.

"Hey." Her voice was happy as she answered, but there was something below the surface that was a bit off. Frustrated? Shaken?

"Hi. How's your afternoon going?" He cradled his phone on his shoulder so he could unlock his car and put the laptop back in his trunk.

"It's been good. I walked around for a while, went in a few of the shops, and now I'm at the bookstore…where I've been the majority of the time."

He swore he could hear the pages turning over the phone. He'd been impressed at how the inside of her apartment already looked like a small library. She had several floor-to-ceiling book shelves, with her treasures packed to the brim, but neatly arranged. There were other random groupings of books spread throughout the home, but all organized in a way that said she couldn't stand to see something of such importance the least bit out of place. Many of them were filled with sticky notes where she'd found favorite scenes or quotes. It was clear that when she wasn't writing, she was reading.

"Adding to your collection?" he teased.

"How can I not? I keep remembering books I've read in the past and have been looking for. And there are lots of new books that sound interesting."

He laughed. "I'm glad you're enjoying yourself. I guess I never thought to spend so much time in a bookstore. I go in, get the book I want, and leave."

"Well, you should try it sometime. It's so fun to look around, do a bit of reading, wonder how many you could buy and still keep your utilities on…"

"Yeah, I'm gonna come get you now. Not sure I'll ever see you again otherwise." He was already walking across the street toward the store.

"Probably a good idea," she agreed.

He smirked as she met him outside the store with a reusable bag full of books. "You came prepared, I see." He gave her the kiss he'd been wanting to since her tease outside the police station, and she grinned up at him with a shrug.

"How'd the presentations go?" She poked him in the ribs, and they started walking toward Old Town Auburn for dinner.

"Really good. Got some great feedback and ideas for changes. And it was cool to see the Auburn guys again."

"I'm glad," she said, taking his hand as they walked through the town square.

Something about the gesture felt like she was looking for comfort, so he looked down at her face, brushing her hair behind her ear so he could see her eyes.

"Everything okay?"

"Uh, yeah."

He could tell she was struggling with what she was going to say. This morning she'd been fine. What had happed in the last few hours?

"Well, not okay." She sighed and stopped walking.

He stopped, still holding her hand, but studying her eyes. Something was causing her pain, and he wished he could fix it. He waited quietly until she was ready to go on.

"I ran into an old friend from San Francisco, across the street there," she pointed. "It threw me. She and I were close at first, but I always felt like she had a thing for Kurt. I think she may have had an affair with him. She's living in Sacramento now. I think she might have moved here because things with Kurt didn't go well. She said she'd never leave the Bay Area. Seeing her took me right back there, and I hate revisiting those memories if I don't have to."

"I'm sorry." He squeezed her hand. "Can I do something to help?"

She shook her head, looking into the distance. "I don't think so. I guess I have to be able to deal with my past when it comes up."

They walked on in silence. He didn't know what to say. He liked to make things right. It was part of his job, and it pissed him off when he couldn't do it in regular life.

They stopped in front of Old Town Pizza. She looked up at him. Did she look a little guilty?

"Is there something else?" He pulled her close.

She sighed, a distant look in her eyes. "Abigail, my friend, told me something about Kurt, but I think she was wrong. I don't want to go over it. I want to enjoy my time with you."

He nodded, a surge of anger going through him, but he tried to keep his expression neutral. He wished there was a way to find some evidence on that asshole. He shouldn't get to keep living in Kassie's life. He wanted her to tell him what this Abigail lady had said, but he didn't want to push her. She'd tell him at some point.

CHAPTER 10

On Monday morning Kassidy went for an early run. She hadn't been able to run much since moving back to Sacramento, and it felt good to free her mind for a while. She tried to listen to her music and focus on her breathing, but the encounter with Abigail kept swimming into her thoughts. She couldn't think about it too long, or she'd start feeling that old familiar panic again, but it was so hard to push the experience away.

There'd be no reason for Kurt to be in Sacramento. Even if his company did some business here, some of his underlings would take care of it. Abigail was still into Kurt. He had probably axed her from his life, and she couldn't let go. Kassidy knew how charming he could be – and how intimidating. Kassidy hadn't sensed any fear from Abigail, only curiosity.

But even if he had been in Sacramento, what did it matter? He hadn't tried to contact her, and she knew he wouldn't. She wanted to believe he didn't know she lived here, as she had never told him, but with his connections, she was sure he knew. Logically, it didn't matter if he was here. Except it did, because he terrified her.

And then there's the fact that you didn't tell Brett what Abigail said.

She felt guilty about that, but it was too awkward. Besides, she didn't want him thinking she was paranoid about her ex – that she couldn't move past him. She had been nervous about starting something with Brett, but she was fast realizing she wanted it. She didn't want to screw it up.

When she got home, she showered and got dressed quickly. Then she drove to Mercy General Hospital on J Street in East Sacramento. She was working on a profile piece for *Sacramento Magazine* about a prominent Sacramento restaurant owner's brain aneurism recovery. After weeks in the hospital, and a major surgery, Jack Murphy had been lucky enough to survive. It was several months later, and he was returning to the hospital to thank the staff. He had agreed to sit down with Kassidy for an interview.

He was not only a restaurateur, but was heavily involved in the Sacramento community, had been married for twenty years, and had three teenage sons. A photographer for the magazine met her there and took some candid and posed photographs for the piece, including photographs of the man and his family in heartfelt conversations with the medical staff.

"I don't know about you, but I ran the spectrum of emotions about my life on a daily basis before this happened to me," Jack reflected. "I loved my work, but sometimes it felt like too much, like everyone was demanding something of me. I sometimes went down the bitter road of thinking people only wanted me around so I would give them money. I loved my family more than anything, but raising kids who are trying to become their own people and find their own ways in the world is hard. I was taking everything for granted, just trying to survive each day.

"This was a wake-up call for me. Being alive every day is a privilege. Not easy to be sure, but still a privilege. My work and the dedicated people involved in my restaurants are gifts. Being married to such a powerhouse woman and watching my boys grow into young men is something I need to try to stop and cherish more. I almost lost all of it."

Kassidy also spoke with the hospital's chief medical officer. He related how overjoyed the hospital staff was to be part of Mr. Murphy's extraordinary recovery, and that the best reward for all of them was to see the man doing so well.

"It really speaks to the strength of the human spirit that the result of such a cruel and traumatic situation was the positive change in Mr. Murphy's outlook on life. He knows this could have ended in a very different way. He's had to work hard and go through a lot of pain to get where he is now, so it's impressive that he still feels he's the better for it happening," the physician said.

"Working with people who survive horrible conditions like this must be such a rewarding part of a doctor's, or any medical provider's, career," Kassidy commented as their interview ended and she packed up her recorder and notebook.

"Everyone is a survivor of something, Ms. Turner. Yes, you're right, this is a very rewarding part of our job. But sometimes I find it's more important that we as medical professionals remember that all people have overcome, or are currently dealing with, any number of difficult things. Many aren't obvious when looking at the person. Many aren't diagnosable conditions or diseases. I think remembering this and considering it in our treatments and interactions can help us all be better health care providers, and people."

The words ran through Kassidy's mind long after she left the hospital. Could she be considered a survivor? She didn't feel like one, but maybe she was in a way. There must be so many people out there with fascinating survivor stories to tell. Not only medical ailments, as the physician mentioned, but survivors of all kinds of things. Wouldn't it be interesting to tell their stories?

***

Brett called Kassidy early Friday morning. He was shaking as he held his phone. His heart wouldn't slow, so he was taking deep breaths. He'd changed and scrubbed his hands and arms raw, but he was sure he could still smell blood. Faces flashed through his mind. Faces he wished he could forget for a little while. He wondered if he'd ever sleep again.

She picked up after several rings. It was early. He'd woken her. She sounded like she was mostly still asleep. He felt bad, but he needed her. She was the closest thing he had to family here.

"Brett?" she mumbled. "Are you okay?"

"Hey. I'm sorry to call you so early. Can I come over?" He couldn't answer her question. He wasn't. He didn't want to say so.

"Of course. Where are you?" She suddenly sounded much more awake.

"I'm close. I'll be there soon."

He had to force himself to climb the steps to her apartment. He was so exhausted, but so wired. She was waiting for him in her pajamas at the top of the stairs, worry written all across her face.

"Your shift isn't over for another couple hours," she said as if the obvious needed to be stated in order to give the situation some sort of normalcy.

"My lieutenant told me to leave early," he mumbled. He felt as if he could curl in on himself.

She closed and locked her door, putting one hand on his arm. She moved it up to his hair in a comforting gesture. He saw her eyes widen as she spotted something on the side of his face. That confirmed he hadn't gotten all of it. Maybe that explained the smell.

"Brett?" She'd gotten a wash cloth from a cabinet in her hallway and put it to his face tenderly.

He felt himself start to shake again and grabbed her into a hug, the wash cloth falling to the floor. She put her head to his chest and wrapped her arms around him. He wouldn't let himself cry. It'd been years since he let himself fall apart like that. But his body protested by shaking more violently.

She pulled him over to the couch. "Sit. I'll be right back." She teleported to her kitchen and back, holding a glass of water out to him.

He tried to drink some, but mostly stared into it, calming himself down.

"What happened?" she murmured, sitting down next to him.

"I can't right now," he answered, shaking his head. How could he ever put something so horrific into words? He never wanted her to have to imagine what he'd seen the night before.

"That's fine. You're safe and here now. That's what matters to me." She put her arms back around him and he leaned into her. This was what he needed. What would he have done without her in this moment?

"You'll stay here and get some rest," she said with conviction and got up, pulling him after her. He felt like he was dead on his feet, but he followed after her.

She pulled back the covers on her bed and nearly pushed him into it. He wanted to smile at her, but even that felt like it would take too much effort. She laid down next to him. His mind was suddenly like a fog. He still saw their faces, but his eyes were so heavy, even they couldn't keep him awake. He was sure he'd welcome them in his nightmares. He never slept in this many clothes, but there was no way he had the energy to remove them.

She curled into him, rubbing his right arm and along the side of his back. It felt so good to have her this close. He wanted to kiss her, explore her body with his hands, but his mind was already drifting into dream images.

He jumped awake in a cold sweat, struggling to get his drenched shirt off. For a moment he forgot where he was and looked around him. She was still in the bed next to him, and she barely stirred. Kassidy's apartment. He was fine. He checked her bedside clock. Only an hour had passed. He couldn't remember what had woken him, and that was okay. He settled down, finding different designs in her popcorn ceiling. He pictured himself on a beach. He was relaxing with her on the sand, and he had nothing to worry about. He finally felt sleep claiming him again. How long would it last this time?

***

Mind groggy, she slowly opened her eyes. She was facing him, but he was on his back, his arm thrown over his face. The blanket was pulled up over his waist, and his shirt had been discarded somewhere. Her thoughts started to wander to images of their two bodies together, and she felt herself blush. She peered at her clock. It was just after eight. She fought the urge to jump out of bed. She never let herself sleep this late. She padded as quietly to her dresser as her apartment's creaky floors would allow. She whirled around to make sure she hadn't woken him, but he hadn't moved. She crept into her bathroom and showered. After she was done, she switched on the news at an almost non-existent volume.

A recap of their top stories gave her the answer: a drive-by shooting in a neighborhood in Brett's beat around nine-thirty the night before. A mother and her three children had been caught in the gunfire.

"Although police and fire responders are reported to have arrived within minutes of the shooting, the mother and two children were pronounced dead at the scene. The third child was taken to UC Davis Medical Center, where he is listed in critical condition." The anchor read the story with genuine concern on her face. She went on to say the woman's husband was a truck driver and had been working, but had arrived at the hospital early this morning.

Kassidy wiped a stream of tears from her cheeks. Her heart ached for that man. He'd lost so much of his life in a such a short, horrific moment in time. She turned to look toward her bedroom. She knew Brett had been there. She couldn't imagine the multitude of feelings he must be having. She wished she could take them from him.

She tiptoed to the doorway of her bedroom. He had kicked the blanket almost all the way off now. He was lying on his stomach, his head under the same arm. She was tempted to go lay next to him and pull him close. But if there was a chance he was getting any kind of sleep, she didn't want to interrupt that. She knew he usually slept into the afternoon.

Besides, her laptop and too many articles waited. She was able to lose herself in that for a few hours and then she heard the floorboards creaking in her bedroom. He came around the corner, looking like he'd been caught in a hurricane. He pulled on his shirt, and she scolded herself for her quick feeling of disappointment.

More important things going on right now, you jerk!

"Good morning." She gave him a small smile from her couch, putting her laptop on her coffee table. She tried to gauge his emotions, but exhaustion was all she could see on his face.

"Morning. Thanks for letting me crash here."

"Of course. How are you?" It was a stupid question, but she wasn't sure what else to say.

"I'm okay." He studied her face for a moment. "You must have watched the news."

She nodded slowly. "I'm so sorry, Brett. I can't imagine…"

He sighed and didn't make eye contact with her. "Yeah. I was one of the first ones there. I tried to stop the bleeding, but there was so much…" A noticeable shiver ran through him and he took a deep breath.

She got up and pulled him onto the couch, sitting down next to him. She got as close to him as possible, which calmed him down a little. She took both his hands in hers.

He stared silently at their hands for several long minutes before he took another deep breath. "I've gotten used to a lot of weird and somewhat disturbing things. Sometimes I feel like I've become pretty jaded. But there are some things you never get used to."

"I'm sure. I don't know how you could."

They were quiet for a while. Then she remembered he might be hungry.

"Do you want some coffee and breakfast?"

"That'd be great," he said without hesitation.

"Do you have to work tonight?" she asked, pouring him a cup of coffee and cracking some eggs into a bowl.

"No, my lieutenant doesn't want me to come back until after my regular days off. And no overtime. I also have to set up a session with a counselor. I guess they've never seen me that shaken. I hate that they saw me like that."

"I know, but I'm sure it affected everyone there more than you realize, Brett. With little kids…I'm trying to say I'm sure you won't be the only one needing to talk to someone. You're all human."

He nodded, taking the bread she passed him and starting the toaster. He took several long swigs of coffee and was silent as she cooked.

"Do you want to spend the day together? Maybe we can take it easy? Watch some movies? Whatever you want."

"Aren't you busy with your articles?" he replied, trying to stop a yawn.

"I'll forever be busy with my articles," she said with a sigh. "But I don't have any deadlines until next week, and since it's Friday, most sources probably won't get back to me today. I'd like to be with you."

"That sounds nice," he said, taking a plate of food from her. "Do you mind if we go to my place? You can meet my socially-anxious cat."

"Sure. I can't wait to see this cat," she replied with a laugh, and he smirked back.

She packed a few things before they left, assuming she might end up staying the night. She left her car and they drove over in his. He was quiet, but kept a hold on her hand.

As they went through an intersection not far from her apartment, a car turning right squealed around the corner and had to slam on its brakes to avoid hitting them. Kassidy jumped and looked in the rearview mirror, her heart hammering. The driver quickly backed off, giving an apologetic wave.

"You okay?" He gave her a quick glance and frowned in his mirror.

"They need to slow the hell down. There're people walking all over here."

His mini rant took enough time that she didn't have to answer his question. She'd been jumpier since seeing Abigail. Her mind immediately leapt to Kurt, but she checked the mirror again. The driver was a woman. Not Kurt. Just another impatient California driver.

Stop it. There is no reason for Kurt to be anywhere near here. He's not in Sacramento. You're freaking out over nothing.

Still, she was happy when they got on the freeway and the car behind them kept going down the city street.

Kassidy heard meowing as they walked through the front door of Brett's house. There was Isla, caught off guard by her presence. Brett wasn't lying. The cat froze in the middle of the entryway, mere feet from Kassidy.

Kassidy couldn't help but laugh, and Brett's face lit up with the smallest smile. "Kassie, this is Isla. Isla, Kassie is really nice. You should get used to her."

"Hi, sweet girl," Kassidy said, but didn't reach toward the cat. Maybe in time Isla would warm up to her. She'd had several cats growing up, and she missed having one now. The last one she almost considered hers belonged to one of her roommates in San Francisco. It'd been a cute little thing whose favorite pastime was playing fetch like a dog. She was attached to Kassidy, and it had been hard to leave her behind.

His house had three bedrooms, one living area in the front, and a small dining area off the kitchen. It wasn't huge but felt big compared to her apartment.

When they got back to the front of the house, Isla froze by the couch.

"I'm gonna give her some food and then go shower. I won't be long. Make yourself at home."

She sat down on the couch as he padded back to his bedroom. She checked her phone and noticed she already had an e-mail with edits to one of her articles. As she was reading through them, she felt a bump against her leg. She looked down in surprise to find Isla sitting right in front of her, looking up into her eyes.

It was Kassidy's turn to freeze, not sure how she should respond. "Hi, Isla. Are you having a change of heart?"

She reached out her hand, and the cat sniffed it curiously, moving on to rubbing against Kassidy's legs. Kassidy shrugged and tried petting her, and Isla started to purr. She had to keep herself from laughing in surprise, afraid it would startle the cat.

Brett returned a short time later, wearing sweat pants and a t-shirt, which displayed the muscles on his arms nicely. His hair was still damp and his eyes were a little red. Kassidy's heart hurt for him.

His jaw dropped when he saw Isla sitting on Kassidy's lap, still purring. "Uh, what's happening?"

"You have the sweetest cat. She's such a love." Kassidy looked down at Isla and scratched her behind the ears.

"What did you do to her?" He let out a shocked laugh.

"I was just sitting here. She came over to me. She started rubbing herself on my legs and then jumped up. I don't think she's anti-social. I think she needs some time to warm up, and maybe it helps when you're not around."

He laughed again at this comment. "Well, that makes sense, but I think it has more to do with you, Kassie." There was such warmth and meaning in his eyes that she could only smile.

Why didn't I understand before that this is how it's supposed to be?

He flopped down on the couch next to her and they surfed through channels for a while before finding *Happy Gilmore*. Comedy seemed like the thing he needed, so they settled in to watch. Brett slowly sank down into the couch and was asleep before half the movie was over. She watched him for a while as his breathing became slow and rhythmic.

She remembered what the hospital's chief medical officer had said about everyone being a survivor of something. That little boy lying in the hospital bed was a survivor, but Brett was, too. She felt called now to tell the stories of people who had overcome different types of obstacles, dealt with different kinds of hardship. She carefully got up from the couch and took her phone into one of Brett's spare rooms.

He had set it up as an office, but it didn't look like he had much chance to use it. Most of the furniture was covered in a fine layer of dust. Pictures of people she was sure were his parents and sisters sat in frames on shelves on the far side of the room. The largest photograph showed his parents, sisters, their significant others and Brett grouped together on a beach. It couldn't have been taken long ago, because Brett looked around the same age. He looked so happy in that picture. She sighed. It was clear how much he missed his family.

She called her editor at *Sacramento Magazine* and left a message. Her idea for a survivor story came tumbling out of her, and she was sure the voicemail would cut her off. She hung up, excitement coursing through her.

She got an almost immediate call back. "I love the idea!" her editor gushed. "I'll put out a call on our website. I'll give them a voicemail number here you can check and also give them our general email. We can forward anything your way. Let's see what we get."

Kassidy was thrilled. She couldn't wait to see who reached out.

CHAPTER 11

Brett had mixed feelings about October. In October, Sacramento weather tried to cool down – sometimes even tried to rain. He missed the beating sun. Summer was his favorite time of year, and while California fire season meant the state desperately needed cooler, rainy weather, he missed that heat every year.

This October had also brought a few sessions of therapy. Not something he was keen about, but something he recognized he might need after the shooting. Things at work were going fine, but he still felt like his lieutenant was keeping a sharper eye on him. He'd already been to visit the surviving boy once in the hospital. He had a lot of work ahead of him, but his father's company had raised a chunk of money to help pay medical expenses and was allowing him to have some time off to be with his son. Brett had donated his overtime pay for the months of August and September to the family, and he wanted to give more.

The end of October would bring the beginning of the detective hiring process, starting with an interview panel. Excitement and anxiety filled him when he thought about this. He felt good about his odds, but he wanted it so much at this point, what would it feel like if he didn't get it? He loved patrol, but would it still be enough if he was passed over for detective?

And there was Kassidy. She had become his light, keeping him focused and grounded. They'd been dating for over a month, and with their busy schedules, he tried to spend as much time with her as he could. Fall was her favorite time of year, so that was a point in its favor.

Kassidy was so giving, wanting to be there for him and support him whenever she could, but she was also exhausted most of the time, because her work was running her dry. He didn't want to push her to look for a permanent job, one that might offer a little more stability, but he wished she felt confident enough to do that herself.

She had bounced back from her meeting with Abigail, although she'd never told him what the woman said about Kurt. She hadn't run into the former friend in Sacramento, so that must have helped. Sometimes though, she'd get a distant look in her eye, and he wondered what she was thinking about. When he tried to ask, she'd smile and mention some article. Her latest series about survivors was going well, with one already published and many more interviews in the bag. She was on the lookout for the next inspiring person to shine a light on. He loved hearing her talk about these stories, because her face would literally brighten and she would pace the room, using her hands while talking. He'd never seen her so excited.

One afternoon, before he had to work, they strolled downtown streets, scoping out spots for a late lunch. Leaves were starting to fill gutters, making sure Sacramento residents knew the season really was changing. These late lunches had become routine for them since he slept through mornings and worked nights. Late lunches gave them the most amount of time together before he had to get ready for work.

She suddenly froze at the sight of two people approaching them. "My parents."

"What?" He tried to see who she was talking about, but since there were a number of people walking by, he wasn't sure who she meant.

"How are they randomly in downtown Sacramento on the same street as us at the exact same time?" She stopped walking.

"GPS tracking?" He grinned.

"Sometimes I wonder, to be honest." She sighed. "Should we duck into the next building?"

"Kassie." He couldn't help but laugh. Was this self-sufficient, determined woman really worried about him meeting her parents?

"I guess you're right. I told them we were dating, but they're…a lot sometimes."

"It'll be fine." He squeezed her hand. He wanted to be utter confidence for her, but if he'd been sitting down, his foot would have been tapping. He hadn't been in a relationship for a long time, so it had been a long time since he had to pass milestones like meeting parents.

"Kassidy!" Her dad spotted her first and waved.

Brett saw her mother's face light up at seeing them together, identical to how Kassidy's lit up when telling him about a story. Next to him, Kassidy groaned and Brett chuckled, putting his arm around her waist.

"Hey, kiddo." Her dad gave her a hug, and her mom was positively glowing.

"Hi, Dad, Mom. I didn't think you ever came downtown." She sounded so nervous, and Brett wished he could take that all from her. He wasn't basing their relationship on what her parents thought.

"We usually don't, but we decided to get out and do something different today. We had lunch, and now we're taking a walk." Annie Turner frowned at her daughter, but instantly changed her expression to a smile when she made eye contact with him.

Kassidy nodded in a casual way, but her body still felt tense. "Sorry, Mom, Dad, this is Brett. Brett, these are my parents, Matt and Annie Turner." Her smile was easy when she looked up at him, and he couldn't help but return the gesture. God, it was exciting to have her look at him like that.

"Nice to meet both of you," Brett said, offering his hand. While Annie's joyful feelings about him were written all over her face, Matt clearly held a mix of conflicting thoughts. He was friendly, but there was no trust in his eyes. Brett couldn't blame him.

"It's nice to meet you, too, Brett." Annie grinned. "We've heard so much about you."

Kassidy tensed again, and Brett could tell which parent got to her easier.

"Kassidy mentioned you're a police officer," her father added.

"Yes, sir. I've been with Sac PD for about five years. Before that I worked for the Orange County Sheriff's Department."

Matt nodded, looking satisfied with his answer.

"So, what are you two up to today?" Annie asked, still smiling at Brett.

"We're about to have lunch. Brett works nights, so…"

Okay, now Brett wanted to tease her for feeling the need to justify why they were eating lunch so late.

Her mother nodded, unfazed. And then, without skipping a beat, "Brett, you should join us for dinner soon. We'd love to get to know you better – if your schedule permits it of course."

"That'd be great. I have regular nights off every week," Brett answered without hesitation. Kassidy squeezed his hand, but before she could say anything, he continued, "I have this Sunday night off if that works."

"Yes, that works fine." Annie didn't even glance at her husband to confirm.

Matt was grinning at his daughter, and Brett had to hold in his laughter. Kassidy was shooting daggers at her father with her eyes.

"Kassidy?" Annie was frowning again, trying to get her daughter's attention.

"Sorry, what?" Kassidy turned back to her mother.

"I said, I think Simon and Carla would like to join us. Does six-thirty work?" Annie raised an eyebrow at her daughter, even with the smile still on her face.

"I…yes, I think so," Kassidy stuttered.

"Great. We'll see you both then. We'll let you get back to your lunch hunt." Annie was basically beaming, and Matt smirked at his daughter as he waved goodbye.

"What happened? I think I blacked out for a bit." Kassidy was slightly pale.

Brett laughed out loud, any tension he'd had now drifting away with the retreating figures of her parents. "It'll be fun. I'm sure they want to know more about me."

"Well, they should know you're a sweet, brave man who has no idea the third degree he's in for." She sighed. "And did you notice how she threw my brother and sister-in-law in there? Does she plan their social calendar?"

He pulled her chin up and gave her the type of long, slow kiss he looked forward to when they were together. When they pulled apart, he could feel her heart thumping in her chest, and he had to slow his breathing.

"Okay, well, I can barely remember my own name now, so I guess it's all good." She laughed and pulled him forward in search of food.

He couldn't wait for them to be alone.

***

"He wants us to terminate Timothy Connell!" Mary fumed, slamming a folder down in front of Christopher.

"I can only guess you mean your favorite client, but who is Timothy Connell?" Christopher picked up the folder to peruse its contents in a bored sort of way.

"A major technology competitor of Kurt's. I'm sure they've met several

times, but Kurt has no beef with him other than the fact that he's competition." She paced the room.

"Mary, sit down. You make me dizzy when you pace. So, he wants him terminated. You said the boss gave you a warning about Kurt's requests. Just arrange it."

"Timothy Fucking Connell, Christopher! The man might as well be the next Steve Jobs. We can't terminate him. How does he think we'd even pull that off?"

"Because we're the best at what we do, and that's what he's paying for. Not to mention, we've terminated people at that status before. It's all about the plan you come up with and who you put on the job." Christopher shrugged.

"With the notoriety and wealth that man has, the investigation would be ruthless. They wouldn't stop until they found something."

"Mary, you've developed airtight scenarios hundreds of times before. You don't have time to develop a suicidal story, so it can be an accident. Even people with notoriety and money get in accidents." He sighed in frustration, as if she was taking up his time with meaningless conversation.

"This guy's gonna have security," she grumbled.

"So, your operatives infiltrate that security. You've done this before. I know you're holding a grudge against Kurt, but you do realize your life is at stake? You do actually understand that?"

"I'm not an idiot, Christopher. But this doesn't make sense. There will be too much attention surrounding this. And now he's killing off his competition? It's asinine! We can't do this."

Christopher was silent. He appeared to be working again.

"I'd like to approach the boss about it, but he's been brainwashed by Kurt's wealth. In the past he would have nixed this. I'll have to delay it by saying how complicated it is to plan. Once Kurt fucks something up somewhere and the boss gets his shit together, it'll be canceled." Mary kept talking, even though Christopher pretended to ignore her. Mary knew better. Christopher could never ignore drama.

He leaned forward suddenly, staring directly into her eyes.

"You know if you don't arrange this, someone else will. They'll give it to someone else, and you'll be terminated."

"At least when it comes back to bite the organization, it won't be connected to me. And the boss is not going to terminate me for this. I've been one of his most valuable project managers for years. He's kissing Kurt's ass now, but he'll snap out of it after a while."

She tried to sound confident. She was tired of Christopher's arrogant bullshit. And she was *confident. There was no way in hell the boss would ever have her terminated. He liked to scare people into doing what he wanted. And the money Kurt gave him was a large, yet temporary, distraction. He valued her, and that ran deeper than any pot of gold. She was sure. Wasn't she?*

CHAPTER 12

On Friday night Kassidy called the voicemail the magazine had set up for her survivor stories. She'd gotten a flurry of messages in the beginning, mostly from people calling to nominate others for her series. Things were slowing down now. There were only two messages that night. One caught her interest immediately, because she hadn't received a message like it yet.

"Hi, my name is Alexis. I'm not sure if I should be doing this, so if you want to call me, I'd like to meet and talk in person before I agree to be in your article. I'm a rape survivor, and I've never told my story. I want to talk to you…if you're interested."

She left her number. The area code was from the Bay Area. Kassidy listened to the message two more times, making sure she had the number right. Something was nagging her. It couldn't be. Her first name was given in the call to readers. Did Alexis recognize it? Was someone finally willing to come forward? No. She squashed that idea. It would be too big of a coincidence. There were too many people with that area code. The odds of this woman being Kurt's victim were slim.

Saturday morning, she dialed Alexis's number, but it took several rings before anyone picked up.

"Hello?" came the quiet answer.

"Hi, Alexis? This is Kassidy Turner from *Sacramento Magazine*. I got your voicemail and was hoping to talk to you about your story."

"Hi, Kassidy. Thank you for calling me." If Alexis recognized her name, she didn't give any indication.

"You said you'd like to meet in person to talk first? Do you have any time this coming week?"

"Yes. Would Tuesday morning work? Can we meet at McKinley Park?" She didn't sound like she would be flexible with the plan.

"Sure, that sounds good. I can text you when I get there." Kassidy wanted to be somewhat in control of the meeting. She liked to give people the benefit of the doubt, but it was good to be careful.

"Okay. See you Tuesday, Kassidy." Alexis ended the call. But not before Kassidy detected a note of something in the way the woman said her name. She wasn't sure what it was, but it was there. It didn't sound dark. Maybe hopeful?

***

Sunday arrived quickly, and Brett's nerves had kicked in.

Calm down. It's only dinner with her parents...and brother and sister-in-law. She'd have met yours by now if they lived close. You've been through actual life and death situations. This is not something to be nervous about.

But those thoughts didn't help. He hadn't had to do anything like this in a long time. He tried to tell himself that if he wasn't dealing with the trauma of the shooting and confronting it head on in his therapy, his nerves wouldn't have such a hold on him. But he wasn't sure if that was true.

He didn't talk to Kassidy about the shooting. She knew the basics, and he wouldn't wish more details on anyone, certainly not her. His therapist worked with law enforcement clients on a daily basis, so the experience wasn't as shocking to him.

Another person might have pulled back from work after that kind of experience, but Brett had thrown himself into it even more, as if he needed to prove he could give well above what the job asked of him. He'd gone back to taking the kind of overtime he had before he'd met Kassidy. She was understanding, because she'd been busier than normal with her regular articles and the more-demanding survivor pieces. Things would change when he became a detective, so he should get as much out of patrol as he could.

He picked her up late Sunday afternoon, and she met him with an intense kiss, not even bothering to close the passenger door when she climbed into his car. He was double parked with his car running in front of her apartment.

"Maybe we could hang out alone tonight?" Her meaning was clear, a sultry look on her face.

They hadn't slept together yet, not that they hadn't talked about it and been tempted to, but since they both felt this relationship was leading them to a future together, they had decided there was no need to rush. They would know when the time was right. But with that kiss and expression, he would like nothing more than to slam the car into drive, find whatever parking spot he could and carry her up to her apartment. He was already picturing her body beneath his as he had so many times before.

He shook his head and had to take few deep breaths. "That's not fair, Kass. I know what you're trying to do, and you will not be safe later." He ran his hand along her inner thigh and her breath caught as she leaned in to kiss him again, running her hand through his hair.

He reluctantly broke away. She was not making this easy. "We're going to dinner. You're not getting out of it."

She sighed, sitting back in her seat with a groan. "You're a guy. Can't you think like a guy?"

He laughed. "Sorry, lady. I'm used to people trying to play dirty."

"Dating a cop was a bad idea," she muttered and he grinned back.

He took her hand. "It'll be fine. No matter what they throw at me, I won't run away."

"You shouldn't make promises you might not be able to keep," she pouted, and he laughed at the pitiful expression.

"It's great to see you," Annie Turner gushed as she opened the door, hugging her daughter. Brett could see the pained expression on Kassie's face, and he looked away to hide his smirk.

"Hi, Mom."

"Nice to see you again, Mrs. Turner." Brett shook her hand, but she also pulled him into a hug.

"Please call me Annie." There was a beam of light flowing from her face. "Would you like anything to drink, Brett?"

"I'm fine for now. Thanks." He smiled as she ushered them inside.

"Mom, can I have some…" Kassidy started, but Annie didn't hear her. Kassidy frowned and threw a glare at Brett, but he made sure to be look elsewhere when he felt her eyes on him.

Annie led them into the family room, where Matt Turner was chatting with who must be Kassidy's brother, Simon, and his wife Carla. The house felt warm and full of life. There was soft music playing in the background somewhere, and he swore he smelled both cooking meat and cookies. Kassie might have to deal with coming over here more often.

Matt shook his hand firmly, but there was that same cautious look in his eyes. His daughter was misused in the past, and Brett was sure it would be hard for him to trust the new person in her life. Simon and Carla both stood to introduce themselves and shook Brett's hand. Carla hugged her sister-in-law with a huge smile.

"Thanks for coming out." Her father motioned toward the love seat that sat perpendicular to the couch and large stone fireplace.

"Thanks for having us. We were looking forward to it," Brett lied for both of them.

They sat down and Annie returned from the kitchen, bringing glasses of wine for Simon and Carla.

"Do I live in a sitcom?" Kassidy muttered, and Brett squeezed her hand.

"Dinner will be ready in about ten minutes." Annie smiled and sat down in an antique armchair. "I hope you like steak, Brett. Kassidy told me you eat meat." She sounded a little unsure, as if her daughter might have given her false information. Kassidy sighed.

"She was right, and that sounds delicious. Thank you," he said with what he hoped was a charming grin. Kassidy bumped his arm gratefully with hers.

"So, Brett, you said you used to work for Orange County. What made you want to move to Northern California?" her father asked with interest.

He sat up straighter in his seat and felt Kassidy shift. She was nervous for him. He wouldn't tell them about the divorce, but there were actual reasons he had wanted to move up here. "It was a few things. I was born and raised in Orange County, so I wanted to experience another part of the state. I did some research on different departments, and I liked what I read about Sacramento. The summer weather and proximity to the ocean sounded ideal. We lived in Costa Mesa until I was in eighth grade, and then we moved to Santa Ana when my dad got a new job. I don't like being too far from the ocean. Overall, I liked how centrally located Sacramento is."

"Was it a culture shock for you? I don't know if Kassie told you I lived in Riverside until I was fifteen. Then my father passed away and we moved up here to be closer to my mother's family. It was definitely an adjustment for me."

Brett was instantly more at ease. Another person who had grown up in Southern California. It was like the universe had given him something to make this meeting easier. "I didn't know that," he responded with a grin to Kassie, who shrugged her shoulders with a feigned guilty expression. "It was an adjustment, for sure. We only ever visited San Francisco once when I was in fifth grade, and besides that, the farthest north I went was Fullerton for college."

"That's still in the northern part of Orange County," Kassidy explained to a confused-looking Carla, giving Brett a playful shove.

Easy laughter filled the room, and Kassidy's sigh of relief was loud enough for Brett to hear.

"Kassidy, did I tell you we ran into one of your friends when we were downtown?" Annie broke in. The timer sounded in the kitchen. Matt went to turn it off and retrieve the meat, while Simon and Carla made their way to the dining room.

Kassie had been leading Brett toward the dining room, but stopped so suddenly, he nearly ran into her. "Oh, really? Who?"

"Your friend from college, Abigail. She was out with a couple friends and she stopped us. It was right after we ran into you. She remembered us from the couple times she visited with you. Such a nice girl. She said she was living in Sacramento now. Have you been able to see her?"

Brett noticed Kassie's face had lost color, but she tried to smile weakly. "I-I did run into her once, but we must have different schedules. I haven't seen her downtown."

"She gave me her number to pass on to you in case you didn't have it anymore. I'll give it to you before you go."

"Okay," Kassidy murmured at her mother's retreating back.

Brett pulled her chin up to look into her eyes. "You okay? You didn't look so good for a sec there. Having the same feelings as when you saw her?"

"Yeah, but I'll be fine. It's strange that I'd run into her in a completely different city and then she sees my parents downtown. Small world, I guess." She took a deep breath and smiled up at him.

"Yeah. Do you want to talk…" he started to say.

"No, that's okay. I'm still working through a lot of my San Francisco stuff. Therapy helps a lot."

"Give yourself time. It wasn't that long ago." He kissed her lightly.

Dinner was much the same in terms of easy conversation. There was even a chance to impersonate Luke Skywalker after Simon mimicked Han Solo. Kassie rolled her eyes, but laughed. Yep, Brett liked this family.

The drive back to Kassie's place was mostly quiet, as she stared out the window, looking lost in thought.

"Thank you for tonight. You were right. It went well, and I appreciate you being up for it," she said with a soft smile as she looked up at him, linking her arm in his.

"No problem." He grinned. "It was fun. I was hoping they wouldn't despise me too much."

"Not possible." She rolled her eyes and kissed him at the door. "Do you want to come in?"

"Absolutely. We have some unfinished business."

"What?" She laughed as she closed the door behind them.

"I said you wouldn't be safe later," he said, pulling her close and drawing her into a painfully slow kiss. He ran his hand from her thigh up the side of her rib cage. She let out a small gasp and her breaths became more ragged. His hands slipped up under her shirt, rubbing her back and toying with her bra clasp.

She pulled him even closer, her fingers sliding through the belt loops of his jeans. His heart felt like it would explode from his chest. He pushed her long hair aside and caught at her earlobe with his lips. She was shaking in his arms as their kiss became more heated. She pushed him up against the wall, and he smiled against her lips. She undid the buttons on his shirt, running her hands along his chest. She removed the shirt all together and hers soon followed. His head swam. He needed her now. He started backing her toward her bedroom, and she didn't protest.

"Brett Green, is this the right time presenting itself?" Her voice was a murmur, a mixture of lust and mirth.

"Yes," he answered matter-of-factly, and she laughed as he picked her up, her legs around his waist, and carried her the rest of the way to her bed.

CHAPTER 13

Kassidy parked her car on the side of McKinley Park and texted Alexis to meet her by the soccer field, which was quiet that morning. She found a bench and waited. She was five minutes early, so she had time to test her recorder in case Alexis felt comfortable being interviewed.

A short-haired brunette, who had to be around Kassidy's age, approached her from the right, looking nervous.

"Kassidy?" She stopped a few feet away.

"Yes, Kassidy Turner. Hi, Alexis." Kassidy smiled and extended her hand as she stood up.

Alexis shook it lightly, and Kassidy motioned toward the bench. Alexis sat down, looking around them. There were people in the park, but no one in their immediate vicinity.

Kassidy studied the woman. Anxiety was written on her face, but there was determination in her eyes. She didn't recognize her at all, not that that meant anything. "I think it's very brave of you to be willing to speak to me. Do you want to tell me a little about your story? Or do you have questions about the series itself?"

"I want to tell you, because you deserve to know."

"I'm sorry?" Kassidy's heart beat sped up.

"It was Kurt. The man who raped me was Kurt. It was close to three years ago, in his office. I was working late. I'd seen him looking at me throughout my time at Reliant, but I knew he had a girlfriend. I had no idea what he'd already done to so many women before me." She stopped talking for a moment, staring at her hands, which were clenched in her lap. "Afterward…he threatened to make my life a living hell if I ever told anyone. He fired me not long after, with more threats. The only person I ever told was my mom. She begged me to go to the police, but I was afraid he'd come after me and her. My mom is the only family I have left. I couldn't do anything that would harm her.

"My name, my real name, was on that list my coworkers gave you over two years ago. After it all happened and I was fired from Kurt's company, I got the hell out of San Francisco. When the story broke that you went to the police and I saw that no one had gone forward with you, I freaked out. I knew a man with power like Kurt's wouldn't let himself be taken down. He threatened to ruin my life, and I believed he would do it. I changed my name, my hair, how I dressed. I didn't feel safe.

"I'm sorry, but I didn't come here to be a part of your series. I live in a Sacramento suburb now, but my mother lives in the city of Sacramento. She signed me up for *Sacramento Magazine* when I moved, trying to help me feel more connected to the area, because I was so miserable. I was on their website the other day, and I saw your name. With the spelling, I thought it had to be you, but I needed to meet you in person and get your last name to be sure."

Kassidy couldn't believe her suspicions had been correct. She hadn't heard from any of Kurt's victims in years. It took her several moments to compose herself.

"If you don't want to come forward, why did you want to talk with me?" Kassidy tried to make her voice as empathetic as possible. It was a legitimate question, not judgement.

"Kurt's a dangerous man, and he's been on the move a lot lately. I came here in hopes of keeping you safe," she said, the volume of her voice dropping so that she was barely whispering by the end.

"On the move?" Kassidy could feel panic building inside her, and she tried to squash it down.

"Everyone who works for him knows he doesn't like to travel outside the Bay Area. He likes to stay tucked away in his opulent little part of the world," she spat the words out, giving her clear opinion of Kurt's lifestyle. "He would have other people take care of all work requiring travel. I have a couple friends who still work for him, and they've been keeping me updated. He's been traveling to Los Angeles frequently, and every now and then to…Sacramento. They don't know why."

Kassidy's heart plummeted into her stomach, and she took several deeps breaths, closing her eyes and concentrating on the tangible things around her. She wouldn't have a panic attack now, not here.

When she opened her eyes and was able to speak again, Alexis looked more than a little worried.

"Sorry, I have a lot of anxiety regarding my experience with Kurt."

"God, I'm sorry. I understand how that feels. I was just…" Alexis looked as if she wanted to reach for Kassidy's hand, but thought better of it.

"No, it's okay. Is there any evidence that Kurt's doing anything wrong?"

"Not that I know of. The people I know inside his company have been trying to keep close tabs on him, but if he's doing anything shady, he's covering it all up. They're afraid of losing their jobs and being blackballed, so they don't want to dig too deep."

"Alexis, I can't get involved in that. I already tried once, and…" Kassidy trailed off. Alexis knew that story.

"No, no. I'm not asking you to. I don't know what Kurt is doing, but he's up to something. And since he's been in Sacramento, I wanted you to know. I didn't want it to be a surprise if he contacts you."

Kassidy nodded. She tried to appear outwardly calm, although her mind was racing. He wouldn't contact her. He had no reason to. He'd already ruined her reputation and pushed her away from the city she loved. "Do you keep in touch with any of his other victims? Any of the others from that list?"

"No," she answered, casting her eyes down at her hands, which she was clasping and unclasping in her lap. "I tried to get away from that life as much as possible. I think a lot of them moved away. I'm sorry. I didn't want you to be caught off guard."

"It's okay. I appreciate it. Can I keep your number in case I need to get in touch with you? You can call or text me anytime."

"Sure, that's fine. Thank you for meeting with me." Alexis stood, giving Kassidy what looked like an attempt at a reassuring smile.

She was gone then, walking back across the park. Kassidy sat back on the bench and, heaving a huge sigh, tried to calm herself down. She closed her eyes and looked up toward the sun, which was partially blocked by the trees surrounding her. He wasn't going to contact her. Who knew what he was doing in Sacramento? Maybe he wanted more control over all parts of his business. Sounded like Kurt. She opened her eyes and looked around the peaceful, green landscape surrounding her, feeling the cool breeze on her face. Would she ever be free from her past?

***

"What is Abigail doing?" Kurt fumed.

"I have no idea." Mary kept her tone even, not taking her eyes from her computer screen. She was doing her best Christopher impression, although Christopher was doing what he usually did when Kurt was around: listening. Mary was done with Kurt. She was strictly business with him now, not giving him any more of her words or time than she had to. Kurt might be approving her projects, but he still needed her, because she was the one who actually knew

how to plan those projects, something he would never understand.

"Your operative hasn't given you any information?" He stared at her, but she kept her eyes on her screen.

"I've told you what he told me. She ran into Kassidy in Auburn. He heard Abigail tell Kassidy she saw you in Sacramento. Kassidy freaked out. They parted ways. Kassidy hasn't seen Abigail since. Abigail then ran into Kassidy's parents seemingly by coincidence, but it doesn't appear you were mentioned. I'm not in constant contact with the operative following Kassidy, because she reports directly to the boss. The updates I receive aren't very informative."

"At least I know I can trust his operative," Kurt replied with a sneer.

Mary said nothing.

"I need you to find out what Abigail is trying to do," he said after a moment, his voice frustrated.

"How did you end things with her? Would she have any reason to want to retaliate?" Mary made eye contact with him as if it was an afterthought.

"She'd been around since Kassidy. I should have cut her loose sooner. She wanted to…" he stopped, a deep frown stretching his face. "She wanted to get married."

Mary had to cough to cover up a laugh. It came out as a choking sound.

Kurt gave her a dark leer. "I told her our time together meant a lot to me, but I wasn't planning on getting married."

Mary raised an eyebrow. She wanted to ask him if Abigail actually fell for that bullshit, but she stopped herself. "So, maybe she's not over you. She ran into Kassidy and her parents, and there's no proof she said anything to Kassidy about you, other than that she saw you in Sacramento. We'll keep watching her. No issue."

"That's supposed to make me feel better with your track record?" He stood and strode from the office.

"Jackass," she muttered as the door closed behind him. From across the room, Christopher almost appeared to smirk.

CHAPTER 14

Brett stepped out of the station into the afternoon light. He breathed a sigh of relief into the chilly air. Halloween was next week, and the sky was overcast for the first time in months. The threat of rain and cold didn't fill him with the usual gloom. Enduring life and new opportunities hung in the air. Nothing could ruin this day.

Kassidy's key was in his hand as he strolled from his car to her place. He spent most of his time there now, unless either one of them had crazy schedules. Then he and Isla would pack up and go home for a few days. Isla hated going back and forth, but everything was forgotten when she was able to jump onto Kassie's lap again. The cat was obsessed.

Today was no different. As he let himself into her apartment, he laughed at Kassie sitting at her dining table, trying to write, and Isla sitting on her lap. But she wasn't curled up and sleeping. She was bumping her head and rubbing her tail against Kassie's chin, begging for attention. Kassie never wanted to kick Isla off her lap, but she wasn't having much success writing.

"Okay," she sighed, picking Isla up and heading for the couch. "You win, pretty girl. How did it go?" She beamed at him as he sat down next to her.

"It was great. I feel really good about it." Brett thought back on the timed panel interview he'd just completed and how easily it had flowed. Next, his supervisor and peers would fill out evaluations about him. If everything continued to go well, he would have an interview with a lieutenant. He was hoping to hear he made detective before Christmas.

"That's awesome. I'm so proud of you. I bet you're glad that part is over. I've never seen you tap your foot so many times as you did over the last few days," she teased, giving him a cheesy grin.

He responded by tickling her until she could barely breath. Isla jumped off the couch, judging him with her eyes.

"You're in trouble." Kassidy laughed, trying to coax Isla back onto the couch, but she sashayed into the kitchen to get some food instead.

Kassidy laid down next to him, her head cushioned against his leg. He sat back, putting his hand on her hip. "I got some other really good news this morning. Mateo's dad called. He was discharged from the hospital. He's still got a lot of physical therapy ahead of him, but he finally got to go home."

"Oh, that's great." She sat up, putting her hand on his cheek. "That must put your mind more at ease."

"Yeah, for sure." He stared into her dazzling eyes. How had she become the most important person in his life in such a short amount of time? He gave her a deep kiss, and she sighed, leaning her head against his chest. Before he realized or could stop it, he felt his foot tapping.

"What's going on there, Green?"

"What?" he asked, trying to sound like nothing had happened.

She pushed herself away from him with a smirk. "You know, the only outward sign of nerves you ever exhibit. What's up?"

No sense trying to deny it. She knew him better than that. He turned toward her, and she looked worried for a moment. He kissed her again. "Kassie, I love you."

Surprise settled in her eyes. "I thought I was going to say that first.

Then I started wondering if it was too early, like I was breaking the rules."

"What rules are those?" He chuckled, his lips finding hers again, and his fingers finding the buttons of her shirt.

Her breathing quickened. "You know, the unspoken rules of a relationship. Timeframes of when you're supposed to do things..." She sighed as he worked to remove the shirt. "Oh, forget it. I love you, too, Brett."

"That's a good thing," he responded with a murmur, wanting to show her his feelings now instead of talking about them.

***

November 8 was not a good day for Kassidy. She woke up that morning with a giant headache, but she had two interviews scheduled, edits to make to two articles and another article due the following day, so she couldn't take the day to try to feel better.

She called Alexis to check in, see how she was doing and if she had heard anything new, but the call went straight to voicemail. She left a message asking her to call back.

Kassidy had no reason to believe Kurt would contact her. She didn't think he even knew she lived here. But the thought of him setting foot in Sacramento made her skin crawl, and she'd had to talk herself down from several panic attacks. She'd had some meetings with her therapist, which had helped. Keeping her life as calm as possible was important. Chances were slim she would run into him.

Maybe he was only here once or twice.

She hadn't told Brett about the meeting with Alexis or the information the woman had given her. Maybe she should have, but she didn't want to add another thing to his plate. It would probably all lead to nothing, and she could tell him about it later, after he made detective.

She took some aspirin, and by the time she left her apartment at ten o'clock, the edge was taken off, but the constant ache still nagged at her. She was working on a story about competitive scholarships for high school seniors, and that morning she was set to interview a local CEO about the scholarship he created for prospective engineering majors. She arrived for the ten-thirty meeting ten minutes early, but her source wasn't there. She waited for fifteen minutes, then thirty, but he didn't show. She called his cell phone and he answered on the fourth ring.

"I'm sorry, Ms. Turner. I completely forgot about the interview. Can we reschedule for next week? I have a couple things going on today."

She swore to herself. She had emailed him the morning before to remind him of the interview, because he had asked her to. He had never responded, but she assumed he would be there. When would she learn? She should have called him, texted him, sent a plane with a banner flying behind it.

"It's okay. I understand things happen. My article is due Saturday. Is there any way we could meet tomorrow or Friday?" She tried to stay polite and professional, but it wasn't easy. It wasn't like he hadn't known about the interview, regardless of whether he had gotten her email. She had set it up with him over the phone a week ago.

"I'm sorry," he sounded more than a little distracted. "I'm pretty booked the rest of the week. Can I call you Saturday morning? Would that work?"

Inside she was seething. This was the part of her job she couldn't stand – sometimes having to rely on unreliable people.

"That would be fine. Would 8:30 work?"

"Yes, that should work fine. I'm sorry again." His voice was genuinely apologetic, but rushed.

"Okay, I'll call you then." As she said this, she was already trying to think of another source for the story. She didn't want to take a chance on him again. She wouldn't miss her deadline.

She made a distinct effort to eat a good lunch and drink plenty of water in between that time and her second interview at one o'clock. Usually she had to sleep off headaches, but in between her failed interview and the next one, she was working on edits, writing, and returning the call of another source. She didn't have time for a nap, and she doubted she could have fallen asleep if she did.

It was when her one o'clock source was fifteen minutes late that she began to wonder what she was doing. She loved being a journalist, and she liked the freedom of freelancing, but really, why was she killing herself for less pay, no benefits, and all the stress of a staff reporter?

She sighed. Tomorrow would be a better day. She had to get through this day. She could get to bed early and sleep off the ache in her head, and that would help. And maybe she was ready to start searching for a staff job.

Luckily, her source did show up, and the woman was apologetic for being late. Guilt seeped into Kassidy for the feeling of annoyance she couldn't quite shake. During the interview, the woman had to take two phone calls, but she answered Kassidy's questions with tons of detail.

As she said goodbye to her source, Kassidy was starting to think the day was looking up. She was only about five minutes from her apartment when her car started making strange noises at a stop light. Then it started resisting as she tried to accelerate.

"What the hell? No!" she groaned, slamming her palms on her steering wheel. "I was so close!"

She punched on her hazards and managed to drive to her mechanic, backtracking away from her apartment.

She didn't want to call Brett. He was picking up some overtime hours before his regular shift tonight and had to make a trip home first. He was probably getting ready to leave her apartment, and she didn't want to bug him. After she checked in, she called her dad. It was two-thirty.

"Hey, Kassie. How's it going?" He picked up after the third ring, causing Kassidy to breathe a sigh of relief.

"Hey, Dad. I'm at the mechanic. My car started making horrible noises and then I could barely accelerate. They're checking it out now, but I don't think I'll be able to take it today. Is there any way I could borrow the Ranger? I need to get home to work on my articles, and today has been…frustrating…" She knew her voice sounded a little frantic, and she tried to calm herself down.

"Sure, no problem. Mom and I will meet you there as soon as we can." His reassuring voice made her feel better, and she was able to slow her breathing.

"Thanks so much, Dad."

Her parents arrived around four-fifteen. She was having trouble keeping herself from pacing by the time they walked through the door. Her mechanic's office was small, and there were several people crowded in there. The noise, stuffiness, and smell of motor oil was making her head swim.

"Sorry, kiddo. Traffic was horrible. There was some kind of accident on the freeway." Her dad handed her the keys to the truck.

"Are you okay?" Her mom gave her a hug. "How's Brett?"

"I'm fine, but they're not going to have the work done until tomorrow, because they're swamped today. It looks like the fuel pump needs to be replaced," she said with a sigh. "Brett's fine. So far things look good for him making detective. I think he's going to really miss patrol, though. He's still taking a lot of overtime hours."

"That's great." Her mom beamed. "I'm sure that'll be a big adjustment, but a good step for your future together."

Kassidy only nodded. She felt bad for wanting to rush her parents, but her bones felt antsy, as if they might jump out of her skin.

"Do you have enough money to pay for the repair?" Her father got down to business.

"Yeah." She shrugged, trying not to make the money a big deal.

Her dad shook his head and held out another check. Kassidy eyed it.

She wanted to take it, but she felt like such a child. Most of the money was already coming from past gifts they'd given her, which she had stored away in savings.

"No, Dad. I'm fine, really."

His eyes were interrogative, like Brett's could sometimes be. "Let me know if you need more," he finally said and put the check back in his wallet.

She nodded, even though she had no intention of doing that.

Her mom did not look satisfied, and she sighed to herself.

Here we go.

And as if Annie Turner had read her thoughts: "Kassie, why don't you take a little break? We're worried about you, rushing around with so much on your mind. You have more deadlines in your life than any one person should have."

"I know it seems that way, but this is what I'm meant to do, and I love it." She decided to play into her parents' hopes for her. "If I'm ever going to get a permanent job at a publication again, I need to continuously show I can meet my deadlines. Today has been an off day, that's all."

They accepted that answer in silence, but neither looked convinced.

"Okay, thank you. I love you both." She hugged them, trying to avoid any more questions. "But I really have to go. I'll call you when I get my car back."

I'm a horrible daughter. They care about me and want me to be okay. With all the help they've given me, I should spend more time with them.

The guilt was strong, but she couldn't deal with it now. She had to get to work. She'd find time for that guilt another day.

She didn't love driving her parents' Ford Ranger, but she was grateful that it was available to her when she needed it. Thank God her dad taught her to drive a stick shift when she was a teenager, so it only took her a few minutes to get used to.

She made her way home through rush hour traffic and immediately sat down on her couch, throwing open her laptop.

It was almost five o'clock, and she feverishly typed, edited and emailed for the next four hours, only stopping to answer a short call from Brett wishing her a good night before he went to work. Even with all the stress of the day, his voice still calmed her.

She felt like she had done enough by nine o'clock, and her stomach was rumbling. She hadn't eaten anything since lunch. There wasn't much to eat in her apartment. She needed to remember to go shopping tomorrow. She decided to treat herself to dinner out. She deserved it after this day. There was a place she liked over by Arden Fair Mall. She'd get a burger and fries and it would be perfect. She grabbed the Ranger's keys and was out the door.

CHAPTER 15

What a shitty day, *Mary growled to herself.*

Kurt signed off on all of Christopher's priority projects, but only two of hers. The asshole had some kind of real vendetta against her now. He knew the Timothy Connell termination had been delayed, but she felt her story of how long it would take to plan was believable, and even the boss accepted it. She was taking care of all of Kurt's other requests, and keeping a close eye on Abigail. The operative following Kassidy didn't have any concerns. She didn't know why Kurt was so pissed.

Her real estate ventures were going great, but with Kurt denying most of her projects, she wasn't moving much of the organization's work forward. She didn't want the boss blaming her for this, so she'd been calling him all day. He never called her back. It was the first time he had ignored her in their many years of working together.

As she stormed out of one of her buildings in the Arden area, she noticed she had a voicemail from him. Finally! However, when she listened to it, her heart fell and she felt her face go white.

"I've received the updated report regarding the denial of so many of your priority projects. Mary, I don't understand where your work ethic has gone. Something is deeply affecting you these days. Your project plans are sloppy, and

I can't have someone like that in such a high position within this organization. Call me tomorrow so we can discuss how you will turn things around. But this will be the last chance. If you don't improve, I'll have to find you a new position...although it will come with a serious demotion."

She seethed with anger. She was working her ass off. She'd never stopped. Her work now was no different from her work earlier this year. Kurt's disgusting, flashy money was the problem.

She slammed her phone down on her passenger seat and pushed the ignition button on her Mercedes-Benz SUV, peeling out of the parking lot.

***

Kassidy turned toward the mall, heading for the freeway that would take her home. Traffic was light, and the mall was already closed. There was a definite chill in the air and Kassidy had cracked the truck's manual windows, reveling in the feeling of autumn all around her.

The sound of screeching tires to her right broke her from her dream. Another street was merging with hers, and she saw a black SUV trying to get around a Ford F-150, but the truck driver wasn't having any of it, speeding up to keep the SUV from passing.

She felt it coming before it happened. She tried her best to stop, to let them pass her by, but it was too late. She felt the impact as one of the vehicles hit her truck on the passenger side. Her body tightened in panic as her air bag exploded open. She threw her arms up in front of her face in an instinctual attempt to protect herself as her head hit her window. The small truck was spinning now. The spinning didn't stop as she felt another impact, and her world was a blur of noise and fear.

She didn't remember coming to a stop. She could hear yelling outside the truck. Someone was banging on her window. She turned her head to the left, and a shocking pain met her as she saw a man on the other side holding his phone to his ear, a scared look on his face. She turned her head to the right, more pain, and couldn't quite understand the way the inside of the truck looked. She didn't see her purse where it had been on the seat, and the seat itself looked contorted.

Her door hadn't been locked, and the man talking on the phone cracked it open, calling to her, "Are you okay?"

When she nodded as best as she could, he instructed, "Stay put! I called 911!" Her ears were ringing, and he sounded far away.

She felt something besides the throbbing of her head, something on the side of her face, tickling like a hair would. She was afraid to think too much about what other pain she might be feeling, and she couldn't make herself move.

Then the man raced off toward another sedan that looked like it was sitting in the middle of the street. She couldn't see through her windshield, as it was mostly shattered, but she could see blurs she assumed were people moving quickly near her truck through her left window. She could hear more yelling now as she took several deep breaths. Now her left arm ached, but in her groggy mind she wasn't sure how bad the pain was. She tried to touch the left side of her head, but flinched at the sticky feeling of hair mixed with what had to be blood that met her there.

Then she heard sirens in the distance.

Panic bubbled up inside her. What had she done to her parents' truck? Her head and arm were throbbing now, and she was trying to assess whether her legs were working. They seemed to be. She attempted to open her door more, but made the mistake of trying to use her left hand, and her arm strongly protested. She took some more deep breaths as the panic built. She sat back in her seat again, reaching for any calm she could grasp.

She listened to the activity going on around her. The sirens were too loud, and the world outside the truck sounded like chaos.

***

Brett was one of three officers to arrive on the scene of a multiple-vehicle accident in front of the mall. There were a decent number of onlookers milling in the road, so Brett began asking them to move to the sidewalk as his other colleague checked on the occupants from one of the sedans involved.

To most people a scene like this would look like pure insanity, but he had learned to compartmentalize each piece of an accident, making the injured a priority, getting extra people and cars out of the way and taking reports. He made his way through the scene, making sure those he spoke to were okay and letting them know ambulances were on the way. He stopped to check on the driver of a second sedan. Her car was totaled, but she was standing outside it. She was shaking and said she was on the phone with her husband. She had some scrapes, but was moving around and didn't have any other major injuries.

He told her she could take her time and that he would come back, but she calmed down slightly as she told him what happened.

"The drivers of the SUV and big truck were engaged in some serious road rage. The SUV hit that small truck." She pointed at a Ford Ranger not far from them.

He glanced at the small truck. He needed to get over there. The driver looked like he or she was moving, but they were still inside, which worried him. He wasn't sure if anyone had checked on the person yet.

"The small truck hit my car, and I hit that other sedan. I swear I saw the SUV back up and hit the small truck again, but that doesn't make sense, so I'm probably wrong. The small truck was spinning, and it hit my car again. I can't believe I'm standing here."

As he spoke to the driver, he saw another officer walk up. "Hey, Callahan! Can you check the driver of the Ranger? I haven't seen them come out of the truck, and I think Rightner's only been able to check on the other sedan and the F-150."

"No problem." The officer nodded and began walking in that

direction. But before he could get far, he was stopped by another woman, who must have come from one of the vehicles. She sounded angry and tried to pull Callahan toward the SUV, motioning wildly at the vehicle. Brett sighed and, reassuring the sedan driver, started toward the Ranger.

The paramedics had already arrived, and they rushed around checking those involved. There were a fair number of injuries – even the SUV driver looked a little banged up – and it was obvious speed played a factor in the crash. If they had all been going the speed limit, it wouldn't look this bad. He was grateful there weren't any kids involved. He wasn't sure how his brain would handle another injured child.

The right side of the Ranger was completely smashed, and the front didn't look much better. The back of the bed also appeared to have some damage.

The windshield was shattered, and he couldn't see well through the driver-side window, as the door was partially open. When he was within feet of the truck, he caught his first good glimpse of the driver. Long, dark hair. He felt his heart drop and confusion took over, immediately followed by a rush of adrenaline. It couldn't be her. How the hell could it be her?

He wanted to yell as he sprinted the rest of the way to the truck, but he couldn't form any words. His heart was slamming in his chest. Why was she driving that truck? What was she doing here?

She was slowly moving different parts of her body, as if taking piece-by-piece inventory of its damage, but her head was leaned back against the seat, her eyes closed. Her movements looked strange, and he wanted to get her out of that truck. Her door was cracked, so someone must have checked on her, right? He threw it the rest of the way open and was pretty sure he was calling her name. He reached over to unbuckle her seat belt. He breathed an enormous sigh of relief as she opened her eyes, looking at him in confusion. The left side of her head was bleeding.

"Brett?" Her voice was quiet, but sounded clear enough. "Are you really here?"

"Yes. Are you in pain anywhere besides your head?" He wanted nothing more than to get her out of there, but he was afraid to move her. He had some gauze with him and held it to her head.

"My left arm hurts. My legs are working. I think everything else is okay." She sounded woozy. He looked around, spotting two of the paramedics and waving wildly at them. He was sure he looked frantic. He didn't care. They started jogging his way.

"Paramedics are on their way," he said as she tried to get her legs out of the truck. "Careful, Kassie. Go slow." He held onto her carefully, as if she might fall from the vehicle at any moment. The rest of the scene around them disappeared as he kept his full attention on her.

"This is so embarrassing." She was shaking, but was climbing out of the truck whether he liked it or not.

"If you needed more of my attention, you could've told me. This was a little extreme," he said, trying to keep a straight face.

"Oh, my God, Brett," she responded, rolling her eyes, but she couldn't keep a small smirk from her face.

The paramedics reached them and started examining her injuries, asking her basic questions about herself and where she felt pain. Kassie didn't like a lot of attention, and Brett could see her wanting to resist, but was relieved that she let them do their jobs.

He couldn't wait any longer to ask the question burning in his mind. "What were you doing driving that truck, Kass?"

Her voice was hard to hear as she responded, "My car was being weird, so I took it to the mechanic. This is my parents' truck. It's been a really shitty day actually. And now their truck…" She tried to turn to look at the other side of the vehicle, but winced. Tears began running down her cheeks.

He quickly took her right hand. "You're okay, and that's what matters. Your parents aren't going to care about the truck when they know you're okay."

"Ready to go?" one of the paramedics questioned, having pulled a gurney up beside the truck.

"Brett, I don't want to go to the hospital. Do I have a concussion?" She turned to the paramedic, who cast an unsure look at Brett, not sure what the relationship of the two people was.

"I believe you might, ma'am, so they'll need to confirm that. You also need stitches on that cut, and your arm is broken."

She stared down at her limb, as if it had betrayed her.

She shook her head and looked pleadingly at Brett. "I have too much to do right now, and hospital visits cost a lot of money. I really think I just need to rest."

"Kassie, no. You need to go to the hospital." Then he continued, trying to give her empathy. "I can help you with the money."

She said nothing, but stared at the activity all around her. Tow trucks were arriving on the scene. A couple ambulances had already left with other patients from the accident.

"We can talk about that later, but you need to go to the hospital. There is no way I can let you go home. Please." He kept firm eye contact with her.

She sighed and nodded her head. "Okay."

She waved away the gurney with a horrified look, so Brett helped her walk toward the ambulance. His heart had slowed now, and he was focused on getting her out of there. All of a sudden, the agitated woman he'd seen pulling Callahan toward the SUV was in front of them, blocking their path.

"Maybe next time you should watch where you're going!" Her voice was frantic and full of rage.

"Excuse me?" Kassidy responded in a weak voice, startling at the yell.

"Ma'am, you need to back up." Brett stuck out his arm, putting a barrier between the woman and Kassidy. Anger flashed in him, and he had to work hard to keep from yelling in her face.

"Officer, I had gotten around that truck and was merging into her lane, and she was sitting there, like she'd forgotten how to drive! What were you doing exactly? Thinking about your day?" The woman raged on, and Brett could already see Callahan and Rightner approaching her.

"Ma'am, I understand accidents are very upsetting, and of course we will get all sides of the story, but you need to back up *right now*," Brett kept a professional tone at first, but the end of the sentence came out in a growl. He saw Kassidy's surprised expression in his peripheral vision.

The woman's face was contorted with hate, but she backed up slowly and let them by. The two officers were behind her now, and Brett noticed she looked very different the moment she turned around to talk to them.

"She looked familiar," Kassidy mumbled.

"What?" Brett moved his head closer to her. The accident scene wasn't exactly quiet, and he barely heard her.

"She looked familiar, but I don't know why."

"Maybe someone you talked to for an article?" he suggested, trying to keep her distracted as he led her toward the waiting ambulance.

She shook her head slowly and winced again. "I don't think so. I just…can't place her. And I don't think that's what happened. I wanted to stop when I saw her and the F-150 coming, but she was already right beside me as the streets came together. I didn't have time to brake."

"Don't worry about that right now. We'll talk about it later." They had arrived at the ambulance, and she grimaced.

"I'm not hurt enough to ride in an ambulance. I can have someone come pick me up."

He almost laughed. This woman he loved was certainly stubborn to a fault. "You're riding in the ambulance, lady. I'll have to be here for a while, but then I'm going to try to get off early and join you. Which hospital?" he asked and one of the paramedics from before stood waiting for her response.

"Sutter. Brett, you have to work." She was clearly tired and wanted to get away from the accident scene.

"Uh, I'm your boyfriend, so I'm supposed to join you at hospitals after you've been in horrible car accidents. Didn't you read that part of the contract?" He grinned, helping her into the ambulance.

Her smile was weak, but it was there.

"Try to call your parents when you get there," he said before they closed the ambulance doors, and he saw the grimace return to her face. Then he remembered he hadn't seen her carrying her purse or her phone.

CHAPTER 16

After the ambulance arrived at the hospital's emergency room and she was checked in, she sat down to wait. It was a busy night, and she was surrounded by people she felt were in much more of a need than she was, but the ache in her head and arm reminded her that she was there for a reason.

Since the ambulance ride, she'd started feeling dizzy and nauseous. The fluorescent hospital lights made her head hurt more. She was sure she had a concussion.

It was nearing midnight, but she knew she should call her parents. She found a payphone and dialed their landline, because they usually turned their cell phones off at night. She sat down in the chair directly beneath the payphone, its short cord straining with the stretch.

"Hello?" her mom answered, her voice groggy.

"Hi, Mom, it's me." She couldn't make her voice any louder than a whisper.

"Kassidy?" Her mother was more alert now. "What's wrong?"

Kassidy sighed. "First of all, I'm okay, so please keep that in mind. I was in a car accident tonight…in the Ranger…I was driving home by the mall, and I was hit by an SUV…or a bigger truck, I'm not sure. Then I think I hit one or two other cars – or maybe they hit me." At this point, she could hear her mom waking up her dad, and there was some noise in the background. She could hear her dad asking questions that her mom wasn't relaying to her. "Anyway, I hit my head pretty hard, and my left arm while I was spinning. So, I'm at Sutter downtown right now."

Her dad had the phone now. "Kassidy, are you in the emergency room now?"

"Yes, but you guys *do not* need to come here. I'm fine, and Brett said he was going to try to get off work early. He was one of the responding officers at the accident. I wanted to let you know about the Ranger, and I didn't want you to get mad at me later for not telling you right away."

"Your mother is currently pulling me out of the house, so I have to go," her father responded.

"No, Dad, really. It's late. I wanted to let you know what happened." She started tearing up again at this point, thinking about their smashed truck.

"Gotta go, kiddo. I think your mother may already be driving down the street. We'll be there as soon as we can. "

The call ended and Kassidy leaned her head back against the wall, wincing at the slight impact.

Her parents were there way sooner than they should have been. They found her in the waiting room, although a nurse was calling her back to a triage area.

"Should I even ask how you got from Folsom to downtown Sacramento in less than twenty minutes?" Kassidy frowned as her mother gave her a careful hug.

"Traffic was light. It's late." Her mother pulled her away to study her face, which still held the paramedics bandage. "You're getting a black eye on this side."

"Seventeen minutes light?" Kassidy raised her eyebrows as she sat on the examination bed.

"Yes." Her mother was looking at her arm, but not getting in the way of the nurse taking Kassidy's vital signs.

Her father's face was hard to read, and she flashed back to seeing him for the first time after everything happened with Kurt. He'd clearly held so many emotions, and this was as similar an expression to that one that she had ever seen him make.

"I'm sorry about the truck. I'm pretty sure it's totaled," she murmured and felt tears stinging her eyes. She knew it was totaled. She might as well say that.

"Don't even think about that, Kassidy. You're okay. That's what matters." Her mother brushed some hair back from her face. Kassidy smiled at her. Even though the woman drove her crazy most of the time and had a hard time giving her approval, it was obvious she loved her.

After the nurse finished with her vitals, she was ushered away for some scans. When she got back to the room, Brett was waiting with her parents. He was still wearing his uniform and she caught a glimpse of the worry written across his face before he managed to get rid of it. He gave her a gentle hug, and she leaned into him for a moment.

The emergency room physician confirmed a mild concussion. Her left forearm was fractured, but not enough to need surgery. She received a wrap and sling for that and was told to follow up with her doctor, who could refer her to an orthopedic specialist. He stitched the gash on the left side of her face and one on her right knee, which she hadn't noticed before.

"You're going to be in much more pain and feel much stiffer tomorrow…well, today." The doctor glanced at the clock on the wall. "Be prepared for that. Don't push yourself too hard. It will take time to recover."

"Did you tell him something while I was out of the room?" Kassidy smirked at Brett.

Brett shook his head innocently with a laugh.

"No, he didn't, but I did," her dad chimed in.

The doctor tried to hide his smile, but didn't do a very good job, and Kassidy sighed.

She barely heard her parents say they would check in with her later that day as Brett helped her to the car. Her eyelids felt like they were being pulled down by boulders.

She crashed into her bed like she hadn't slept in years, but she couldn't get comfortable enough to fall asleep. Her left side ached, but when she tried to lay on her right, her knee throbbed. After tossing for a while, she sat up, leaning back against her headboard. Brett created a barrier of pillows around her to try to keep her as still as possible. The clock showed her the passage of time in hour increments each time she opened her eyes. The glowing numbers of five-seventeen burned into her mind as she fell into a deeper sleep.

***

Brett checked his phone for the millionth time. Eleven-seventeen in the morning. He'd barely slept. He had set her up in the middle of her bed to give her as much space as possible, so his bed for the night had been the couch. He checked on her six or seven times, making sure her breathing was normal. She'd been awake two of these times, but was groggy, so hadn't really acknowledged him. She was in a new position every time he went in her room, so he knew she wasn't sleeping well. All the movement had pissed Isla off. The cat tried to sleep on his feet, but he had to keep kicking her off. He knew she wanted to be with Kassie, but he wanted to keep things as quiet and still for her as he could, so he made sure to shut her door behind him.

He was sitting up on the couch now, watching the muted TV. His eyelids started inching closed. He'd already had two cups of coffee, but maybe he needed more. A loud groan from her room had him leaping off the couch, causing Isla to jump into the air like a cartoon cat.

"Hey." He kneeled down next to her, not wanting to move her by sitting on the bed. "How are you feeling? How's your headache and your vision?"

"My headache is still there, but I think it's a little better. My vision is fine. I've heard people say they feel like they've been hit by a truck, but I never understood it until now," she responded, shifting onto her back from her side.

He sighed with concern, pushing some of her hair away from her eyes. "Can I get you anything? Are you hungry? You should try to eat something before you take your pain meds."

"I can't even tell if I'm hungry," she said, her voice cracking.

"Okay, I'll make you some toast and we'll see how that goes. I'll bring you some water, too." He got up in time to see Isla jump on the bed.

"Hi, sweet girl." Kassie smiled at the cat, who was staring at her, looking more like her old anxious self.

When Brett came back with the toast and water, the cat was curled up and purring, Kassidy petting her with her right hand.

"That didn't take long," he said, grinning. He sat down on the bed as carefully as he could.

"Do you know what happened last night?" She turned her head to face him as she took tentative bites of her toast.

"It's looking like a road rage incident and that the SUV hit you, which caused you to hit at least one of the sedans. It was a chain reaction."

"Was that the angry lady?" she asked, her voice so different from that of the vibrant woman he knew.

He nodded. "Witnesses, one of the sedan drivers, and the F-150 driver are all telling the same story of the SUV driver trying to get around the F-150. The F-150 driver didn't want to let her by. When she finally chased him down and managed to get around him, she swiped him and then hit you on the right side as the two streets were merging together.

The SUV driver is still denying it. She says you were stopped in the road, she slammed on her brakes, but couldn't avoid hitting you. Don't worry though, no one is corroborating her story. You said last night that she looked familiar. Do you remember where from?"

She was quiet for a few moments as she thought. She shook her head, frustrated.

"No. I don't think it's from any time recently, but I know her from somewhere." She winced as she tried to sit up more.

"Do you want some of your pain medication?" He wished he could take the pain from her somehow, or do something more for her. As someone who was constantly trying to fix problems, he didn't like feeling this helpless.

She grimaced. "I don't like taking that stuff. I'll take some Tylenol for now."

He nodded, grabbing some from her kitchen.

"What happens now?" she asked when she had taken the pills and drank the whole glass of water. He knew she was thinking about her parents' truck again, but he wouldn't be talking to her about that right now.

"For now, you need to rest, and if you're hungry for anything else, I'll get it for you."

"Brett," she murmured, her voice full of frustration.

Kassidy liked to be in charge, but she was going to have to accept some help now. And one of the ways he planned to help her was waiting until she was better to burden her with bad news.

He kissed her on the forehead. "Your parents called earlier. They already talked to their insurance company, and they want you to let them handle that right now. All you need to think about is resting and getting better. In a couple hours you can call your doctor about getting that referral for your arm."

"But the truck…it's totaled, right?" She closed her eyes, and he knew she was fighting tears.

He was silent, and she didn't ask again.

Her eyes snapped open. "My phone!"

So much for keeping bad news away. "They found your purse, but your phone…"

"Was flattened?" A few tears escaped and ran down her cheeks. "Everyone I ever talk to for articles, all the editors from the different publications, everyone who needs to reach me, has that phone number. And having to buy another phone…"

He wiped her tears away. "You can email your editors tomorrow and let them know what's going on if you feel up for it. Or I can help you. And it'll be easy to get another phone with the same number. I can help with that, too." He kept his voice calm, rubbing her good arm. "Until then you can use mine. We'll figure it all out, but the first step is you resting as much as possible."

"You know I don't know how to rest," she grumbled. "I want to figure out how I know that lady. Do you know her name?"

"No, I didn't take her report. Maybe your parents have it from the insurance stuff."

She nodded and sighed in frustration.

CHAPTER 17

"You hit her car. Kassidy Turner's car. Then you backed up and hit her again," Christopher said in as animated a voice as she had ever heard him use.

"I didn't mean to hit her again. I was trying to get around her. I wasn't planning on stopping. And it wasn't her car. I've seen pictures of her car. This was a truck. I didn't know it was her," Mary growled in reply.

"Even if that's true, do you think Kurt will believe that? That the boss will believe it? They'll think you're trying to sabotage her monitoring again. The operative was only a few cars behind her. She will make it sound like you were targeting Kassidy."

"I had no idea she was there! I was trying to get around that asshole in the F-150. When I finally did, he sped up and I hit him, which caused me to hit her. I had no fucking idea it was her until I approached her and the cop!"

"Which makes the story even better. Her cop boyfriend was there and saw you, too. You yelled at Kassidy Turner and her cop. The operative saw it all."

He smiled. Christopher the sociopath actually smiled. She wanted to stroll across the room and punch him in the face. Instead, she continued working on the hand-written report she was preparing for one of her projects.

"I feel like you want to get caught, Mary. Like you're looking for a reason

for the boss to have you terminated." Christopher leaned back in his chair, staring at her.

"He's not going to have me terminated, asshole!" she screamed across the room. "The cop has no idea who I am. He didn't recognize me."

"But did Kassidy recognize you?" He was, of course, unfazed by her outburst, pushing her ever closer to the edge.

Her mind started racing again, as it had every other hour since the accident three days ago. She tried to remember Kassidy's face. Was there recognition there? She'd been pretty beat up and out of it, but Mary had no way of knowing if her identity stuck out in the woman's mind. She used a pseudonym on her insurance, as she did with most of her official and legal accounts, so even if someone shared it with Kassidy, she wouldn't know it. She'd only met the woman a couple of times at the most. There'd be no reason for Kassidy to remember her.

She tried to calm herself with these thoughts, but she still hadn't heard from the boss or Kurt, so it was hard to be calm. She knew the operative would have reported to the boss right away. Maybe John wasn't concerned. Maybe the operative hadn't colored the accident in any particular way. Maybe she had only given the facts.

God, Mary, don't be delusional, *she thought to herself.*

She wanted nothing less in that moment than to continue the conversation with Christopher, but he would tell her if he knew anything. Christopher didn't have an empathetic bone in his dark, twisted body, but he never lied. He never felt the need to.

"Have you heard anything from Kurt or the boss?"

"No. I'm sure they're saving that pleasure for you."

***

The week after her accident, Kassidy had a phone appointment with her therapist, because moving around too much was still painful, and she wasn't allowed to drive yet. Brett had gone back to work after taking time off to help her. Her parents had already driven her to a few doctor appointments, and she felt guilty asking them again.

She had a cringe-worthy blue cast on her arm, and it went up past her elbow, so she didn't think she could even drive with it. At least she had a new phone, which Brett had helped her order and set up. She was starting to work on a couple articles again using voice-to-text, much to Brett's chagrin, but she would never ask him to stop working, so she knew he wouldn't ask her to.

"These last few weeks have been some of the most frustrating of my life. I know I need to heal, but I can't let my work slide. I can barely afford to live as it is. My parents have asked to help, but I'm almost thirty years old. I shouldn't be taking hand-outs from them."

"Kassidy, these are special circumstances," Lina said. "If they want to help, it's okay. It's not hurting your overall goal of independence. And I know you love your work, but my suggestion would be to give yourself a bit more time. Another week even. Then, after that, if work helps you create your new normal as you heal, get back to it. Your editors can be understanding for another week."

Kassidy sighed. "I'll give it a try. Other things…my parents want me to move back in with them for a short time. They want to take care of me. I feel bad saying no because of everything they've done for me, but I don't want to. I want to be here in my home. I want Brett and Isla with me, and they wouldn't be there."

"Don't do that. Your parents are great. Wonderful. If they want to help you financially, that's awesome of them. But I don't think you should uproot your life right now. You need to stay in one place and heal. You need to feel as comfortable as possible. I know your mom loves you, but you don't have an…easy relationship. And you haven't lived with them since you moved back to Sac. I think the adjustment would be too much for all of you. If you can stay in your apartment, do that," Lina responded without hesitation, as if she was taking a test she already knew the answers to.

"Driving is the other thing. I can't right now, and might not be able to until I get my smaller cast, but I'm not sure I'll ever…want to again. A couple nights after the accident, when I was sleeping better, I started having nightmares. There are these gigantic vehicles ramming into me, but I'm not in the truck or my car, I'm at my desk at the *Chronicle*. Then sometimes Kurt is there and he's calling me all those names again. Sometimes he's driving the vehicle that hits me. I don't know how Kurt became connected to the accident in my dreams."

"It could be because your meeting with Alexis came shortly before the accident. Both things have caused you stress, emotional and physical. The driving will take some time. I've had a lot of clients who think they will never drive again after car accidents, but most do. Give yourself some grace with that. Have you spoken to Alexis again since your meeting? Has she been prominent in your mind?"

"I tried calling her the day of my accident, but the call went straight to voicemail. I asked her to call me back, but she hasn't. She was worried about Kurt, about his power. And yes, Kurt can ruin reputations with the snap of a finger, and he's a disgusting person for what he did to all those women, but I don't know what he could do to her now. She wasn't going to go to the police. So, why would he care to hurt her?"

"You said she was studying his travel, that people in his company were keeping her informed. Maybe she suspected something specific, but didn't want to get into it, so she played dumb? I don't know, but that would explain why everything is so mixed up in your dreams. Leave Alexis for now. She'll call you when she's ready. Worrying about Kurt will bring more stress your way. He's never contacted you, and if he does, go to the police, Kassidy. Have you talked to Brett about any of the Kurt stuff?"

Lina asked the question Kassidy had hoped she wouldn't.

"No, I don't want to put that on him. It's so awkward, and it's probably nothing, so I don't want to bother him with it. If anything happens, I'll tell him."

Lina was silent for a moment, which was unusual for her. "I think you should tell him, Kassidy. Awkward, yeah probably, but it's kind of a big deal, especially since your wounds from Kurt are still raw. He should know what's going on, both because he's your boyfriend, but also because his job could be helpful if Kurt does contact you."

Kassidy acknowledged this, but knew this was the one suggestion Lina made that she wouldn't take. She needed to get beyond Kurt. He could come to Sacramento without her falling to pieces. There was no evidence he was involved in anything shady. She didn't need to bring Brett into this.

Two nights later, Kassidy was laying on her couch, binging episodes of *M*A*S*H* with Isla snuggled securely on her feet. She'd taken Lina's advice and put her articles on hold for another week. Her editors had all been pretty understanding. She felt disconnected, but having time to rest her brain and body felt nice. She'd been thinking about Alexis, but hadn't called her again. If she wanted space, Kassidy needed to give her that.

It was about eight o'clock, and Brett had already left for work. Her phone rang. She didn't recognize the number, but most numbers she didn't know were sources. Maybe it was someone she had already called for an article.

"Hello?"

"Kassidy?" The voice was hopeful, and Kassidy froze.

"Abigail? Uh, hi. I didn't know you had my number." She had changed her number when she moved to Sacramento, so how had she gotten it?

"Oh, yeah. Sorry, your mom texted me the other day. She said she forgot to give you my number, so she sent me yours. I've been wanting to get in touch with you since Auburn."

"Oh, okay." This made sense. Kassidy and Abigail were really close in their San Francisco days, so she was sure her mom didn't think twice about giving Abigail her number.

Calm down, Kassidy.

Abigail wasn't a bad person. They didn't have to be close now, but it didn't hurt to catch up over a phone call.

"Yeah, how have you been? How's the new company?"

"It's going great. The Sacramento business community has been super welcoming. This was a good move for me," Abigail gushed. "How are you? How is your writing going?"

"It's good. I'm doing a lot of freelancing right now. I have to take a little break though. I was in a car accident a little over a week ago, and I got kind of…banged up." Kassidy didn't feel the need to expand on her injuries.

"Oh, no! I'm sorry. Let me know if you need anything. I can stop by with supplies. Whatever you need."

"Okay, thanks." Kassidy felt guilty, but at this point she wanted to end the call and get back to Alan Alda's thought-provoking scene.

"So," Abigail wasn't going to let that happen yet, "have you heard anything from Kurt?"

"What?" Kassidy's jaw dropped and her phone nearly had the same fate.

"Remember how I told you I saw Kurt in Sacramento? I was wondering if he reached out to you. He hasn't reached out to me," she said, and Kassidy heard the faintest note of anxiety in her voice.

Kassidy was stone silent. She wasn't sure if this conversation was really happening. When she spoke again, her words were measured and slow. "Why would Kurt reach out to me after what happened in San Francisco? He told the most hateful lies about me, Abigail. Tried to ruin my reputation. Why would he care to have any contact with me?"

"I know…I was just wondering. I didn't know why he would be here otherwise. I told him I was moving here, but…" She sounded more frantic than anxious now.

"Abigail, were you in a relationship with Kurt while he and I were dating?" she blurted. It was obvious now that they'd been together, but Kassidy had told Abigail about Kurt's horrific actions and affairs. Abigail had been as shocked as she was. Had Abigail been with Kurt the entire time?

Abigail was silent for a full minute. "Kassie…" Her words faded away.

Kassidy sat up quickly, startling Isla. "I don't understand. You were my friend. You knew about everything he did. How could you…" She got up and started to pace. "I have nothing to do with Kurt! I don't want anything to do with him! He's never going to contact me, so please don't ask me again. I don't know how he ended things with you, but I think you need to move on. He's disgusting, Abigail! He's done horrible things!"

"Kassie…I know he's made mistakes. Everyone has. But I was with him for years."

Years?

Kassidy wanted to be shocked. She was definitely outraged, but not shocked. Not after everything Kurt had done. Not after she'd realized Abigail was pining for him.

"I know what you went through…everything you believe he did… but that wasn't my experience," Abigail continued. She became a different person as she said these words. Calm, a little condescending. Who was she?

"Everything I believe…Abigail, please don't call me again." She ended the call.

Her heart slammed in her chest, and her mind raced. She took several deeps breaths and closed her eyes, trying to bring herself down from the mountain of rage and hurt she was standing on. Was her entire life in San Francisco a farce? Kurt had already ripped out her heart and all-but shredded her ability to trust. She'd thought Abigail was a best friend, but that was another lie.

CHAPTER 18

"We haven't talked about Thanksgiving yet." Brett poured Kassidy a cup of coffee and brought it to where she sat on the couch.

"Thanksgiving?" She looked at him in confusion.

"Yeah, it's coming up. Did you make plans with your parents?" He wasn't surprised by her confusion. The accident had been a lot, but she'd been more distracted the last couple of days. When he tried to ask her about it, she blamed it on her recovery.

"Umm, I guess so. I go to their house every year. They haven't said anything yet. I bet my mom is wondering if you and I made plans. Or maybe they don't want me to have to think about it right now."

"Makes sense." He looked down at his coffee mug, watching the steam slink into the air, feeling the warmth on his hands. Maybe he shouldn't have brought this up.

When he looked up, she was studying his face. He wanted to forget the whole thing and kiss her instead, but he knew he'd already been caught.

"Why, did you make plans with your family? Didn't you tell me you try to go down there for Thanksgiving?"

"Uh, yeah. Most years."

"So, you're going this year, too?" Her eyes squinted a bit, and he felt like he wasn't supposed to look away.

"So, before this," he motioned at her cast, "they were kind of hoping I would bring you. I meant to talk to you about that, but didn't before... Anyway, they understand that can't happen now, so we vaguely talked about Christmas."

He cleared his throat and looked out the window. He hadn't gotten away with anything. Here it came. His Kassidy being who she was.

"Brett," she murmured, and when he looked back, her eyes were dark, "you're still going to see your family, right?"

"Um." He ran his hand through his hair and gave her a smile he knew looked pathetic. "No. I'm gonna stay here with you."

She sat up straight and moved closer to him. "No, you need to go see your family."

"Kassidy..." He so rarely called her that anymore, it felt awkward. He kept that nervous, pathetic smile on his face, hoping it served as some kind of distraction.

"I know how much you miss your family, and this is one of the only chances you have to spend any real time with them. Didn't you say you ask for this time off at the beginning of every year – to make sure you get it?"

"Yeah, I do, and this year I'll be able to spend my time off with you." Before she could protest, because he could see it written on her face, he continued, "Yes, I miss my family, but you were in a ridiculous accident, and I love you. I want to spend it with you. You're my family here."

Her face blushed at this, but she wasn't giving up. "I don't want to be the reason you don't see your family. I don't want you to resent me for that." The sentence ended on a frantic note.

"Kass, I made the decision because I want to be here. You know I wouldn't resent you for that. What's really bothering you?"

She sighed and motioned toward her arm, but he wasn't going to take that excuse this time. He knew there was something else, something that started a couple days ago. He stared at her until she had to look away.

She turned so her whole body was facing him, and placed her cup down on the coffee table. Her face had gone white. He felt his foot wanting to tap, but forced it to be still.

"When I ran into Abigail in Auburn and she told me about moving to Sacramento, she also told me she thought she had seen Kurt in Sacramento. She wasn't sure, but she thought it was him. She was really interested in why he was here. It wasn't seeing her that freaked me out, it was the thought of him being here. I didn't tell you, because I thought it was stupid and something you didn't need to deal with. Remember when my mom said they ran into Abigail downtown and she had her phone number for me?"

He nodded, anger brewing in him at the thought of Kurt being anywhere near her.

"Well, she forgot to give it to me, so she texted Abigail later and gave her mine. Abigail called me a couple nights ago when you'd already left for work. She asked me if Kurt had reached out to me, because he hadn't contacted her. They were in a relationship, which I kind of suspected, but…she confirmed they were in one when Kurt and I were together."

"What?" He sucked in a breath. His ability to handle rage would be a very useful skill in this moment.

"I guess they're not together anymore, but she's not over him. I told her Kurt would not be contacting me. I knew I had to end the call when I brought up what a disgusting person he is and she started defending him, making it clear she didn't believe anything I said had happened. She was there when it all happened. She was one of the only people I could talk to about it. Her support was fake if they were already together. At the end of the conversation, I asked her not to call me again."

His mind reeled. "Kassie, you need to tell me stuff like that. That's a big freaking deal, and you were carrying that around on your shoulders along with all the other shit you're dealing with from your accident. If you feel unsafe…"

"No, I don't. It freaks me out that Kurt's been in my city, but I never told him I was moving here. He's already chewed me up and spit me out, and he's doing fine. He has no reason to contact me."

He brushed her hair away from her forehead, following the gesture with a kiss. She sounded like she was trying to talk herself into believing the words coming out of her mouth. "Okay, but if you ever see or hear anything from him, tell me. You don't need to deal with that on your own."

***

Mary stared at her ringing phone on the desk next to her in the silent office. She not only had the ringer up loud, but had left vibrate on. When it had started ringing, she'd almost jumped out of her seat. Maybe she could ignore it, say later that she had left it at home. He wouldn't believe her. He knew she never let her phone out of her sight. John knew so many things about her that a boss never should.

She felt a rush of adrenaline as the phone stopped ringing. She was in control of her life. She didn't have to answer because John called. He had ignored her for weeks. The accident was at the beginning of November and now Thanksgiving had come and gone. It was almost December and he was calling her. She was busy. She'd call him back later.

The phone rang again. She could almost feel the vibration in her bones. The back of her neck broke out in a cold sweat, but she let it ring. When it stopped, she got up to get another cup of coffee. She heard her phone ding as she sat down. A text from John lit up her screen.

Answer your phone. This is the last time.

As the phone started ringing for the third time, her heart raced. Did she dare? She'd never been defiant with the boss before. She'd never had a reason to be. As the ringing continued, she felt her resolve cracking. She knew that, ultimately, he wouldn't be ignored. And talking to him on the phone would be safer than seeing him in person.

She swiped her phone to answer, putting John on speaker.

"Hello?"

"Did you have fun with your little game?"

"What? Your other calls? Sorry, I had stepped away. My phone isn't glued to me."

"We both know that's not true. Take me off speaker." His voice was almost a growl.

"I'm the only one here," she said, motioning around the office as if he could see her.

"Take me off speaker," he repeated, and she could barely hear his voice.

She did as he asked. As she put the phone to her ear, she was a combination of scared and excited. It felt good to rebel, but she knew what could result from his anger.

"The accident," he said as if that was all she needed to hear. She noticed his inflection of the word also suggested the crash had been the opposite of accident.

"Yes. I've been trying to call you about that since it happened."

"I know. Do you know who else has been calling me since it happened? Kurt Leonard." She could hear the anger and irritability rising in his voice. "Apparently, the operative assigned to Ms. Turner now reaches directly out to him before contacting me, even though she is my employee. Mr. Leonard is providing her with additional funds to speak to him first. He found out about the "accident" before I did. He is threatening to pull his funding from the organization."

"He won't do that, John." Mary kept her voice calm and sure. "He doesn't have anywhere else to go. I brought him in. He has no other contacts. I doubt he'll contract with some cheap hire-to-kill group. They would be too sloppy. And you have to believe that the accident was just that. How would I have known that moron was driving that truck? That's not what she usually drives.

Turns out it's her parents'. And there is no way I could have recognized her enough in that moment to back up and hit her again because of who she was."

"Unless you had been following her."

"What?" This idea floored her. When would she have time to follow that worthless woman?

"Mr. Leonard suggested the idea." His voice was so cold now.

"Of course, he did! He's trying to turn you against me, John! The man is bored, pissed at me, and has nothing else to do! He wants you to get rid of me so he has no one speaking up against him! He's got more control in this organization than I do, and he started as a client! Don't you see what he's doing?"

"Don't ask me if I know what's going on in my organization!" he yelled, and she heard what sounded like his fist slamming down on his desk. "You need to get your shit together, Mary! I don't know what made you do what you did that night, but it's done now. You *are done. I will be finding a new position for you at the beginning of the new year. Finish up your active projects in December."*

"No! You can't do that! I've worked my ass off for you for years. Open your eyes, John! You're so obsessed with money; you can't see what's going on around you!"

"Goodbye, Mary," he answered, and the call ended.

She stared at her phone in shock. She was still alive, but she might as well be dead.

CHAPTER 19

He pulled his arms in closer to his body as he gripped the grocery bag handles. Man, it was cold. He hated winter, and while the calendar might say there were a few days of fall left, it was the middle of December, and no one was falling for that crap. The gray sky had opened up as he searched for a spot near Kassie's place, so now it was also raining as he trudged down the street to her apartment. For whatever reason, he'd never been able to stand jackets or coats with hoods, so he didn't own one. His Dodgers cap didn't do much to keep him dry, but at least it was something.

His entire family was flying up from Orange County for Christmas. He and Kassidy had planned to go to them, but his mom had insisted Kassidy should stay home to be more comfortable. She assured him it would be no trouble for his parents and siblings to travel this year.

Kassidy was in physical therapy for the injuries to her neck, back and leg, and, from what he could tell, it was going well. Her long cast had been replaced with one that only covered her forearm, so she was able to drive again, although her confidence wasn't quite there. But she was able to work more, which resulted in a considerable change for the better in her daily attitude. The swelling on her face and all stitches were gone, and he could see that she felt better about herself. He'd asked her a couple times about Abigail and Kurt, but she hadn't heard from either one of them.

If I could just make detective, he thought to himself as he walked. He hadn't heard anything yet, and his patience wasn't in top form.

As he made to climb the stairs to her apartment, his phone rang. He took a deep breath as he looked at the screen.

About five minutes later, he burst through her front door, a grin on his face. She was sitting on her couch, laptop situated, tea cup in her hand. Her eyes were wide with surprise, and Isla sat up quickly from where she'd been laying on the couch.

"No one should look that happy about going to the grocery store," she said with a small laugh, putting her computer and cup on the coffee table.

"I did it! I made detective!" He put the bags of groceries down inside the door, throwing his wet cap on a hook.

"Brett, that's awesome! Congratulations!" She was off the couch in seconds, throwing her arms around him. He managed to remove his soaked coat, and she kissed him, dancing him around the room as she embraced him.

This was what he had needed in his life for so long, and sometimes he still couldn't believe he had it. He kissed her forehead and savored the moment.

"But are you going to be able to adjust to working regular-person hours?" she teased.

"Yes, because it means we get to go to bed together every night."

"Every night? That's a lofty goal." She wiggled her eyebrows up and down.

He laughed and kissed her deeply. He didn't have to work that night, and he wanted to celebrate. "Go get ready. I'm taking you to The Melting Pot."

"Ooooo, fancy." She did a little jump, her expression one of pure joy.

She'd told him more than once how much she loved the fondue restaurant in downtown Sacramento. She ran to her room to change.

He beamed at her retreating figure. He never wanted to do life without her.

***

Mary slogged through her final projects. She had no motivation. What was the point? She couldn't imagine what type of tedious, low-level work the boss would assign her to after the holidays, but she wasn't planning to stick around for it. Her real estate business was thriving now. She didn't need the organization anymore. But she wasn't going to tell him that yet. Employees never left the organization, so she wasn't sure how she was going to do it. But she was going to make it happen.

It was nearly nine at night by the time she pulled into the parking lot of a multiple-story office building near Cal Expo. She'd sold the building several months before. Last year, she'd completed a termination project involving two of the new owner's debt collectors. With no debt collectors, he kept his life. So, while on paper he owned the building, she still controlled it. The organization was also giving him a stipend for allowing it to funnel some of its money through his business, so he couldn't really complain.

This building held a special place in her heart. One day it would help her destroy Kurt, and he would never see it coming. She had to bide her time a little longer. The more she had on him, the better. She had found a woman named Alexis after months of searching. The woman had changed her name after Kurt raped and fired her, and she'd buried herself deep to keep him from finding her again. Alexis was an avid member of a local painting group, and Mary had joined to get close to her. Over time, she would convince Alexis to go to the cops. She didn't care if the organization terminated Alexis after she went forward; she needed one of Kurt's victims to step up. That would be the icing on the cake of damning evidence she planned to provide the police.

She waved at the evening security guard stationed in the building's foyer. When she rounded a corner into the large atrium in the middle of the building, she ran into him.

Her voice sounded more unnerved than she would have liked as she tried to regain her composure. "What are you doing here?"

"You forced me to come to you. You're not returning my calls." Even though the light in the atrium was dim, she could still see the sneer on Kurt's face.

"Yeah, that was on purpose, asshole. I'm sure the boss told you I'm being demoted. I'm finishing up what I have, and then I won't be dealing with you anymore. Now get the hell out. I have some work to do before Christmas, and I don't want to be here late." She motioned toward the door, wishing one of the security guards would start doing their rounds.

He didn't move.

"If you had done your job properly from the beginning, you wouldn't be getting…demoted. I don't know why you have this sick obsession with me, Mary. You brought me into the organization because you wanted me to be close to you, but you sabotaged everything I asked you to do. I'm not sure how you got the position you're in. Or did you only treat my projects like this?"

Any fear she had been starting to feel was replaced by anger as her jaw dropped. "What the hell are you talking about? I'm not obsessed with you! I haven't given a shit about you since college. And you must be talking about Kassidy. I'll admit, the first two people I hired to follow her weren't great, and maybe I did that on purpose on some level, but every other single project I completed for you was done well and on time. All the monitoring. All the terminations. All the research and planning. Perfect.

"So, is it that you're obsessed with Kassidy? Wishing you hadn't let that go? Too bad she's found true love with her cop now. She was too repulsed by your disgusting habits to ever stay with you anyway. Not like that Abigail woman. I can see her causing you a lot of problems in the future. You let that go for too long.

"And where in the fucking hell do you get off questioning my position? You

have no idea what you're talking about. You have no idea the scale of work we do. I have been working in this organization for years, and I've done things you couldn't even dream of in your worst nightmares. And I have done them well. The boss has always had confidence in me. It wasn't until you showed up that it all went to hell. Now, get out of my building!"

He still didn't move, and she wished she could rip that repulsive look off his face. "I have no interest in Kassidy Turner. I'm assuming she will become more of a problem at some point, as well as her boyfriend, and then I will have them both terminated. So far Abigail is harmless, but she will most likely end up terminated as well. I have to keep myself and my company safe, Mary, and with the money I'm giving your boss, he is more than willing to help me do that."

"But you understand that John's your boss now, too, right? You're reviewing projects, so you work for him. And if something was to come to light that made you too big of a liability, his mind would clear quickly, and no amount of money would make you a friend of this organization." She seethed through gritted teeth.

He laughed – a slightly strangled sound that raised the hairs on her arms. "I don't have a boss, Mary. I don't answer to anyone. And nothing will come to light, because your lovely organization is making sure that doesn't happen. I have to wipe things completely clean."

"Things can never be wiped completely clean. You've assaulted, raped, and killed a lot of people. You may not have used your own hands to do the killing, but you still killed them. You've created a lot of ghosts, Kurt, and those ghosts will come back to haunt you."

He studied her face for a moment with his intimidating eyes, the same eyes he used to scare all those women. She stood her ground. He didn't scare her. He didn't.

"Are you making some kind of threat, Mary?" he asked, his voice like ice.

"No. I'm stating the truth."

He slapped her hard across the face. "Stop playing games!"

Shock filtered through her as she gripped her cheek. What the hell? Did he really hit her? Anger raged through her. Anger at everything he had done since the day they met. Anger at how he had never taken her seriously, never been interested in her like he was interested in bimbo women like Kassidy and Abigail. Anger at how he had destroyed her life and still wanted to rub her face in it. She wanted to hurt him now. To scare him.

"I have everything, Kurt. Documents, photos, videos, audio. Everything your sick mind has ever thought to create while doing your disgusting deeds. I have every piece of documentation for every one of your projects. I've kept them all."

"You're supposed to be destroying all evidence as you go." His face was blank now, but anger still lived in his eyes.

"I know, but I decided it might be better to hang onto it." She stood up straight, staring into those eyes.

"Where is it, Mary?" he asked, and she heard the smallest falter in his voice.

"Go to hell, Kurt. I'll enjoy watching you take that trip."

He stepped forward and grabbed her arm. "What did you do with it? Which disgusting building are you hiding it in?"

She grabbed his hand and twisted it back, and he pulled away from her with a growl. Her heart was racing now.

"And I shared it with Kassidy. She has copies of everything, and she is going to share it with her cop. You're too late, Kurt. Even if you find everything I have, you're too late!" She tried to sound convincing.

He stepped back as if she had hit him. "You're lying. You've never spoken to her."

"But didn't you and John think I was following her? Didn't you think I caused that crash on purpose? I was trying to get close to her. The crash wasn't ideal, but it gave me a reason to talk to her later."

"That's bullshit. I don't believe you." He turned away from her to look down one of the dark hallways that led away from the atrium. When he looked

back, there was something in his eyes Mary never thought she would see.

"Like hell, you don't. I can see the paranoia on your face." She wanted to laugh. Her, scaring Kurt Leonard. One of the most powerful men in the country. It felt good.

"That's okay. If you won't tell me where it is, I'm sure my friends here can find out. If I'm going to hell, Mary, you'll be there to greet me."

She was confused for a moment, but then someone grabbed her, and she turned quickly in the tight grip. She recognized the two men standing there. They were operatives with her organization. Her heart stopped. This was her termination.

Her mind went blank for a moment, but then she started to fight. She tried to grab for the knife she kept in her purse, but it was ripped away from her and tossed to the side. She screamed, calling for the security guards, who were nowhere to be seen.

She looked into Kurt's eyes as time slowed and the men attempted to hold her. She managed to get away from them for a few seconds and land some kicks and punches. She started to run, but they were agile and strong, and they soon overpowered her.

Kurt turned to walk away, saying nothing to her. There was no remorse on his face, only calm. But she had seen his eyes, and they told a different story. Kurt was scared. Kurt was breaking. She might not see another sunrise, but he wouldn't be far behind.

She flailed, kicked, screamed, and tried to bite as the men dragged her down that same dark hallway she'd seen Kurt studying moments before. The light faded away and with it, the retreating figure of a man who, once upon a time, she would have done anything for.

CHAPTER 20

It was just past eleven at night, and Kassidy had already managed to crawl into bed. She was getting back into her full work schedule again, but it wasn't easy to keep up. She was still in pain sometimes, and her cast, albeit smaller, was annoying to type with. She was drifting into a dream in which she was walking in a field, when a strange feeling hit her, almost like waking up to an earthquake, when gravity feels both less effective and heavier for several moments. She swore she heard some kind of noise, but since she was still trying to pull herself from her dream, she couldn't be sure. Within minutes, as her tired mind was trying to drift back to sleep, the streets around her filled with sirens. She sat up and listened, pulling her knees to her chest. She checked her phone. Nothing from Brett. It might not have anything to do with his beat. She laid down again, Isla jumping up on the bed from wherever she'd been before. Kassidy pet the cat, who felt anxious, trying to slow her mind.

It didn't work. She thought long and hard about turning on the news in case they were already covering whatever it was, but she really needed to sleep. But she tossed most of the night, wishing she had turned on the stupid news. Her alarm sounded at six-thirty, but she shut it off and managed to fall asleep.

Her eyelids were heavy as she forced them open, feeling Brett get in bed next to her. When she managed to focus on the clock, she saw it was already after nine. There went a good part of her morning. Thank God her first interview wasn't for an hour, and it was over the phone.

She stretched and breathed in deeply, concentrating on the air around her. She coughed, reacting to the smell of smoke. Her brain leapt to attention as she turned to face him, remembering the sirens from the night before. He tried to smile at her, but he looked more than exhausted.

"It's late…Did you just get here?" By now she was used to his hours, and he usually got to her place between seven-thirty and seven-forty-five in the morning, depending on how much paperwork he had at the end of his shift.

"About twenty minutes ago," he answered with a large yawn. "I'm sorry if I stink. I took a shower, but I feel like the smell is one with me now. I left my uniform in my trunk, so you wouldn't have to smell it, but I guess it doesn't matter." He yawned again, and his eyes stayed closed for a while before he opened them.

"What happened? I woke up around eleven, but forced myself not to watch the news."

"And then tortured yourself for not watching it?" He chuckled, knowing her too well. "An office building near Cal Expo exploded."

It took her brain a moment to register his words. "Exploded? How? Was anyone hurt?"

He moved closer to her. She took his hand under the covers. "Two nighttime security guards patrolling the building died. Well, the second is presumed dead. They haven't located her body yet, but she was supposed to be at work. They don't have record of anyone else being there.

"There were two college kids hanging out on the side of a building in the adjacent parking lot, and the blast threw them. They were taken to the hospital with pretty serious injuries. I'm not sure how they are now, unfortunately. The two closest buildings also sustained some damage.

"It blew out three cars' windows, and the cars crashed into each other. Those occupants were also all sent to the hospital. The back of the building faces a vacant lot, so at least no harm was done there. The preliminary thought is there could be something faulty in the gas line going into the building. PG&E responded and is going to investigate.

"The property manager showed up, and he said the female security guard, the one who hasn't been located, was written up a while back for cooking in the cafeteria's kitchen during her shift, which she didn't have permission to do. He thinks she might have left the gas on and then something caused a spark.

"I don't think anyone's buying that, but the remains of the building will have to cool a bit first before they can investigate. They're still making sure the fire's extinguished now. There's not much of it left unfortunately, and it may be hard to get a for-sure cause. No one reported smelling gas in the days leading up…" His words drifted away. His eyes were closed, and he'd thrown his arm over his face, which she'd learned was his comfortable way of sleeping. But she was still so curious.

"So maybe foul play of some sort?"

"Possible," he murmured.

She sighed, feeling for those families now grieving their loved ones and those recovering in the hospital. "At least it didn't happen during the day, when the building probably would've been full. Not that that makes it any easier for the families of those who did die."

He made some kind of noise, but didn't say anything.

Thinking of the people in the hospital made Kassidy think about her survivor series. She'd submitted one right before her accident, but hadn't worked on another since. She needed to get back into that. She wondered where Alexis was and if she was okay. She'd never heard back from her. Maybe she should call her again.

She was sitting up now, and she smiled down at his sleeping form. Hopefully he'd be able to sleep until the afternoon. They'd discovered it was more difficult for him to sleep as long as he needed when she was home. It was like his brain couldn't handle the fact that she was up and doing things. She'd be lying if she said she wasn't looking forward to him working during the day and for fewer hours. She loved Brett, and it was clear he loved her, but Brett also loved overtime. He'd promised he'd cut back on it when he started as a detective, and she couldn't wait for those days.

***

Christopher could breathe in Los Angeles. He belonged in this city or in one like it. He often had to stay in Sacramento for weeks at a time, but Los Angeles was his home. He craved crowds, noise, activity. He liked to blend into it all and observe, partaking when he chose. It provided him with endless amounts of entertainment. Of course, Manhattan was his dream. A much different culture, but so full of everything. He'd requested to be transferred there many times. He was used to working with Mary now, and her tornado-like personality was interesting enough, but he would leave for Manhattan in a heartbeat.

Christopher wasn't surprised to see Kurt standing near a back wall of the boss' office when he was ushered in that afternoon. Mary was right. The relationship between those two was tight. Christopher had only ever seen the boss act so chummy with Mary, but Mary didn't have millions of dollars to contribute.

"Christopher. Thank you for coming." The boss motioned for him to sit down.

Kurt said nothing, but nodded as Christopher took a chair on the other side of the boss' massive desk.

Christopher returned the gesture. He never felt the need to make small talk or act like he cared more than he did in professional settings. The job was all that mattered. He pursued recreational relationships elsewhere.

"I'll come right to the point. I have a proposition for you that I hope you'll accept. It'll mean a promotion, and you'll be working with some of our top operatives and project managers. I know it's a position you've wanted for some time." The boss held his fingertips together in front of his face, which resembled a cold, gray stone.

Christopher made it clear he was listening, but didn't respond. He didn't play games. He wanted people to learn to be straightforward.

"A project manager position opened in the organization's third Manhattan office, and I suggested you fill it. My New York counterpart is impressed by your experience. You've made incredible progress in California, and you've proven you should be in a more fast-paced environment."

Christopher nodded, but kept his expression neutral, casting the quickest of glances at Kurt, who looked anxious about something. He narrowed his eyes the smallest amount and turned his gaze back to the boss.

"We need you to complete one more project here. Once that's done, you will be immediately transferred," the boss continued.

Of course, *Christopher thought to himself. "What is the project?" he asked out loud.*

"The termination of Abigail O'Rourke."

"Mr. Leonard's former lover?" He allowed himself to raise one eyebrow only slightly. "That is surprising. I was under the impression Mary was handling all of Mr. Leonard's cases, except Ms. Turner."

Christopher noticed Kurt flinch at Kassidy Turner's name. What had he missed?

"We thought you would be better for this project. Mary has demonstrated the inability to stay objective when it comes to Mr. Leonard's projects. In fact, we're going to house you in a different office in Sacramento while you plan and execute. We can't have any distractions," the boss explained.

"And we'd like it to be something quick. There isn't time for a drawn-out plan. Something like a car accident or suicide," Kurt said, stepping forward.

Christopher studied Kurt for a moment and then turned his eyes back to the boss. He didn't know John very well, but he knew how to read the man's face. John's jaw was clearly clenched, his eyes dark, but he said nothing in response to Kurt's comment.

Interesting. Do we have some ill feelings developing here? *Christopher thought to himself. The next time he talked to Mary, he would have to find out what she knew.*

It was clear the "proposition" the boss spoke of wasn't so much that as an order, but Christopher decided to ignore that. "That would be no problem. I can get started with the plan right away. I look forward to the move to New York. I appreciate the opportunity."

"You deserve it. You've more than proven yourself here. I know this project will be flawless. We'll be in touch to provide you with the information you need."

Christopher nodded and stood, understanding the meeting to be over.

"One more thing." Kurt stepped forward again, failing to hide the anxiety in his voice.

Christopher stopped and clocked the boss' expression again. The man's annoyance was bubbling just under the surface.

"Yes. We had something to ask you." The boss sat forward in his chair, his face changing. Whatever the question was, he wanted it to look like his idea to ask.

"And it's important that you're truthful." Kurt was trying to look taller than he was, but Christopher was not a short man, and he wasn't easily intimidated.

Christopher blinked at Kurt and turned back to the boss.

"You and Mary worked closely together for years, and she may have confided in you about things she didn't tell anyone else. We're aware she was keeping an unapproved collection of various documents and other evidence regarding Mr. Leonard. Do you know the whereabouts of that collection?"

A secret stash? Interesting.

"You could ask Mary." He knew full well it was a ridiculous statement,

but he was testing an idea.

"We tried that. She wasn't helpful." Kurt looked a little jumpy.

"Mary had to be disciplined for her string of project-related inadequacies. She was transferred without much notice and didn't update us on its location," the boss explained in a monotone voice.

Christopher had the distinct feeling he would never be speaking to Mary again.

"So, Mary never discussed this with you?" The boss fixed his stare on Christopher, measuring his body language, but Christopher never felt the need to perform for anyone, so there was nothing to measure.

"Not that I recall," he shrugged in response. "I believe that is something I would remember."

The boss continued to watch him for several more moments, and Kurt fidgeted in the background.

"Thank you, Christopher. You can go. I'll be in touch." The boss nodded with what looked like a smile on his face, but it was a little off somehow. Christopher doubted John was capable of an authentically friendly expression.

Christopher nodded and walked casually from the office.

Mary, I tried to tell you, *he smiled to himself, shaking his head as if musing over the follies of a small child.*

CHAPTER 21

Brett's parents, sisters, and their families flew into Sacramento International Airport on December 23. The rainy day didn't faze Brett. The ridiculous airport traffic was like nothing. The crowd of anxious people milling through the terminal felt like a World Series championship parade. He hadn't seen his family since the summer. It was an electric feeling having them in his city.

Still, he tried to play it cool for Kassie. He knew she was nervous enough, and he didn't want to make it worse.

"You're like a kid at Disneyland," she laughed at him as they waited at the bottom of the escalators. His sisters' flight came in first. He realized he was rocking back and forth on his feet.

"No idea what you're talking about." He checked his watch again.

She rolled her eyes and pulled his Dodgers cap down to his nose. "I'm talking about you checking the arrivals board at least five times."

"That's normal behavior." He grinned, keeping the hat like it was for a few moments before running his hand through his hair and placing it back where it should be.

"Uh, yeah."

He noticed she was also checking her watch, and crossing and uncrossing her arms, and pushing her hair behind her ears.

"They're going to love you." He put an arm around her shoulders.

She leaned into him and nodded, but didn't say anything.

Brett's sister Elise was the middle sibling. She had a glowing, graceful personality, which put those around her at ease. She, her husband, and their son came down the escalator first. Brett grabbed her into a hug, fluffing his baby nephew's hair. She broke free with a wide smile and hugged Kassie.

"We're so excited to finally meet you." Elise adjusted the baby on her hip, her smile never leaving her face.

Thank God for Elise, Brett thought. The older of his two sisters was a master at smoothing over anxious situations.

Kassie shook hands with Elise's husband, Terrance, and gave their nearly-six-month-old son, Isaiah, a soft smile. The boy looked less than amused, but Kassidy made a silly face and he cracked a little smile before turning away again.

This is going pretty good so far. Brett felt a sense of relief wash through him. He shouldn't have worried.

Brett's youngest sister, Lily, and her husband, Brandon, had flown with Elise and Terrance. Lily's personality was like a small explosion. He couldn't remember many times throughout their lives when she wasn't talking. She tried to win every argument. It made perfect sense that she'd become an attorney. She was already chattering about their trip as she hugged Brett. When she turned to Kassie, her natural light dimmed a little. She still smiled and shook her hand, but said only a few words.

Brandon was quiet and relaxed – the complete opposite of his wife. Brett figured this was how their marriage worked. His brother-in-law also shook his and Kassie's hands, and Brett wasn't sure if the man noticed his wife's unusual behavior.

Elise was chatting with Kassie, so Brett caught up with Lily, who was already making her way to baggage claim.

"What's up, Lil?" he asked, taking her carry-on bag from her, even though she protested.

"Nothing. It's great to see you, big brother." She gave him a grin, stopping as they reached the conveyer belt. Everyone else was meandering toward them, so they would be alone for a few minutes.

"You always were good at changing the subject."

"How much do you know about Kassidy? You've been dating for what, a few months?" she asked, acting like she'd missed his comment.

"Uh, yeah. I know her really well." He suddenly felt himself getting defensive. "I've told you about her."

"I know, but you didn't tell me about the stuff in her past." Lily turned to him, crossing her arms.

"What?"

"I Googled her, Brett. I know what happened in her past, with that guy in San Francisco."

"You Googled my girlfriend? Why the hell would you do that?" He was more confused than angry, and he checked behind him to make sure Kassie wasn't close.

"Brett, did she tell you what she did?"

"She told me what happened, yeah. All that she 'did' was try to bring him to justice." He frowned as she turned to watch the conveyer belt, which had begun its sluggish march.

"There was never any evidence. None of the women ever came forward. He'd broken up with her, and the articles I read made it sound like she was after his money. She'd been living with him, and she didn't want to give up that lifestyle. They even interviewed a couple of her friends from college. They confirmed she'd told them how much she liked having anything she wanted available to her."

He stared at his sister, finding it hard to believe the words coming out of her mouth. "Lily, that's bullshit. Those women were too scared to go up against that guy, because he's got a lot of power. Does that surprise you in today's world? I don't know who those 'friends' were, but I'm guessing they wanted attention. And, if she loves money so much, why is she dating a cop?"

Lily again failed to respond to most of what he said. "It's that cop I'm worried about. The Me Too movement is huge now, Brett. Why haven't any of these women come forward?"

"I don't know. I wish they would, because I'd like to nail that guy to the wall. It's not like you to judge someone you don't know," he hissed back quickly as Kassie came up behind him.

Lily frowned at him and turned to grab one of her suitcases.

"You okay?" Kassie asked, her eyes studying his. He planted a smile on his face and put his arm back around her.

Shit.

"Yeah. The airport's getting to me." He didn't like lying to her, but the truth would hurt her more.

"When do your parents arrive?" She squinted back toward one of the arrival screens.

"In a couple hours. They need to pick up their rental car," he nodded toward his siblings, "and then they're going to their hotel so Isaiah can nap. I can take you back to your place if you'd like to get some work done." He was starting to wish the day was over. Elise was acting like herself, but had Lily told his parents what she'd found? He didn't need them believing lies about Kassidy. He wanted to pick them up by himself so he'd have the chance to talk to them.

"I'm done with work until after Christmas. I don't mind coming back to get them."

Of course.

When everyone had their luggage and the sisters picked up their rental car, Brett and Kassidy grabbed his car so he could guide them to their hotel. His parents would be staying at his place.

"I don't think Lily likes me," Kassie said in a matter-of-fact voice when they were alone in the car.

Dammit.

"That's not true, Kass. She's an attorney. She's high strung and has trust issues. That's how she is at first." He heard the bitterness in his voice, which he had meant to hide.

"Wow. I never knew you had a thing against attorneys." She turned in her seat so she could face him, brushing stray hair away with her casted arm. "You've never described her that way before."

"Yeah, I don't see her that way, I guess, but it takes her a while to warm up to people," he shrugged in response.

Not true. The woman treats strangers like friends.

By the time they arrived back at the airport to pick up Jill and Andrew Green, Brett had a headache and wasn't saying much, but he held Kassie's hand tightly. His mom was a lot like Elise, and his dad was a logical person. They wouldn't believe any of the crap Lily might have shared with them. Brett wanted to guard Kassie from her past. He wanted to go back and erase those dark moments, but protecting her from them now was the best he could do.

He saw Kassie give him questioning looks in his peripheral vision, but he hoped she thought it was just nerves.

His parents were kind to her right off the bat, and Brett felt relief wash over him. Who gave a crap what Lily thought if his parents treated her well?

"She's lovely, Brett." His mom squeezed his arm as she looked over at Kassidy and Andrew, once again waiting for luggage. "Lily mentioned something last night. She read some news articles about Kassidy?"

Freaking dammit.

"Yeah." He ran his hand through his hair. "Kassie's last boyfriend did some pretty messed up stuff. Kassie discovered the truth and tried to go to the police, but there was no evidence. He's this high-powered tech guy in San Francisco. He dragged her reputation through the dirt, and she moved back to Sacramento to get away from him. Lily believes the crap they wrote about her in those articles – that she was after his money and wanted to get back at him for breaking up with her. You should have seen the way she treated Kassie earlier." Brett was seething by the time he was done, but he noticed Kassie and his dad were on their way back, their hands full of luggage, so he tried to calm down.

"She's worried about you, Brett. Lily likes to have this air of complete confidence, but she doesn't do well with you being so far away."

He was surprised by this, but his anger wasn't so easy to drop. "Okay, but she shouldn't believe disgusting news stories over what I tell her."

"I agree," his mom reassured him, and then Kassie was at his side.

"Something's up with you." She slowed him as they followed his parents out of the terminal. "Things went great with your parents…"

"They did. It's nothing, Kass. I'm tired. Looking forward to the lights?" He took her hand and tried to give what he hoped looked like a charming grin.

He had the night off, and their families were getting together to walk the Fab 40s light display in East Sacramento. Every Christmas season, the residents of 40th-49th Streets strung their houses and trees with holiday lights, and Kassie got a faraway look in her eyes when she talked about it. She described the different houses she loved and the feeling she got hearing strangers wishing each other "Merry Christmas" amidst the sounds of a school band and children's choir. Brett would do anything to give her that kind of joy.

She watched him for a moment. He knew she didn't believe him, and he felt a wave of guilt, but he wouldn't tell her the truth. In a couple days, Lily would see how wrong she was.

***

Kassidy was so used to Brett staying over that it felt weird not to have him there while his parents were at his place. He'd taken Isla with him, because his mom wanted to win the cat over. She was alone in her apartment for the first time in months, and she didn't sleep well. In the past, she'd loved having her own space, but that wasn't the case anymore. Even when it was only Isla there, the company was nice.

Brett had to work Christmas night, so everyone was going to Kassidy's parents' house for lunch that day. His parents were driving their rental car, so Brett picked her up on his own. She pulled him into the apartment and kissed him like she hadn't seen him for weeks, wishing they had more time to themselves.

"Merry Christmas, Kassie," he said, keeping his lips close to hers.

He pulled a rectangular package wrapped in dark red and gold paper from behind his back. She knew right away it was a book, but she hadn't asked him for anything. She unwrapped it, and it took her a moment to understand what she was seeing. It was a book she already owned in a tattered paperback, because she had read it a million times. *To Kill a Mockingbird.* It was a book she loved, a book that had changed her life, but this copy was different.

She caught her breath. "Brett, is this a first edition?"

He nodded, watching her with a small smile.

"But a first edition of this book..."

"Because I know you'll worry about price, I have a friend in Orange County who collects and sells rare and first edition books. He found this for me and gave me an incredible discount. That's to set your mind at ease. I know how much this book means to you. It's signed by Harper Lee..."

She jumped across the small space between them, kissing him again. "Thank you." She didn't think she could have received a more perfect gift.

"I'll take that to mean you think it's an acceptable gift, but maybe I should try harder next time," he said in a serious voice.

She rolled her eyes, placing the precious book on her coffee table and grabbing his gift from where it had been leaning against the side of her couch.

He didn't say a word as he unwrapped the framed artwork, which had the feel of a mini mural, but would fit perfectly on a wall in his house. It was a stylized painting of several of the major scenes from the original three *Star Wars* movies. The paint had the appearance of metal.

"This is incredible! Where did you get this?" he asked as his eyes took in every piece of the painting. She wanted to pat herself on the back.

"I'm friends with one of the downtown mural artists. I gave him some input and asked him to create something for me. He's as big of a *Star Wars* nerd as you are," she teased.

"It's awesome. Thank you." He returned her embrace, but could barely take his eyes off the painting. "We're kick-ass present givers."

She laughed and gave him a playful shove, taking her coat off the hook by door.

As they made their way down the stairs, Kassidy glanced at a car parked just feet away. She recognized many of the vehicles parked near her apartment, because they belonged to her neighbors or people who lived nearby. She didn't recognize this one. A woman was struggling to get several packages into her car. She succeeded as Kassidy and Brett made it to the bottom of the stairs. Brett was in front of her and was already turning left, the opposite direction of the woman's car.

Kassidy meant to make nothing more than quick eye contact, maybe offer the woman an empathetic smile, but the woman stopped and held Kassidy's gaze. Her face was like a stone. She stared until Kassidy turned to follow Brett. Who the hell was she? Why the evil look?

Kassidy turned once more to look over her shoulder, but the woman was back in her car now, pulling out of her spot. As she looped her arm back through Brett's, she wanted to ask if he had noticed the woman, but the peaceful look on his face told her otherwise, so she didn't bother.

Calm down, Kassidy. She had nothing to do with you. She was someone having a bad day. Enjoy yours. There aren't enough days like this.

CHAPTER 22

"You have nothing to worry about. If they were somewhere in that building, they have already been destroyed, and I have operatives checking all her other properties. Her house was cleared. I believe she was bluffing, but if there is anything to find, we'll find it." John sat back in his chair, the general state of annoyance he lived in when Kurt Leonard was around was growing, spreading through him like a deadly disease. There was strong evidence Kurt was breaking, drowning in the immoral situation he had created for himself. John had wanted to keep him happy as long as possible, to bring in as much revenue as he would throw their way. But if Kurt fell apart, he would be more of a liability than he was worth.

"I hope so, because if I go down, this organization goes down with me." Kurt scowled.

John's anger developed into full-blown rage. He stood from his desk and gazed out his window in an attempt to calm down. Money or not, this man had to go. He turned around when he felt he wasn't going to leap across his desk and strangle Kurt. He settled in his chair, folding his hands and resting his elbows on his desk. He took Kurt in. The man was used to living in a world where he could say and do anything and everyone else cowered at his feet. This was not that world.

"What an interesting thing to say, Mr. Leonard. Do you believe this is the kind of organization that can be squashed by one disgruntled man who was careless in his life choices? You must understand that this is one piece of a nation-wide conglomerate, and certainly not the strongest piece. We are an organization that has itself tightly wound through all aspects of this country's political, business, entertainment, and drug cultures, subtly controlling those cultures as necessary." He wiped all expression from his face, and Kurt was quiet.

"Perhaps Mary didn't make you aware of our extensive power when she first brought you to me, as it's our policy not to give new clients too much information when they start working with us. But as a man who was signing off on high-priority projects, I assumed you would have gained this knowledge. Of course, we are very grateful for your generous contributions – they have gone to support projects across the country. And we have completed the requests you paid us to complete, although at times they were clearly unnecessary. But, please keep in mind, this company is worth many billions of dollars without your funding. You should in no way think anything that happens to you has any impact on this organization.

"You should also keep in mind that I allowed you to carry out the termination of one of my best project managers. Your methods were… interesting, as I believe they will only bring attention your way, but I allowed them regardless. Yes, she had become the proverbial thorn in my side as of late, because she was too distracted by you and her real estate business, but she was one of the best. Still, I recognized your funding was far more important to this organization than one project manager. Yet," and here he paused until he saw Kurt squirm, "her absence, and the absence that Christopher's transfer brings, will put me behind in my Northern California projects. Christopher's transfer is only necessary because we need to distract him from looking into Mary's disappearance, and we must start fresh with a new team in Sacramento. I'm sure all of this will work out fine, but I hope you understand the stress it causes me and our California chapter. You should keep everything I just told you in

mind before you open your mouth and let anything else spill out."

Kurt couldn't hide his shock, but after several moments he appeared to be attempting to regain his composure.

"Since I've already paid you, I'm sure you will do everything in your power to locate Mary's evidence, if you don't confirm it's all been destroyed."

This was an acceptable statement, so John nodded.

"I would like to request the terminations of Kassidy Turner and the cop she's dating. These would need to be priority projects, because I'm not sure if Mary shared the documentation with Kassidy." Kurt sat up straighter in his chair and spoke with a tone John assumed he used with his employees.

John stared at him again for several minutes. He was done with Kurt Leonard.

"Again, I believe Mary was bluffing. Most likely, she was trying to add to your paranoia. I'm afraid we don't have the project managers to coordinate any more of your requests at this time, Mr. Leonard. We appreciate the business you've given us, but you and I are going to part ways now."

"What?" Kurt eyed him, shifting in his chair. "But these terminations need to be completed right away. If Mary got to them…"

"Mr. Leonard," John stood up behind his desk, pushing a button to open his office door, "if that had happened, you would be hearing about yourself on the news by now. The operative I assigned to Ms. Turner has noted no difference in their daily activities, except spending time with the boyfriend's family for Christmas."

Two of John's personal security guards loomed in the office doorway, waiting if needed.

"I…I could pay more than before." Kurt sounded frantic now.

"Unfortunately, your funds are no longer needed here. Have a nice day."

"You're dropping me? You can't fucking do that!" Kurt screamed, slamming his fists down on the desk. John had turned to his computer screen and gave no reaction. His security moved forward, towering behind Kurt.

Kurt turned quickly, taking them in. He gave John one more glare and stormed from the office. John sighed. Now he would have to arrange for an operative to follow Kurt. Who knew what kind of asinine issues he would cause in the future? He wished Mary was alive so he could berate her for making the mistake that was Kurt Leonard.

***

Brett's family stayed in Sacramento until December 30. Although Brett hadn't been able to get much time off, he soaked up what time he did have. He was already making plans for his summer vacation – a trip to Orange County for Isaiah's first birthday. He was glad Kassie loved the beach, because he planned to spend about ninety percent of his time there, forgetting anything that didn't involve sand and ocean.

"It's been great having them here," Brett sighed, leaning back in his chair, taking Kassie's hand. "They've driven me nuts on several occasions, but it was worth it. And they've gotten along great with your folks."

His and Kassie's families were finishing up a farewell dinner at Zocalo, one of his favorite Mexican restaurants in Sacramento, the night before their flights.

"You're so at ease when they're around." Kassie gave him a small smile. Then she added quietly, "Have you ever thought about moving closer to them?"

Her eyes were conflicted as he studied them. She wanted him to be happy, but she wanted him to say he didn't think about moving.

"Maybe someday, but I've made my life here for now." He squeezed her hand and gave her a small kiss.

She nodded, but her eyes remained concerned. He realized she was looking over his shoulder at Lily, who was sitting two seats away from him. The two hadn't exchanged many words, not for Kassie's lack of trying. Brett felt like a child, wondering if their mom would notice if he shoved his sister.

After dinner, everyone made their way back to Brett's house for coffee and dessert. As Brett handed his mom a piece of pie, he noticed Kassie pulling Lily aside. His sister's arms were crossed and she looked less than interested, but Kassie looked determined.

Good job, Kass.

His girlfriend was more perceptive than most, and she'd noticed things with Lily hadn't gotten any better.

The two women ended up sitting down and talking for about forty minutes. Everyone else was distracted with various conversations, so they had the chance to do so. Brett looked over at them every now and then. Their expressions boomeranged between pissed and calm, but Kassie held her own, and the talk resolved itself. They didn't hug or act like best friends as they parted, but they looked more comfortable with each other.

"How did that go?" he asked as Kassie came to stand by him.

"It was good. I got a chance to explain my side of things, and she opened up a little more about her feelings. She didn't really want to hear what I had to say at first, but I was persistent. I don't think we'll ever be soul mates, but it's a lot better now. She worries about you, Brett. She doesn't like having you up here."

"I've heard that before. I get it, but it's not a great excuse for her to dislike you."

She shrugged. "I think she sees me as someone keeping you tethered here – like maybe you'd move back home otherwise. That made it easier for her to believe what they wrote about me in those articles. Now that we've talked, I think she'll trust me more as time goes on."

When his family was gone, the expected funk he felt after reunions settled on him, and his natural reaction was to push himself back into work as much as possible. So, he picked up an extra shift during the day on New Year's Eve. He'd be starting his detective duties on January 2.

"You could start a one-man-band with that foot, Green," Kassie teased as they waited for the ball to drop on the TV in her apartment on New Year's Eve.

"It's hard being terrified and excited at the same time," he grinned in response, forcing his foot to stop tapping.

"I know, but it's a new year – one I think we both need, and you're going to do great. A new adventure awaits the Squirrel Thwarter!"

"Oh, my God, I thought you'd forgotten." He smacked his palm to his face.

"I'll never forget that." She stuck out her tongue, but when he was silent for a moment, she added, "You love me."

"Damn right," he responded as he pulled her into a kiss. No matter what happened and what other stress he had, she would be there. Everything would be fine.

CHAPTER 23

Kassidy woke up at two in the morning to another anxious feeling she couldn't quite pinpoint. She wondered if she'd been having a nightmare. She listened for a moment. The world around her was too quiet. But with the time, that shouldn't be a surprise. She felt Isla laying on her feet at the end of the bed, and she could hear Brett's quiet breathing next to her. Everything was fine. Why did something feel wrong?

The news was on by six, almost right after she opened her eyes. She could see how tired the reporter was. She was standing outside the site of the building explosion near Cal Expo. Countless police cars sat in the background. The building had already been fenced off, but there was fresh police tape as well.

Right before two o'clock that morning, police were alerted to someone moving around at the site. When police arrived, they exchanged gun fire with several people. Two of the mystery assailants were killed; one was injured and taken into custody.

A police department spokeswoman could not comment on who the people were, mentioning that the investigation was ongoing. She indicated police believed the suspects were there for a specific reason, as witnesses said they appeared to be searching the site, and they brought gun power to defend themselves.

Kassidy heard Brett's cell phone ring and then his muffled response. He was in and out of the shower in about five minutes. He flew to the kitchen, where he started some toast for himself, attempting to both eat an apple and pour coffee while he waited. She got up to help him with the coffee. She'd gotten her cast removed, and it felt so good to have total use of both hands and arms.

"Was it on the news?" he questioned without having to be specific.

She nodded. "What's the deal with that building?"

"Hopefully we can figure that out. I'm gonna work the case with a couple members of my team." He looked energized as he grabbed the travel mug of coffee and juggled his still-hot toast from one hand to another, trying not to burn himself. He gave her a quick kiss.

"I'll call you later. Love you." Then he was gone. It was the fastest she had ever seen him move.

She had already eaten dinner that night when she heard a key in her lock. She was sitting on her couch working on two different articles, with one of her favorite podcasts playing in the background, but her curiosity about the explosion site had been getting the better of her all day. She looked up, imagining he would be exhausted.

She was shocked to see he had as much energy as he had that morning. He flopped down on the couch next to her after giving her a kiss. Isla jumped on his lap, and he scratched under her chin.

"So, what's so important about that building that random goons would be sneaking around its burned-out shell?" She turned to face him, crossing her legs under her.

He laughed. "Goons. I love you."

"What? It's a popular word in the cheesy 70s and 80s shows that hold a special place in my heart." She gave him a small smile, but was waiting to see what he'd say about the building.

"Oh, I know. You'd leave me for Jim Rockford in a second."

"Of course, I would," she replied, playing into his tease. "So…"

He smirked at her. "I don't know what's so special about that building. We're working on that. These guys weren't your everyday crooks – a synonym I will use in place of goons. They were there for a reason. They had guns at the ready, and from what the responding officers told us, they shot those guns well. Luckily, there were more officers, so they were able to overpower them. Strange that whoever sent them wouldn't have thought about how heavily people would still be watching that site. The cause of the fire hasn't even been officially determined, and the department has already had to chase away several wannabe investigators."

"Clearly these weren't more of the same. Maybe they were a diversion for something else? Or an expendable part of a bigger crime. If they achieved whatever they were there to do, great, but if they didn't, maybe it didn't really matter." She sighed, wishing she could write this story, but it'd been assigned to the staff writer at the *Bee* who covered the explosion.

When he didn't say anything, she turned to see what he was doing. He was staring at her, a proud smile on his face. "Maybe you should be the detective."

She flashed him a goofy grin. "I've covered my fair share of crime over the years, and they were just ideas. However, I think I'd make a damn good detective."

"I know you would."

"I wonder if the guy who survived will say anything. I wouldn't imagine so," she said, thinking aloud again.

"We'll find out soon. He could be discharged from the hospital in a few days."

***

Brett had never felt so exhilarated but so exhausted in all his life. He missed patrol, so he picked up a little overtime on weekends, but the cases he was working as a detective were constantly swirling through his mind. As a patrol officer, he'd been more of a triage step in the process. Getting to follow the timeline of crimes, hold interviews, and uncover evidence was giving him a sense of fulfillment he hadn't realized he needed. Sometimes he felt way too green, but his team was supportive and wanted him to grow for the betterment of the team.

The schedule was the thing giving him the most trouble. He'd worked graveyard since the beginning of his career, every now and then picking up a swing shift, but he couldn't remember the last time he'd started a shift so early in the morning. Getting used to sleeping at night was really throwing him off. It was great to be with Kassie as they ended their days and every morning as they started them, but his unreliable sleep also caused him to snap at her a few times during his first couple weeks.

"You're on an opposite schedule," she would shrug in response to his apologies, as if it didn't bother her, but he didn't believe that. "I think you need to give yourself time. You've worked nights for forever. Your body will adjust and then it'll be fine."

I'm lucky she puts up with my crap.

The guy who'd been arrested after the shootout at the explosion site wasn't talking, and they weren't having much luck in terms of evidence. They looked into the building owner and the two previous owners, but nothing strange stood out. The woman who'd owned the building prior to the current owner, a MaryAnn Richards, was out of town visiting family according to her voicemail, so they had to wait to talk to her. They had never located the body of the female security guard, but she had never gone home, so they assumed her remains must have been destroyed in the explosion.

In the meantime, there were plenty of other cases to focus on, as well as those reliable overtime hours.

Kassie was pushing herself harder than ever on her articles, and he wondered if her sleep was much better than his. He knew she hated the stress, but also felt she still had something to prove regarding her reputation as a reporter. He wanted to say something, but who was he to talk when it came to being obsessed with work?

The Friday evening of his third week as detective, he walked into her apartment while she was leaving a voicemail for someone. Her tone sounded distressed, so he tried to ask her about it when she ended the call.

She waved it away. She looked like she was in the middle of five other things. "It's this lady I was hoping would be a source for my survivor series, but she won't call me back."

Sources not calling her back was a typical cause of her stress, and he wanted her to finish up for the night, so he let it go.

Over the weekend, they stayed at his house so he could work on some ongoing home improvement projects. They had started talking about moving in together, since he was already at her apartment ninety percent of the time he wasn't working. Her place was too small, but they could find an apartment or house of their own closer to downtown. In case that moved quicker than they expected, he wanted to have his house ready to sell.

Kassie's phone rang Saturday while they were eating lunch in his backyard.

"It's my mom," she said and answered the call. "Hey, Mom. How's it going?"

Brett took a bite of his sandwich and watched her face lose all of its color. "What's up?" he mouthed, touching her hand.

"Are you sure? That doesn't sound like her. Her company was doing great. I thought she was happy here." She stood up and paced the patio, the sound of denial filling her voice.

She was silent for several moments as she listened. "Okay. No, it's okay. It's better to know about it now than learn about it on the news. Yeah, I'm with Brett. I'm okay. I'll talk to you soon."

She put her phone down on the table, her hand shaking.

"Kass, what is it? What happened?" He reached for her again. He would do anything to erase the horrified look from her face.

Her voice shook as she tried to answer him. "Abigail. She's dead. Apparent suicide."

CHAPTER 24

Sunday morning, she was sitting on Brett's couch, Isla snuggled up next to her. She didn't get it. Yeah, Abigail obviously wasn't over Kurt, but killing herself because of it? By her account, her business was booming, and the *Bee* had confirmed that Saturday night in an online article about her death. Yet, she'd shot herself in her office Friday night. It'd first been mentioned on Saturday morning on a couple of the news stations, which was how her mom heard about it. Kassidy hadn't turned on the news Saturday morning.

She'd known Abigail for years and never knew her to have any issues with depression, but maybe she was good at hiding it. Maybe the pressure of her business was too much, even with it doing well.

She sighed and turned to look out Brett's sliding door into his backyard. Things with her and Abigail hadn't ended well, but the woman had been her friend for years, before Kurt even came into the picture. So many conflicting emotions ran through her, it was hard to organize or understand them all.

About an hour before, she'd called Stephanie, needing a long-time friend to talk to. Her high school friends had only met Abigail once, but Kassidy had talked about her frequently during phone calls when she lived in the city. Kassidy gave Stephanie the full story.

"That's insane, Kass. How are you doing with it all?" Stephanie's voice was full of shock.

"I don't know. I feel angry, sad, guilty, really confused. She didn't have any issues with depression or anxiety that I know of, and besides whatever happened with Kurt, her life sounded pretty great. I can't see her killing herself over him."

"With what he did to you, I can't imagine he treated her very well."

"But the last time we talked, she defended him. I got the vibe that she still wanted to be with him." Kassidy sighed, wondering if Abigail had talked to Kurt before she died. Maybe he'd been harsher in that conversation, and she really couldn't take their relationship being over.

"Yeah, it's weird for sure. Maybe the police will find some more answers. I wish I could give you a hug. We need to get together again soon."

"Yes, very soon," Kassidy responded. She missed Stephanie and the rest of their high school group – the friends she had before she let chaos into her life. The friends she could trust.

Brett was at the hardware store after asking several times if she would be okay on her own for a bit. She didn't want to keep him from doing what he needed to do with the little free time he had, and the last thing she wanted to do right now was go to a hardware store. Instead she was trying to piece together an article that had been giving her trouble, and having very little success.

Her phone rang, breaking the silence of the house. She didn't recognize the number, but the area code was from the Bay. She didn't answer. She needed to get through this ridiculous article, and they could leave a message. Several minutes went by with no voicemail. She shrugged.

Probably spam.

When the phone rang again, it made her jump. She rolled her eyes. The house was too quiet.

Get it together, Kassidy.

She checked the screen again. Same number. Might as well answer if they were going to keep calling and not leave a message. She swiped her screen.

"Hello?"

"Kassidy."

The voice was like ice water going down her spine. It made her want to scream and hide, like a frightened child. All that therapy couldn't have helped with this moment.

Kurt.

She must have sat there for at least a minute, but he didn't end the call, and she wondered if she'd even really heard his voice. Her mind raced and she couldn't think of what she should do next.

"We need to have a conversation, Kassidy." His voice was deep and confident, but there was something below the surface – something shaky.

Her brain clicked into action, and she heard herself speaking without knowing how she formed the words, "Don't ever call me again. We have nothing to talk about." She ended the call.

She threw her phone across the couch as if it had burned her. Isla startled and ran out of the room. However, since Kassidy sat and stared at her phone for the next several minutes, the cat made her way back, cautiously settling herself on Kassidy's feet.

Kassidy felt the panic attack brewing, and she began searching for real things around her. She'd managed to slow her breathing and slamming heart by the time Brett got home. A war raged in her brain. She should tell him. He would want to know. But she couldn't. She was afraid and angry. She was in denial that Kurt had called her. Had said they needed to talk. She hated that his disgusting voice still had power over her. He was messing with her now for who knew what reason. He wouldn't call her again. So, she stayed silent. If Brett noticed anything was wrong, he must have thought it had to do with Abigail.

She decided to stay on at Brett's house for a few more days so he wouldn't have to pack up and head back to her place. She also needed to be somewhere other than in her apartment right now. She wanted some separation from her normal life – the life that included her past. She tried calling her therapist, but remembered too late that Lina was on vacation, visiting family in Ohio. She didn't want to talk to anyone else. Unless he ever approached her, she could handle this on her own.

On Tuesday, her phone rang again. She didn't reach it in time, but it was a local number. There was no voicemail.

It couldn't be him again. He's not going to call from a local number.

On Wednesday, late in the afternoon, her phone rang again. It was another local number. She'd been talking to sources all day, so she answered without thinking.

"Kassidy, we need to have that talk." His voice was strange. Anxious, maybe?

"You need to stop calling me. I don't know what sick game you're playing, but we have no reason to talk." She tried to sound confident.

"Actually, we do. I need you to break up with the cop and get rid of whatever you have on me."

She pulled the phone away from her face and literally stared at it for a minute. It was all a joke. Someone was playing a horrible joke on her. She almost wanted to laugh.

She touched her screen to end the call. She put the phone down on the coffee table, feeling like she was in a dream. It sounded like him, but was it? What the hell was he talking about? Her phone rang again, but she recognized the number as a source she'd called earlier. She needed to finish that story, so she answered.

By late Friday morning she decided it was time to leave the sanctuary of Brett's place. She hadn't heard from Kurt again, and she was spending the night at her parents' house to cover a fundraiser in Folsom Saturday morning.

Hey! Since you're staying at your parents', can you leave Isla? She'll hate me for it, but I'm picking up a patrol shift tomorrow, and Sunday morning I have to take her to the vet in Natomas for a check-up. I'll stop by your place tomorrow night for dinner?

Sure! I'll miss her though. And you a little, too.

He sent back several laughing emojis. *I love you, Kassie.*

Love you more.

"Goodbye, sweet girl." She held Isla and gave her several long pets before kissing her head and putting her down on the couch. "You'll be at my place again by Sunday. Don't torture the vet too much, okay?"

Isla meowed and followed her to the front door. Kassidy had to slip outside so the cat wouldn't follow. Isla was still meowing on the other side, and Kassidy wished she could take her.

As she locked Brett's front door, a strange feeling washed over her – similar to the one she felt when she made eye contact with the woman outside her apartment on Christmas.

She turned her head to look behind her and saw a car parked across the road. A man sat in the driver seat. He was looking at his phone and not her. She had never seen the car before, but people were allowed to park in neighborhoods and look at their phones. So, why did she feel like he'd been watching her? She felt a little silly as she walked quickly to her car and drove away. She didn't see the car follow her.

Geez, Kassidy. This Kurt thing is really messing you up. Get yourself back in the real world.

When she pulled up outside her parents' house, she saw she'd gotten a text message. This time it was a Bay Area number.

If you continue to evade me, I will make sure my message gets across another way. I'm going to call you tomorrow morning. Answer your phone.

Evade him? What the hell? she thought to herself, anger growing inside her. She didn't know what his game was, but it needed to stop.

Leave me alone, asshole. I'm going to start blocking all the numbers you call or text me from. Keep harassing me and I'll go to the cops.

There was no response. She blocked all his numbers. She'd had enough of this. She would tell Brett about it tomorrow night.

The next morning, she was enjoying a quick cup of coffee and bagel before running off for her fundraiser story. Her phone rang. Another Bay Area number. She ignored it. He called two more times over the next fifteen minutes, both from different numbers, and she ignored both calls. After the fundraiser, she checked her phone. No calls.

She was annoyed all day. Why was he back in her life after years of ignoring her? Hadn't he done enough to her? She was so pissed, she didn't even want to bring it up to Brett, but she knew she should. She wished the whole thing would go away.

***

Brett made his way down the street to Kassie's place, his hands jammed in his coat pockets in an effort to fight the cold. It'd been a busy day. Tons of people doing random and weird things. He was beat. He wanted to sleep, but he missed Kassie. It'd been strange sleeping without her the night before.

She opened her door, a concerned look settling on her face. He pulled her into a long kiss, his hands resting on the small of her back. She came away slightly breathless, and the look was gone for at least a little while.

Please don't say anything about how tired I look tonight. I want to spend time with you – not talk about my work schedule.

The smell of cooking spaghetti and meatballs hit him, and his stomach growled. He leaned back into her couch and closed his eyes while she was in the kitchen.

He felt her sit down next to him. She smelled like lavender. He wanted her so much in that moment, but he was so tired and hungry. She ran her hand through his hair, rubbing his scalp. He made a satisfied noise and kept his eyes closed. Maybe tired and hungry could wait.

"You look so tired," she murmured. "Maybe you should cut back on your hours."

Crap. I don't want to talk about this now.

"Look who's talking," he tried to joke, but the statement didn't come out with as much humor as he meant it to.

She moved away from him, and when he opened his eyes, she was frowning.

Maybe today was a rough day for her, too.

She'd definitely been off since she found out about Abigail, but he figured that would take time.

"Brett, I have to work as much as I do in order to pay the small amount I do to live in this place. You know that. I don't have the regular paycheck and ridiculous overtime money you have."

"Kassie, I know. I was…"

She got up and went back to the kitchen, which annoyed him. He had been about to say he was being dumb, but maybe they needed to have this conversation now.

"Kassie, you could have that regular paycheck and maybe decent health benefits if you got a permanent job. You'd feel more secure."

"Oh, okay. I'll run out and get one of those jobs really quick." She motioned toward her front door, stabbing at the spaghetti in its pot, rather than stirring it.

"I didn't say anything about it being easy, but you could apply. You could try. Freelancing is killing you. You're scared, Kassidy. You're using that as a crutch."

She didn't say anything, continuing to stare at the spaghetti.

"What is going on with you? You've been acting off for a week. Is it Abigail?" he pushed a little bit, hoping to get something out of her.

She glanced over at him. The look on her face was a mixture of so many things, he couldn't describe it. Most of all, there was yearning there.

Did she need to tell him something?

"Forget it," she replied, her voice full of frustration.

This surprised him, so he didn't try as hard as he could have to keep the annoyance from his voice. "You can tell me if something else is wrong."

She scowled back at him. "No! You come in here looking like death warmed over, and I try to make a suggestion about cutting back to make things easier, and you turn it around on me. And I'm not scared."

His jaw dropped. "You're in freaking denial. And I'm sorry if the thing I love to do is making things too hard on you," he finished sarcastically.

"Oh, shove it, Brett! I meant easier for you. You know I've been nothing but supportive of your job, even when you keep piling on extra hours you don't need to take. You have a normal schedule now, but it's not enough. You have to keep taking more and more. Most of your weekends are still consumed by that job. You're exhausted all the time, but sleeping and having time for yourself and us aren't as important as that job."

Again, it comes down to this. No one is ever going to be able to deal with my job.

"I could say the same about your job," he grumbled back. "You barely let yourself heal after your accident. Right back to work. You put it before your own freaking health, Kassidy." He knew it was childish, but he used her full name again in the hope that it would sting.

"Because I had to!" she screamed back at him.

"I'm done with this. I had an insane day, and I don't need to be screamed at." He grabbed his coat, shoving his arms in the sleeves.

"My whole *week* has been shit, and I don't need to be attacked!" she yelled back.

"Then tell me why your week has been so crappy." He whirled on her. He knew the expression on his face was dark.

She stood, silently staring at him, almost-palpable waves of anger rolling off of her.

"Yeah, okay." He wrenched her door open and slammed it behind him.

His anger renewed itself as he took the stairs two at a time and marched down the street. Why the hell wouldn't she open up to him about whatever it was that was bothering her? He'd never realized she felt that way about his job. He'd thought she was supportive like she claimed, but that had all been a lie.

As he got closer to his car, his anger began mixing with a strange sensation, that of being watched. He stopped and glanced all around. It was dark, and he didn't see anything except parked cars and streetlights. He shrugged and kept walking.

CHAPTER 25

Kassidy felt like crap on Sunday. She was still angry, but she missed him. She wished she hadn't said those things about his job, although her words were pretty representative of her recent feelings. They'd never fought like that before, and she knew a lot of it had been that she was pissed and frustrated about Kurt, Abigail, Alexis disappearing, her accident, everything in the last couple months of her life. Except him. Sure, she wished he worked less. She really believed it would be better for him and them, but she'd felt so light whenever he *was* around. Love with Brett was easy and relaxed, something she had never had before.

She hadn't told him about Kurt. She should have, but her anger turned her against that idea. He asked her to tell him, but she couldn't.

She didn't call him that day. She figured he needed space, and her anger continued to flare up as the hours ticked by without word from him.

Her mind was reeling and her anxiety was bringing its "A" game, resulting in a stomach ache and somewhat manic thoughts racing through her head. Her therapist was still out of town, so she used the coping mechanisms she'd learned. She even resorted to that annoying journal.

On Monday morning, Brett texted her before work.

I'm sorry. We've both had a lot of stress lately, and I think Saturday was us getting that out. But I love you, and I'll call you tonight.

The text was reassuring, but she was editing an article, composing an email, and waiting for one of her editors to call when she got it. She put her phone down and stared at her computer screen, trying to focus on work. Then she sat back with a start. Hadn't she been thinking about how much she loved and missed him? How horrible she felt after their fight? This was exactly what he was talking about the other night. Her job was her freaking life. She would still argue that his job was the same for him, but at least she could make a change in *her* life. She didn't have to wait for him to call that night. He must be on his way to work. She should be able to reach him.

She grabbed her phone and was about to select his contact when there was a knock at her door. Putting her phone down, she cracked the door open to see who it was, only to feel the blood drain from her face.

"You had to do this the difficult way," Kurt Leonard growled, pushing his way into her apartment.

"What the hell?" The words flew from her mouth as he pushed her backwards.

He slammed the door behind him. The shock lifted enough from her mind for her to lunge for her phone and start dialing 911, but he plucked the phone from her hands and threw it onto her couch.

"Get out of my apartment! What the hell are you doing?" She tried to get to the door, but he blocked her way.

It was then she noticed he had a gun. At least, it appeared to be a real gun. Kurt Leonard with a gun – not a sight she ever thought she would see. Kurt couldn't stand to hear people talk about guns, let alone own one himself. He'd told her once he felt weapons no longer had a place in their society, except possibly with law enforcement, but only in the most severe situations.

She'd gotten away from him and was now on her floor, under the window next to her couch. If he moved further in, she could try for her door again. She thought about her neighbors and if they would hear her scream. She was sure they would. But it was a new work week, and all three sets of neighbors worked outside their homes. It sometimes gave her an eerie feeling to know she was the only one in the entire building during the day.

She took in his outward appearance. He was dressed in his usual designer shirt and jeans, but he looked sloppy. His hair wasn't combed, and his eyes looked wild. He looked like he'd held a gun before, but his hand was shaking a little.

"Where is it, Kassidy?"

"Where is what? What the hell are you talking about?"

"Everything she gave you. All the copies. Everything you're giving to the cops."

"I have no idea what you mean. Who gave me?" she growled back.

"Fine, we'll get to that in a bit. First things first. Gotta catch him before he goes into work."

He threw something down on her coffee table, and her own face looking off into the distance caught her eye. The photograph was from two weeks ago. She remembered wearing that green sweater. Brett was standing next to her, giving her one of his cheeky smirks. She could almost see the eye roll she must have been making in return.

"What the hell…"

He threw another down on the table. "This is Saturday. His extra shift."

It was a picture of Brett talking to a citizen on a Sacramento street, the patrol car only a few feet away. It was obvious Brett had no idea the photo was taken.

"This is from that night. He looks pissed. Have a little fight?" He added another picture to the pile. Brett leaving her apartment Saturday night, looking like he would breathe fire at anyone who approached him.

Even through her fog of confusion, it hurt her heart to see that.

"And this is from minutes ago." Kurt shoved his phone in her face. On it were a string of several pictures of Brett, sitting in his car in his driveway. She couldn't make out the expression on his face, because the photo had been taken from the wrong angle, but she could see he was holding his phone. It was probably the exact moment he had texted her.

"I don't...What are you doing?" Her voice came out in some sort of cracking whisper, rather than the yell she was hoping for.

"Showing you I'm serious. I don't know what sort of information you have, but I'm done with this, and it needs to end. The first step is for you two," he pointed at the pictures of Brett, "to be over. And your little disagreement came at a perfect time. He won't help you if he hates you."

"Get the hell out of my apartment, Kurt." She was surprised at the force of her words, seeing as there was a gun pointed at her face. Maybe it was that she knew deep down he hated the weapon. She found it hard to believe he would use it. "I don't know what is wrong with you, but get out!"

She decided to try to retrieve her phone, but he stepped in her way, still pointing the gun. His eyes looked insane, but his hand wasn't shaking anymore.

"This isn't a choice, Kassidy. No matter what you two have, if you're not together and you can't go to the police, that buys me some time. I don't know what your plan is and why things haven't blown up yet, but I'm going to take advantage of that. You're going to break up with the cop." He started pacing across a very small piece of her floor.

"If you could tell me what you're talking about..."

He turned back to her, his face contorted. She'd been heading for her phone again, but froze.

"I have someone watching him right now, and that person can make your boyfriend's life very difficult and painful – I don't care if he's a fucking cop! I also have someone watching you. Of course, that goddamn group dropped me, and I had to hire these disgusting people on my own, but they'll get the job done. I don't give a fuck about your boyfriend. I don't want them to have to kill you, but they will if I tell them to."

"What group? Tell me what…"

"Shut up! Pick it up, and call him. Don't try 911 or this ends now." He motioned toward her phone.

She didn't move.

He shrugged and made a call. "Yeah, if he's not at work yet, make sure he has trouble getting there." He hung up. His phone vibrated, and he held it up for her to see. It was a picture from the vantage point of a car behind Brett's, stopped at a traffic light.

"No, stop! Call him back!" She heard herself yell. Brett should have his gun with him, but if the driver hit him…

Kurt sneered and sent a quick text. He then motioned again for her to pick up her phone.

As if in a dream, she stumbled to her couch, picked up her phone, pulled up her call log, pushed his name from the last time they had talked, and raised the phone to her ear. She could hear the blood pounding in her head, and she felt dizzy.

Although she didn't know what Kurt would do in that case, part of her wished Brett wouldn't answer. But he did. He had her on Bluetooth, so he sounded like he was in a tunnel.

Panic threatened to consume her. She wanted to scream, wanted to tell him Kurt was in her apartment, but that could end his life or hers.

"Kassie? Are you there?" She heard his words and realized he must have already said something.

In that split second, she decided she would do what Kurt wanted, but somehow let him know it wasn't true. She didn't know how, but she would. She had to keep him safe for now.

"Yes, sorry. I'm here…"

"I'm about to get to work, but I'm glad you called. I didn't want to wait to talk to you, but I wasn't sure if I should let you respond to my text first – to see if you wanted to talk." It was the least confident she had ever heard him sound.

She glanced up at Kurt. He was pointing the gun with one hand. With the other, he unlocked his phone and started typing.

It wasn't real. She would fix it. She needed to keep him safe. "Brett, I can't do this anymore," she managed to mumble.

"What?" It was clear he had taken her off Bluetooth and was holding the phone to his ear. He must have parked.

"I'm sorry. It's…too much." And now she was crying, because this was ridiculous, but she had to make it believable. "Ever since the accident, everything has been too much. I haven't…come back from it."

These words were true in a way. But in reality, she didn't want to give up, like these words implied. She wanted to keep fighting and moving forward.

He was quiet for what had to be a full minute, and when he spoke, his voice was full of many emotions.

"I know, but it's a rough patch, Kassie. I love you. That hasn't changed at all. It's a rough time for both of us. And I was an ass Saturday night, and I'm sorry."

"It's all too much for me." She was repeating herself. She didn't know how to do this. She didn't want to do this, but the barrel of that gun was still pointing at her face. And she was sure one was pointing at him.

"Don't do this, Kassie." She could tell he was trying to sound strong, but she could hear a shake in his voice. "We can work through this. Do you really want to do this?"

She had to hold the phone away from her face for a few moments so she could try to calm down.

Repeat it. This isn't real. I'll fix it. This isn't real. I'll fix it.

Kurt was frozen, watching her every move.

"I don't want to…" The words came out. She didn't mean them to.

Her eyes flashed to Kurt. He was typing on his phone. He held it up for her again. Whoever was taking the picture was nearly on top of Brett, but Brett was standing outside his car, his back to the person. She was distracting him. Would they kill him in a police station parking lot? They wouldn't get out of there alive. But Brett would still be dead. She needed to keep him alive.

"No!" She yelled at Kurt. "We can't make this work, Brett, and I'm sorry. This is how it needs to be." Tears raced down her cheeks.

"No, it doesn't. I'll come to your place, Kassie. Right now. We can talk." Brett was nothing if not persistent. He wasn't going to give up.

"You have to work." Her head was starting to hurt. She had to keep him away. He would be safe in that police station.

"I don't give a crap about work right now! I need you. Please, let's talk."

The conversation had to end. She couldn't handle it anymore. "No. There's nothing to talk about. I have to go now. Please do not come over. Goodbye, Brett." The last two words came out in a strangled voice as she tried to hide her tears. She stared at her phone for a moment before forcing herself to hang up.

This isn't real. This isn't real. I can fix this.

Kurt was staring at her, satisfied.

"Call them off!" she screamed at him, tears still running down her cheeks. She collapsed on her couch.

His eyes barely left her as he sent another quick text.

"Done, but here's how it's going to be: you will not contact him. Your calls, text messages, social media, everything, will be monitored. If you try to call the police, tell your parents, tell your therapist, tell anyone, he dies."

"You can't do that," she cried, her despair mixing with anger.

"I can't?" He laughed now. "Did you forget that technology is who I am? Monitoring someone is really not that hard, as long as you have the tools to do it. Also, if you try to see him, I'll know about it, and he dies." He gestured toward her window, and she managed to get there from her couch.

The same car she'd seen outside Brett's house days ago was parked at the curb across the street.

She turned to face him. She was shaking. "Exactly as you said, you're a tech guy. I don't know what the hell is going on, but you won't get out of this. I'll figure this out. He'll figure it out. This won't end well for you."

"Shut up, bitch!" He grabbed her arm and pulled her close to him. He blocked her palm before she could send it straight up his nose to break it. His hold was tight and reckless. "I'm sure he'll be here soon, so we need to address the next thing. The evidence she gave you."

"Again, I don't know what you are talking about." She enunciated every word as he let go of her. "Who is 'she'? And what 'evidence' do you think she gave me? No one has approached me about you in years."

"We'll have to check that, won't we?" he asked as if addressing a child.

For the next ten minutes, he followed her around her apartment, the gun at her back. He made her open closets, cabinets and drawers. He carelessly rifled through everything, throwing her things on the floor. When he found her old journals in the closet and read a small piece of one page, he laughed at her. When his search came up fruitless, he dragged her back to the front door.

"It doesn't matter at this point, anyway. You'll never have a chance to turn it in." His voice was frantic, as if he was reassuring himself. He sent a quick text and waited for the response.

"The cop's on his way. Do *not* test me, Kassidy. I'll be in touch." He pointed the gun wildly at her again, and she ducked. He flung open her front door, slamming it behind him as he left.

She sank to her floor, taking in the mess that was her apartment. Her mind spun, and her heart slammed. She reached for things around her so she wouldn't pass out.

Then there was a strong knock on her door. She knew it was Brett.

"Kassie, it's me. Please open the door." His voice sounded so strange in the fog that was her mind.

It would have been so easy to open the door – to fling herself at him and tell him everything. But would they both die in the process? She crawled to the window. The man was getting out of the car across the street. He was moving as if in slow motion, throwing a cigarette to the ground. He was watching. He looked toward her window, sending her a small nod. He moved his jacket to the side to show his holstered gun. She felt like she was going to throw up.

Brett knocked again, asking her to open the door for the second time after several quiet moments. She could tell he was scared. In the whirlwind aftermath of her accident, she'd heard that same sound in his voice – when he was afraid of losing her.

Tears began making their way down her cheeks again, but she sat still, keeping an eye on the man leaning against his car across the street. His face moved back and forth, watching her at the window and Brett at her door.

She realized she was biting her lip and soon tasted the acidity of blood. Brett tried calling her phone, and she silenced it with a start. If he thought she wasn't inside, maybe he would leave. He left a message. He waited for several more minutes, and then she heard the scrape of the shoes he wore to work as he turned and made his way down the stairs.

She watched him get in his car, which was parked several vehicles away from the man watching them. He sat for several more minutes and tried to call her again. She didn't answer. The man watching them had gotten in his car. Brett started his car and drove away. Another sedan pulled away from the curb and followed. The man parked across the street stayed right where he was.

She couldn't bring herself to listen to the voicemails Brett left. She pulled her knees to her chest and shook with tears.

This isn't real. I'll fix this.

CHAPTER 26

Brett called her every day over the next two weeks. Each time her phone rang, she had to make sure it wasn't him before she answered. He left messages. She listened to them in the beginning, because she felt she owed him that at least. He often sounded distraught and became angry at times, but when one of them was tearful, she had to stop listening.

He stopped by her apartment a few times, too. It was obvious he wanted to fight for them. Once, as he talked through the door, he said he was worried about her. Was she in some kind of trouble?

If only he knew.

Always, the man across the street watched. She wasn't sure if the man ever left. Maybe when she slept? She started trying to be out at night, when there was a higher chance Brett would come by.

Kurt sent her two text messages during the first week. The messages detailed many of the people she had called over the previous two days, as well as anyone she texted. He was letting her know he wasn't bluffing, and it scared the shit out of her.

During these initial weeks, she had two serious panic attacks. She wished she could call her therapist, but she wouldn't be able to explain the panic attacks without explaining what was going on. The first attack happened a couple days after she broke up with Brett. She came across two of his casual shirts. Even though he was at her place most of the time, he often did his laundry at his house, when he needed to go there for other reasons. The shirts hung ready and waiting in her closet after their most recent wash. They still smelled like him.

She started thinking about how she would never be able to hug him again, never smell his scent. He would hate her because of this. She had no plan to get herself out of this. She had no ideas. Her heart rate sped up, and it was harder to breathe. She developed tunnel vision, which was a regular symptom of her panic attacks. Her chest hurt, and she had to sit down on the floor, her back braced against a wall. She felt like she was being slowly suffocated as she gasped for air. But she knew what the feelings were. She could get past the attack. She found specific scents and objects around her. She thought of them, held on to them, willed them to pull her back to reality. In time, her heart slowed and breathing became easier again.

I hate this so much! she screamed inside her head, because she couldn't scream out loud.

She was essentially a prisoner. Kurt and the man across the street let her go about her daily business for her articles, let her run various errands, but she didn't dare interact with her friends or anyone else she knew, because she wouldn't be able to keep quiet. The most she did was text her parents to say she was having a really busy few weeks, and she would call them soon. She did the same for her therapist. It was not outside the realm of possibility, so they all bought it.

The man watching her changed the make and model of his vehicle two times. Otherwise, he was there. She felt like she was living in a nightmare she had had many times before, where an unknown terror was hunting her, and she ran forever, but still never got away. When the monster showed itself in her nightmares, she would wake up. She couldn't wake up from this.

When the third week started, Brett called her again, and then there were no more calls. He stopped coming to her apartment. He had given up.

I'm done with this shit!

She had to figure out Kurt's deal. Who was the woman he'd mentioned? One of the women he molested? What evidence did that woman have against him? Had she been threatening to come forward? Could it be Alexis?

This felt like a good place to start. She only remembered the names of three of the women on the list of Kurt's victims, two of them being the ones who approached her. She Googled the name of the first: Amelia Mazur. No pertinent information.

But when she Googled Sheline Phillips, an obituary came up. Strange. Sheline had probably only been in her mid-twenties when she contacted Kassidy. The obituary didn't mention the cause of the woman's death. Maybe she'd been sick? She looked down a little farther in the search results and discovered, through a story in a small Bay Area newspaper, that Sheline had a massive heart attack and passed away nine months prior, while she was running. Apparently, she had been an avid athlete, but had an undiagnosed heart condition.

Okay, that happens.

Kassidy Googled Lana Gonzalez. She found her obituary as well. She'd died six months ago. Kassidy found another news article from the college town Lana lived in, not far from Sacramento. Lana was killed in a multiple-vehicle accident early in the morning on Interstate 80, not far from home. Kassidy remembered reading about that accident right after it happened, before the victims from several of the vehicles were identified.

Kassidy noticed the article included an interview with Lana's husband, who said his wife left to visit her parents for a couple days. Her parents still lived in Mill Valley, in the Bay Area, and her husband said she liked to leave early to avoid some of the traffic. The Highway Patrol investigated the crash and found the cause to be an intoxicated driver, whose blood alcohol level was well over the legal limit. He caused a chain reaction of cars ramming into each other. People in three cars were killed, including Lana. He survived, but was now serving time for manslaughter. Another article said Highway Patrol officers found open bottles in his car, as if he was literally drinking while he was driving. The man pled guilty and was sentenced right away.

Interesting, but they investigated and didn't find anything other than his intoxication.

The two women died in feasible ways, so Kassidy didn't think she should read that much into it. Still, it bugged her that they were both Kurt's victims and they died within months of each other. She pleaded with her brain to remember the names of some of the other women, but none came to mind. She had no idea where that list was, but maybe she'd written some down in her journal at the time.

Next, she researched Kurt. Nothing very recent came up, except for a feature piece from a few months ago in a well-known online business journal. The story profiled several new top executives in Kurt's company. It appeared he hired them to lighten his load. This didn't sound like Kurt.

The man was a narcissist and worked ridiculous hours when they'd been together – although now she realized he was doing disgusting things in some of those hours. He thought he should be able to do all of the executive work himself, since he was the company's founder and CEO. He had a hard time trusting anyone else – except with travel. He didn't like to travel back then, so he had much lower-level employees do that. According to Alexis, that had changed.

But here were three new (very highly paid, according to the article), executives: two men who sounded like they had tons of experience in the field, and one woman, who had a double master's degree in communications and business. Kassidy had to admit she had no idea what most of Kurt's job entailed, but the trio sounded like they were taking on many of his main duties. Still, none of this was very helpful in terms of figuring out what exactly was going on with Kurt.

She turned on the news in the early afternoon. A reporter was in the middle of a breaking story. A body was recovered from a ravine in the foothills. This in itself was not unheard of, as it had happened several times in the past. Many of those deaths involved members of the homeless community.

This person had not been a member of that community. She was identified as Lilian Martin. It appeared she committed suicide, but when her broken-hearted father was interviewed, he said he couldn't understand it. Lilian worked in Sacramento as a security guard. She was happy with her life. Her father couldn't believe she would commit suicide. Before they found her body, her family thought she was killed in a recent fire. He wondered out loud what she was doing in the foothills.

If Lilian's death was a murder rather than a suicide, it appeared sloppily executed, almost like an after-thought. Kassidy came up with a theory, but she waited for the next report, to see if her idea would be confirmed.

Later that day, a *Sacramento Bee* article reported Lilian had been a security guard at the building destroyed by the explosion. Investigators had never found her remains, but assumed they were completely destroyed in the fire. She was scheduled to work that night. Her family reported she left for her shift at her regular time. So, how did she end up in the foothills?

Something about that explosion, and everything related to it, was off. Did it have something to do with the building itself? Why were those people snooping around the burned-out site? At least researching the building would give her something more to do.

The next day, she pulled assessor records to find out who owned it. The name wasn't familiar and didn't mean anything to her. However, the man was a fairly new owner. The previous ownership was listed under Richards Properties, Inc. Another moment of perusing records led her to the owner of that company, a MaryAnn Richards.

She Googled MaryAnn Richards and caught her breath. The results included a photograph from a *Bee* business article a few years ago. MaryAnn Richards was standing in the shadow of one of her office buildings. She was not smiling. She looked like she'd rather be anywhere but there. Kassidy recognized that face.

Things came flooding back and connecting in her mind. She nearly jumped away from her computer and ran to her bedroom, opening her closet and reaching to a shelf on the top. Aggravated that she couldn't quite get to some of the notebooks she had shoved in the far back corner, she grabbed a step stool from her kitchen and made her way back to her room, her heart pounding.

She threw some notebooks on the ground and sifted through the pages of others, looking for a specific date range. She preferred to use spiral notebooks instead of actual books intended to be journals. She wasn't sure why. She only hoped she hadn't torn out any of the pages in the date range she was looking for.

After everything went down with Kurt, she'd destroyed many of the pages detailing the more intimate things they'd done in their relationship, as well as certain trips and experiences they had together. She'd existed in a state of depression, anger, and anxiety for so long. Only her therapy started bringing her out of that.

She let out a little sound of satisfaction as she found the dates she was looking for, and all the pages appeared to be there. She sat down on the area rug by her bed and leaned back against the frame. She began sweeping through the pages, looking for a specific event. And there she was. Kassidy had met MaryAnn Richards at a gala, but she'd gone by a different name then.

Kurt and Kassidy's relationship was new at the time, and it was easy to feel like Kurt only had eyes for her. She wrote about finding it an attractive quality that Kurt had a close female friend. He told Kassidy they were business partners at times, and they went to college together for a while.

Kassidy rolled her eyes at her naïve past-self. She was sure now that Kurt and the woman had been more than friends and business partners. Who knew what they were while Kassidy and Kurt were together?

She'd recognized the woman driving the SUV at the accident scene, and now she knew why. It was that same face she saw studying her with vague interest at the gala years ago. She was buried in Kassidy's mind – one of the many things she tried to forget since her days with Kurt. But her face floated to the surface now. Had she recognized Kassidy after the accident? She must have. Was she still a friend of Kurt's? Most likely with how close they'd been a few years before. This all explained so much. The aftermath of the car accident. Kurt hunting her down after the explosion. The "she" he mentioned. It was all connected to her, the woman who used to own that building. The woman who went by MaryAnn Richards. Kassidy stared at her journal, once more reading the woman's other name – then saying it out loud.

"Mary Ronson."

About five weeks after she broke up with Brett, the man in the car disappeared. She wasn't sure at first. She thought maybe he changed his vehicle again. She waited a few days, studying each car parked near her apartment. She drove around Sacramento and outlying areas to cover various stories, but no one appeared to be following her.

She hadn't heard anything from Kurt since the first week, but should she expect to? Her mind raced, wondering if she dared call the person she wanted so desperately to call. She wanted to explain everything to him – to make him understand why she did what she did. But she was still scared, so she hesitated. Kurt could still be watching her. But if she never took a chance, she would never see Brett again. She would never be able to tell him the truth about their relationship or her hypothesis about Mary Ronson and Kurt.

CHAPTER 27

Brett wanted to buy a damn shirt. His purpose there was to buy a damn shirt, and he couldn't do it. He was out a couple shirts, because he'd left them at Kassidy's place. As far as he was concerned, he'd never be getting them back. So, he went to the mall to buy a shirt, but all he could think about were the shirts he'd left at her apartment. He thought about her. God, he missed her. But she'd dropped him after one fight. One fight. Then she'd ignored him. He felt like an idiot for trying so hard, but after a couple weeks, he'd been done wasting his time. Now, even more weeks later, he was trying to move forward.

But she drifted into his dreams, and his nightmares, and he couldn't get rid of her. He missed her so much it hurt, and that pissed him off. She was done. Why couldn't he be done?

So, he forced himself to buy a shirt, because he couldn't let thoughts of her control something so stupid. He didn't try it on. He didn't even know if he liked it that much. But he did what he was there to do. He checked his watch. He needed to get back to work.

He was scrolling through emails on his phone as he walked into the cold. It would be spring soon. He couldn't wait for the heat of summer. It was something to look forward to.

He slammed into someone. He looked up, about to apologize, but shut his mouth.

"Oh! I'm sorry!" she said, trying to catch her phone before it hit the ground.

Damn stupid phones.

He didn't know what to do. He stopped, trying to wipe all emotion from his face.

She composed herself and straightened, seeing him for the first time. Her face went white.

"Oh, Brett…"

Kassidy. He said her name silently, because he didn't trust himself to speak.

"I was trying to decide if I should call you. Wait, that didn't sound right. I mean, I was hoping we could talk. I have so much to tell you…" Her words faded away as she watched his face. Her eyes were pleading with him.

I miss you. I love you. I'm fucking mad at you.

He had to hold on to that last thought. "After shutting me out with no real explanation. Your reasons were…bullshit. Now that it's been five weeks, it's okay to talk?" He hated how angry he sounded, but he needed that anger right now.

She looked like someone had punched her in the gut, and it broke him a little more. He had to get out of there.

"The timing is part of everything…" Her words were little more than a whisper.

In that moment, a car drove by in the parking lot, bass booming from its speakers. She jumped and looked behind her. He didn't miss the reaction. What the hell was going on with her?

No, I need to go now.

"Brett…" She moved closer to him, and he had to back up, because he wanted to hug her, kiss her. But she'd made it clear she was done, so he needed to move on. He wasn't going to make a fool of himself again.

"I have to go." He hesitated for a moment, and then forced his legs to walk away from her.

When he got to his car, he looked back. She was still standing there, her back to him. Were her shoulders shaking?

You wouldn't be able to see that from here, idiot. Leave.

When he got out of the shower the next morning, she'd left him a voicemail. He debated erasing it, but listened anyway.

"Hi, Brett. I know you don't want to talk, and that's fine, but I have some information that might be useful for the investigation of that explosion site. Or at least information that might be connected to that somehow. It's actually related to what happened with us…But anyway, I don't know who to talk to in your department, so I was hoping you could give me some direction with that. I don't know who's working the case besides you, but this is a bit much to try to explain to someone over the phone. Anyway, I'm rambling. Please give me a call when you can."

What the hell?

Not what he was expecting, but interesting. There was no way in hell he was calling her back, but he had no doubt she'd found something if she said she had, so he went to his call log and punched a different number.

***

She agonized over Brett calling her back for most of the day. She wanted any excuse to hear his voice again, but she was terrified of dealing with how angry he was. She'd had enough of that the day before.

In the early afternoon, someone called her from a blocked number. She was expecting a few return calls from sources, and she still hadn't heard from Kurt, so she answered.

"This is Kassidy Turner." She was annoyed to hear her voice shaking.

"Ms. Turner, this is Detective Luke Kruger from the Sacramento

Police Department. I believe you called one of my colleagues about some information related to our investigation of the office building site by Cal Expo?"

"Yes." She couldn't help feeling stung that Brett hadn't called her himself, but should she really have expected him to? He'd given her the referral she'd asked for.

"I was hoping you might be able to come to the station to speak with me in the next couple of days. As soon as tomorrow would work if that works for you."

Detective Kruger sounded interested. She wondered if the explosion site still wasn't yielding any new information.

"I'm free tomorrow afternoon, if that's okay," she responded, her nerves beginning to get the better of her

"That's fine. Two o'clock?"

She agreed, and he made sure she had the address.

She hung up the phone and stared at it for several minutes. Her nerves danced. For a second, she forgot about Brett. She really hoped her suspicions about Kurt were correct.

She felt like she was going to jump out of her skin when she arrived at the police station the next afternoon. She sat in her car, trying to get her heart to stop pounding. She wondered if Brett would be there. It would be the only chance she'd have to explain herself. But with the way his face looked at the mall, the words he said, maybe it wouldn't matter if he was there.

She sat in the lobby for what felt like hours, but was really only about ten minutes, before Detective Kruger came out to meet her. He shook her hand and reintroduced himself. His voice carried a hint of a southern accent. He was friendly, but also incredibly tall and intimidating. She pushed her anxiety down as much as she could.

Kruger walked her back to an interview room. Her heart continued to race and then threatened to explode.

Brett was standing outside the room. The butterflies in her stomach became a flock of albatross. He was stone-faced when he caught sight of her, and it was clear his anger hadn't subsided.

He looked so good in his slacks and button-down shirt. She tried not to think about his muscled arms going around her and holding her in a tight embrace.

"Ms. Turner, Detective Green is working this case with me, but based on your…previous relationship, he won't be participating in your interview. Another detective will be joining us in a minute." Kruger's voice was awkward.

So, why is he here if he's not going to stay?

Brett handed a laptop to Kruger and tried to keep his eyes away from hers.

Ah, a laptop handoff. Of course. A logical reason for him to be standing there.

Brett turned to walk away, and her anxiety went into overdrive. If she let him go, she'd lose her chance to explain what happened. This wasn't the ideal place, and she was sure he wouldn't be happy about it, but she had to seize the opportunity to make him listen.

"I'd rather he stayed, if that's okay. It would make me a lot more comfortable. The information I have is also important for him to hear." Kassidy was surprised by the confidence in her voice.

The comfortable part was a lie of course, but based on the many past conversations she'd had with police representatives, she hoped they would do what they could to make her feel safe during the interview.

Brett stopped and cast a brief, unsure look at Kruger. He had to be interested in what she had to say. Did that outweigh the anger?

Kruger thought for a moment, nodded at him, and looked at her. "Okay. I'm assuming you'll explain that."

It was Kassidy's turn to nod.

They all went into the room, and Brett closed the door behind them. The space was small, and even though Kassidy didn't have much of an issue with claustrophobia, she started feeling it creep up her spine. She also knew there would be an audio and video recording of this conversation. She hated that feeling. She liked being on the other side of the recorder, but there was no way around it.

"Now, Ms. Turner, you said you had some information you thought might be helpful regarding the explosion site?"

"Yes," she answered, two sets of eyes staring into hers. "I know this may sound random, but I figured it's important. I think Kurt Leonard was either directly or indirectly involved with the explosion."

"I'm sorry, Kurt Leonard? He's that tech CEO in Silicon Valley. What's his company's name? Reliable? He had some sort of controversy regarding sexual assault a while back, didn't he?" Kruger asked.

"Reliant. That's the name. And yes, he did. I also think the explosion was also somehow related to the previous owner of that building, who was an associate of Kurt's. I believe that associate, and certainly Kurt, were involved in some sort of criminal activity connected to all of this." She sped forward, sure what she was saying wasn't making any sense.

"The previous owner of the building? Isn't that MaryAnn Richards?" Detective Kruger gave Brett a look. Brett's expression didn't change, but Kassidy could see the interest in his eyes.

"Yes, well, Mary Ronson. Her real estate is under the name Richards Properties, Inc., with the owner of the company listed as MaryAnn Richards. I believe that's an alias Mary Ronson uses. She sold that building several months ago. I don't understand why that particular building would be involved if she no longer owns it, but I'm sure it's not a coincidence."

"How do you know about her other name?" Kruger asked, typing on his laptop, but maintaining eye contact.

"When I pulled the assessor record and found her company's name, I looked her up. I found a picture of MaryAnn Richards from a profile piece in the newspaper. I recognized her. I…I was in a car accident in November, and she was also involved. She confronted me at the accident site, and she looked familiar to me then, but I couldn't place her. But I know now. I met her when I was dating Kurt Leonard years ago. He introduced her to me as one of his most trusted colleagues. I wrote her name down in a journal I was keeping at the time, and I described her personality and how she looked. I didn't know much about Kurt at the time, so meeting any of his friends was pretty interesting, and I tried to remember them. I found that journal, and I wrote her name as Mary Ronson."

Her interviewers were quiet for a moment. Did they know about Mary? Had they been able to contact her? They weren't volunteering any information. Instead, they both kept their poker faces intact as they took notes – Detective Kruger on the laptop and Brett on a pad of paper. Leave it to Brett to use a pad of paper. She nearly smiled at the example of Brett's old soul, but then remembered the cold look he'd given her when she first walked around the corner. At that moment, he looked up at her, before glancing over at his fellow detective.

"And you mentioned you think Mary Ronson was involved in some kind of criminal activity. What makes you think that?" Kruger prompted.

"That's a little easier to explain as it relates to Kurt, but there's evidence suggesting Ms. Ronson was in some kind of crisis. After I discovered who she was, I did a little more research. I called an acquaintance who works for the Sacramento office of a fairly large commercial real estate firm. I was wondering if he might know anything about Ms. Ronson, or MaryAnn Richards, as people in Sacramento probably all know her. He did. He had actually known MaryAnn Richards for years.

"He told me she'd been selling off several properties lately, but was trying to stay involved in those properties. Like she still wanted to be in control, but not held responsible. Like maybe she was trying to become less conspicuous in the city. It didn't make any sense to him.

"He noted, and I double checked on the Department of Real Estate's website, that her real estate license was delinquent. This was strange, since she was heavily involved in the commercial real estate market. He said the MaryAnn Richards he knows is organized to the point of obsession. He wasn't sure how she could let that slip.

"I used several different combinations of her real name and alias in my search. I came across a police log recap from a smaller newspaper in a Los Angeles suburb. A Maryanne Ronson was arrested not long ago for public intoxication and destruction of property. Of course, I can't guarantee this was her, but she does own several properties in Los Angeles, and her real estate business has an office there. I'm sure you would have no problem confirming her identity. If it was her, it doesn't match the confident, calculated actions of the Mary Ronson I met, or the MaryAnn Richards my acquaintance knew before.

"And then the accident we were involved in…She was incredibly agitated. She was engaged in road rage with another driver. She looked like she wanted to rip my head off. All of it leads me to believe she must be going through something. I know it's all conjecture at this point, but I think it's worth looking into. It would be a pretty big coincidence if one of her 'former' buildings happened to explode. I know investigators believed it could have been an issue with the gas line, but the death of the security guard shows it wasn't that."

Kruger was quiet again as he wrapped up his typing.

"I haven't heard that you've found any remains at the site, but I have a theory Ms. Ronson's may be there," she cautiously added.

Both men looked up at her.

"My real estate acquaintance said he hasn't heard from her since early December, and they used to talk shop at least once a month. The timing would match. The disposal of the security guard's body was…sloppy. She had no reason to be in the Foothills. They, whoever that is, were trying to get her far enough away. Maybe they had a plan to go back later, but something happened. I don't think they knew she was going to be working that night. Maybe she walked in on something she shouldn't have. They had to get rid of her in a hurry. But I think if they killed Ms. Ronson, she's there. Maybe they…destroyed the body first. Causing an explosion is pretty brazen, but it was probably a way to get rid of any further evidence."

Maybe they had found remains, maybe not. But she felt pretty good about her theory.

"Did you ever think of becoming a detective, Ms. Turner?" Kruger smiled, and she almost thought she saw a hint of the same expression on Brett's face.

"Do you think your contact at the real estate firm would be willing to talk to us?" Kruger asked.

"I asked him, thinking you might want to talk to him. He said that would probably be fine, but he might need to have his company's attorney with him. He doesn't think they will have a problem with it, because he's not speaking on behalf of the firm, but he wants to make sure."

"We understand. If you can leave his information with us, we can reach out to him," the detective responded.

Brett's voice was the one to break through the brief silence. "What led you to believe Kurt Leonard is involved?"

She took a deep breath. She had to get through this. There were things she wasn't willing to tell him with Kruger in the room. Maybe one day, when he'd had time to get past his anger, she would give him all the details.

CHAPTER 28

Brett watched her as she steeled herself to answer his question. He knew Abigail had talked about Kurt a couple times, that Kurt had visited Sacramento. But by the way she braced herself, as if the weight of the world was about to be released, something major had happened with Kurt. He could feel himself getting angry and worked to control it. No matter how upset he was about the break-up, the thought of Kurt having anything to do with Kassidy was enough to send him through the roof.

"About six weeks ago, Kurt showed up at my apartment. He was very different from the person he was when we were dating. He was anxious and desperate."

Brett balled his left hand into a fist and pushed his pen tip down into his notebook with his right.

Keep it together.

"Kurt demanded that I..." Her face went white and she stopped, looking down at her hands in her lap. The room was dead silent as they waited for her to keep going.

"He demanded that I break up with Detective Green," she managed to say, and he could see she was fighting tears.

What?

Once, when Brett was about seven, he'd been running through the grass in his backyard. He'd tripped and fallen chest-first onto one of the football-sized rocks his parents used as a border around a section of plants. For one of the longest minutes of his life, he couldn't catch his breath, the wind knocked from his lungs. It was painful and scary, and it was similar to the feeling he had as Kassidy's words registered in his brain. She was watching him, gauging his reaction. He tried to keep his face neutral. Kruger was like a stone next to him.

"He told me he'd been having us followed, and provided lots of photographs to prove it. He threatened our lives. I hadn't seen or heard from Kurt since I moved back to Sacramento, although I'd heard he'd been here. I don't know how long he'd been keeping tabs on me. He made it clear he had the resources to carry out his threats through the men following us."

Kruger tensed noticeably. Brett felt numb with shock.

"Are you in danger right now, Ms. Turner?" Kruger asked.

Kassidy took a deep breath and shook her head. "I'll explain, but I don't think so."

She took another breath and continued, "He demanded to know what 'she' gave me, where the evidence 'she' gave me was. I'm assuming the 'she' was Mary. I don't know if Mary was working with Kurt, but it can't be a coincidence that we were in an accident together and then Kurt reappeared. I'm sure she recognized me at the accident scene. Somehow Kurt was convinced she'd given me evidence against him. I don't know why she'd have evidence against him unless she was working with him, or maybe their relationship had become acrimonious and she was building a case against him. Either way, I think they're connected and there is something much bigger going on. Kurt searched my apartment that day, looking for the evidence. Unless Mary was full of it, that evidence must exist somewhere." She stopped herself, watching both their faces.

"I know it all sounds crazy," she continued, "but his threats were very real. He told me not to contact Detective Green…Brett…or anyone else I knew about his visit, or Brett and I would die. There has to be something behind all of it." The tone of her voice was pleading now, begging them to believe her.

Kruger nodded thoughtfully. "So, that day you broke things off with Detective Green?"

She clamped her lips shut, but nodded.

Brett couldn't look at her. He had no idea how to process what he'd heard. She wouldn't make up the story about Kurt, and he knew her well enough to know when she got a hunch about something, she was usually correct. But it seemed like a stretch, and she had no evidence of what Kurt and Mary Ronson were supposedly involved in. He passed a look at Kruger, who, to Brett's surprise, looked pretty interested.

"And has Mr. Leonard tried to get in touch with you since then?"

She nodded. "He was monitoring my phone. He texted me during the first week to give me a rundown of who I had called and texted, so I would know he was serious about not contacting Brett. I printed the text messages if you'd like them." She passed them across the table to Kruger's outstretched hand. He perused them as she continued, "I assume he was also monitoring Brett's phone, although he never said that. After the first week, I didn't hear from him. But the man he hired to follow me was always there. I'm also guessing he continued to have Brett followed. The one following me disappeared a short time ago, which is why I don't think I'm in danger anymore."

Brett frowned. He would have noticed someone following him for five weeks.

Although you were so consumed with thoughts of her during those weeks, you didn't notice much of anything in your life outside of work.

She broke him from his thoughts by speaking again. "I have an idea, and I'm sorry it's just another idea, of what Kurt's crimes might be – why he was so desperate to find that evidence. Before I started researching Mary, I did some research on Kurt. I thought one of his assault victims might have threatened to come forward, and that was the 'she' he referenced. I could only remember a few of their names. Sheline Phillips and Lana Gonzalez were two of them. Sheline was one of the women who physically came to me with allegations against Kurt. Sheline and Lana died unexpectedly within months of each other. I believe they were murdered."

"Lana Gonzalez. Didn't she die in that horrible accident on I-80 back in the summer? I remember her. But I haven't heard of Sheline Phillips," Kruger said. Brett raised his eyebrow at his partner. Kruger's memory was like a steel trap.

"Sheline died a few months earlier. According to the article I saw, she still lived in the Bay Area. She was an avid athlete. Allegedly she had an undiagnosed heart condition, had a heart attack, and died while running."

"Allegedly?" Kruger questioned.

"I don't think she had a heart condition." Kassidy sat up straighter, as if defending herself on the witness stand. "I think someone caused her heart attack."

"Do you have any evidence of that?" Kruger frowned. Brett could tell that theory was a bit much for his partner.

"No," Kassidy sighed, "but maybe there will be some in her medical records. I know it's a stretch, and I wish I remembered some of the names of Kurt's other victims, because I would be willing to bet others have died as well. If that's the case, I bet Kurt had something to do with their murders. I don't know how he'd pull that off, but if you had seen his eyes, his face, at my apartment…The man was reeling. You could tell he felt threatened by something."

"Did Mr. Leonard say anything about other potential locations for this evidence? Unfortunately, it would be difficult for any law enforcement agency to make an arrest for alleged murders without it. Lana and Sheline were just two people who died of what could be called 'normal' causes. I agree, it seems strange that two of his alleged assault victims died within months of each other, but without evidence or witnesses…" He shifted in his chair. "There's the possibility of charging him for forcing himself into your apartment, since I'm assuming you didn't welcome him in. And there's the phone tapping and having you followed."

"I understand. I know you need evidence. I don't think Kurt had any clue where the stuff was. If it was Mary's, maybe she was keeping it in one of her buildings." She was quiet for a moment. "I know Kurt has a team of sharks for attorneys. I have the text messages, but they just look like a list of contacts for calls and texts. He doesn't state how he got them or why he's sending them. I don't have tangible proof he was having me followed. I should have tried to take pictures of the guy…And I'm sure they could make up a story about me inviting him in. I feel like they'll chew me up and spit me out. It would be so much better to get him on the sexual assault and murder charges."

Kruger nodded, again looking thoughtful. "I'll think on it and get back to you. In the meantime, in the interest of your safety, call us if Kurt contacts you or if you suspect you're being followed again. Can you leave the contact for your friend at the real estate firm? And would it be okay if we took a look at your journal mentioning Mary Ronson?"

Brett tried to keep his eyes on his notepad. If anything, his anger had grown, and he didn't trust himself to look at her.

"I actually brought all of them," she responded. "This is the one that mentions Mary Ronson, and the rest are in my car. I tore pages out of some of them after Kurt and I broke up, but maybe there will be something helpful there. And I've already written down Craig's contact information." She handed the journal and piece of paper across the table to Kruger.

"Thank you. We can take a look." Kruger stood up and Brett followed suit. "Can you wait here for a minute? We'll have someone walk you out, and you can leave the journals with them."

She nodded, her face sad. He met her gaze briefly, but then looked away.

"Thank you for coming in. I'll call you when we're done with the journals." Kruger shook her hand with a pleasant smile.

Brett stood outside the room. Kruger closed the door behind him. Before Brett could think too hard about it, the words were out of his mouth, "I'll walk her out."

Kruger gazed at him. "You sure that's a good idea?"

"Yeah. I need to talk to her."

Kruger shrugged. "Up to you. Brett," he lowered his voice, "if this thing with Kurt goes anywhere, they might take you off the case because of her involvement." He nodded toward the closed door.

"You think it will?"

"You know there are several Bay Area agencies that've been trying to get that guy for years. There's never been any evidence. If we can find some and she's right about those murders…"

"That felt like a stretch." Or maybe he was biased against her.

"Never know," Kruger responded and walked down the hall.

Brett knocked on the door before opening it. Surprise was written across her face at seeing him again.

"I'm going to walk you out, if that's okay," he mumbled.

She stood up too fast and stumbled, almost running into him. He put his hand out, but pulled it away as she steadied herself.

"Sorry." She looked away from him, grabbed her purse, and followed him out of the building. He spotted her car and walked toward it without saying anything to her.

She fumbled to unlock her sedan, pulling the box of journals from the back seat. She handed him the box, and he realized how close she was. She was as beautiful as ever in that moment, and he tried to stop himself from thinking about what it was like to kiss her.

She looked up into his eyes, and he had to look away. "Kassidy, why didn't you tell me Kurt came to your apartment? Why didn't you tell me what was really going on? I could have helped you."

"I tried to talk to you…"

"Five weeks later. Why didn't you tell me right away?" He couldn't keep the frustration from his voice.

"He was monitoring my phone and having us followed, Brett! What did you want me to do? He would have had us both killed. I wanted to tell you everything, believe me. And I thought I'd be able to find a solution much sooner. I thought I would find a way to tell you what was going on, but I didn't. Now I can tell you everything…" Her voice broke as he interrupted her.

"He may have been monitoring your phone, because he's a technology-savvy asshole who knows how to do that, but a tech guy arranging murders? You should have talked to me. I'm a police detective. This is what I do. I would have known how to keep us both safe if needed. I loved you, Kassidy, and you just…Maybe our fight played a bigger part in this," he commented, because part of him questioned whether the break-up was something she wanted.

"No, it didn't!" Her response was immediate and angry. "That fight was stupid. Yeah, I was pissed, and I know you were, too, but right after you texted me, I was going to call and talk to you about it. Then Kurt showed up. I never wanted to break up with you, Brett." Her voice broke, and she swiped away tears in annoyance.

He didn't know what to say, so he stayed quiet, looking down at the box in his arms.

She found his eyes with hers when he looked up again. She took a deep breath. "So, you don't think he could've been involved in the murders of those women?"

"We don't know that they were murdered. It's two deaths that could be a coincidence. Those weren't outrageous causes. I remember that car accident, too. Several people died, not just Ms. Gonzalez. And undiagnosed heart conditions in athletes happen."

"I know that, but something is telling me this is all connected. I wish

I could remember some of the other names on that list." She sighed. "I'm really sorry I didn't tell you about Kurt right away, but every time you came to my apartment, the guy following me got out of his car and stood there watching you. You didn't see him, but he was watching, and he had a gun." Her eyes were desperate as she said this.

"For what? To kill me in broad daylight? Kassidy, you're saying Kurt was working with people who arranged elaborate murders and blew up a building, but that man was going to shoot me in the middle of the day when there were probably countless people who could identify him?"

He could tell how much his response hurt by the way her face fell. He hated himself and felt satisfied at the same time. Maybe he couldn't stop loving Kassidy, but he could force himself to move on. He had to be in a relationship with someone who trusted and would be truthful with him.

"Brett, I don't know…Let me explain…" She tried, but he didn't need to hear the story again.

"I asked you to tell me if Kurt contacted you. You said you would. I wanted to keep you safe." He shook his head. This wasn't going to get him anywhere. "I have to go. We'll call you about your journals." Then he turned and walked away without looking back. Why did he still want to go back to her? Why did he have to keep picturing that pained look on her face?

CHAPTER 29

She tried to push Brett out of her mind when she got home, because she was livid, and she couldn't waste the rest of the day on that feeling. He dismissed her concerns about the guy across the street, like it didn't matter that some crazy person had a gun he could use to end their lives. He didn't believe her theory about the women's deaths, even though he knew her intuition was pretty on par.

He wouldn't even let me freaking explain the full story! He treated me like a paranoid child. Saying our fight had something to do with the break-up. What an ass! If I could only remember some of the other names on that list! What did I do with the list?

She could still see Sheline's face as she handed over the long list of names. Scared but determined. Kassidy's anger surged as that memory played out in her mind. Each person on that list claimed Kurt assaulted or raped her, and the variety of things they claimed he did in the process made her sick to her stomach.

Alexis!

She'd forgotten all about Alexis. She could have told Kruger and Brett about her. Maybe they could convince her to make a statement. She didn't feel right giving them her number without asking her first. Alexis had never called her back, but she would try again.

"Alexis, it's Kassidy Turner. I hope you're okay. I understand you not calling me back, but you need to know this: I went to the police in Sacramento today. Kurt came to my apartment about five weeks ago, threatened me and my boyfriend. I wasn't allowed to talk to anyone about it. I don't think he's having me followed anymore, so I finally went to them. Alexis, I think Kurt had people killed. Some of his assault victims. I'm trying to remember other names. I only recall a few. Do you remember many? I didn't give the police your number, but if you're safe, it would be so helpful if you would go to them. Please let me know what you think." She rambled through the voicemail, praying Alexis would call her back.

She sat down hard on her couch. She keenly felt Isla's absence in that moment, as she had for the last six weeks. If the cat had been there, she would have jumped on Kassidy's lap, and petting her would have been its own kind of therapy.

She forced herself to think back to that list. She had read each name carefully. She'd met a couple of them during the few times she'd gone to Reliant's large campus of buildings. She'd tried so hard to forget them after she left San Francisco. Now she berated herself for that. She should have remembered those women. She should have kept fighting for them, even if they wouldn't or couldn't fight for themselves. But she'd been too young and scared.

She settled her mind as much as she could and tried to picture the list Sheline placed in her hand. Amelia had been standing close by. What had she done with it after everything was over? Had she thrown it away? She could almost picture herself doing that – another step in trying to erase the pain.

Who were they? Try to remember pieces of names. That could help.

But nothing came to mind. She hadn't come across the list while looking through her journals. Could it be in another box somewhere? She walked back to her room, dragging that step stool with her again.

She began tearing apart the deep top shelf of her closet. Two dilapidated boxes she'd pushed to the back fell down past her head, nearly knocking her over.

"Shit," she mumbled as she sat down in the mess on her floor. She started throwing everything back in the boxes, but a piece of paper crumpled into a ball caught her attention. It couldn't be.

She carefully opened it, the page ripping slightly. It looked like she had opened it, then crumpled it back up, a million times. Some of the names were illegible for this reason, as they'd been handwritten. But several stood out, and it was like she was seeing them for the first time as she stood in Kurt's disgustingly-large house in San Francisco: Yolanda Thomas. Janie Byrne. Alicia Walker.

She ran for her laptop, slipping on the miscellaneous crap still on her floor. She typed in each woman's name with a pounding heart.

Yolanda Thomas had moved to Florida at least a year ago. Dead. Drowned in a large river while having a Memorial Day celebration with friends. Authorities investigated the death. They'd found Yolanda's blood alcohol level to be extremely high. It was a horrible accident.

Janie Byrne. Lived alone in a Los Angeles suburb. Dead. Suicide. A couple friends with public Facebook accounts tagged the woman's page and commented how tragic it was. Janie had lost her job, and they wished they'd seen the signs of her depression. Janie's Facebook account still existed, but it was private.

Alicia Walker had moved back to Nevada to be closer to her parents. Dead. Robbed and stabbed walking back to her car after a late work shift. Kassidy found a heartbreaking news article that included a video interview with Alicia's mother, who could only speak for a couple minutes before dissolving into tears.

She found no mention of authorities putting the deaths together as a trend. But no one knew they were Kurt's assault victims. Sure, they had all worked for Reliant, but not all at the exact same time. None of the causes of death seemed impossible, and the women were scattered throughout the country. Kassidy wondered if any of their still-living colleagues had the same idea long before she did, but were too scared to say anything, fearing they would be next.

All those women. She sat back on her couch, shaking. She was sure there were more. She wished she could have convinced them to come forward with her. She should have tried harder to help them, but there was no way she could have ever expected this. He couldn't have killed all of them, right? That list was disgustingly long. She hoped Alexis was okay.

She grabbed her phone and called Brett. He didn't answer. She let out an aggravated yell and threw her phone on the couch. She called the station and asked to speak to Detective Kruger. He wasn't available, but she was transferred to his voicemail.

"Hi, Detective Kruger, this is Kassidy Turner. I found the list of Kurt's assault victims. I looked into three more of them. They're all dead. There's no obvious evidence of foul play, but I know they were murdered. Their names are Yolanda Thomas, Janie Byrne, and Alicia Walker. Yolanda moved to Florida. Janie moved to Los Angeles, and Alicia moved to Nevada. Please look into this. I know Kurt was behind it. There are so many more on the list, and I'm sure more of them were murdered. I'll bring the list to the station this afternoon." She ended the phone call after leaving her number.

She angrily started a text message to Brett, her adrenaline raging.

I called Kruger. Yolanda Thomas, Janie Byrne, Alicia Walker. Look at their deaths, Brett. These were all women on the list of Kurt's victims. I found the list. I'll drop it off at the station. This is NOT a coincidence!

She sent the message and stood up, pacing the room for a few minutes, calming herself down. She was sure they'd search Mary's buildings now. They'd find the evidence Mary stashed away. This would be the end for Kurt.

As she pulled into the police station parking lot for the second time that day, she heard her phone ding with a text message. She let out a joyful scream when she saw it was Alexis.

I'm sorry, Kassidy. I've been hiding out a lot, but I've been safe. I'm sorry he did that to you. The murders are horrifying news. Please give me the number of who I should talk to, and I'll call them. I'm ready for this to end.

She walked into the station feeling triumphant and free. Kruger was there. When he looked at the list, his jaw nearly dropped. She told him about Alexis, and he gave Kassidy his cell number, which she immediately texted to the woman. She mentioned Abigail's death, and he said he would add that to their list of things to look into.

"Mary's buildings are at the top," he said, scanning the victim list. "We've gotta try to find that evidence, but Alexis's statement will help. Many of these crimes may not fall in our jurisdiction, but we'll work with whomever we need to. We're going to keep trying until we can bring him to justice, Ms. Turner."

Kassidy could have hugged him in that moment, but Kruger didn't look like the type of man who enjoyed a hug from a near-stranger.

Two weeks later, on the morning news, she learned Federal authorities, in cooperation with police and sheriff's offices across the country, had arrested Kurt Leonard overnight on a multitude of felony and misdemeanor charges.

In shock, she stared at the television. She had been so sure this would happen, but it was like a dream. Live footage showed Kurt, surrounded by people she assumed were his legal team, being rushed into a courthouse in San Francisco. Reporters swarmed around him, trying to put microphones and recorders anywhere near his face. Cameras flashed. Kurt looked dazed.

Her mind swam as she tried to listen to the reporter talk about the exact charges...something about organized crime. The words murder and sexual assault jumped out at her. Memories from not so long ago came flooding back – memories from when she tried to bring Kurt to justice on her own. And now she was watching it happen in front of her.

The organized crime aspect sparked her interest. It could explain all the well-planned murders. But how did Kurt get involved?

She sat down, put her head in her hands, and cried, feeling far too many emotions at once.

Later that day, she got a call from two of the assistant U.S. attorneys working the case against Kurt. She would be a witness at his upcoming trial. They wanted to meet with her to discuss the things she'd told the Sacramento detectives. They were interested in the contact she had with Kurt, his threats, and the cell phone monitoring. They said certain hearsay exceptions would also allow her to testify about the women who approached her in San Francisco, as a number of them were now dead. She wanted to ask them about Alexis, but wasn't sure if they could say anything about her.

The attorneys explained Kurt was charged with a number of felony and misdemeanor crimes, but the thing that really stuck out was his violation of the Racketeer Influenced and Corrupt Organizations Act, otherwise called RICO.

Kurt had allegedly committed a number of crimes linked to a highly-elusive national organized crime group with a strong presence in California. Even with how insane he acted at her apartment, she never could have imagined this. Many of the crimes he was involved in resulted in murder charges. Money laundering was a big one as well. Then there were all the sexual assault and rape charges.

As Kurt had done in the past, his attorneys would try to discredit her as a victim and witness. They would make up lies about Kassidy and Kurt's relationship – maybe say Kassidy had rekindled things with Kurt. They'd say Brett found out and was jealous, so he'd threatened the couple. They might say Kassidy asked Kurt to have someone follow her, to keep her safe. The U.S. attorneys weren't worried. With all the evidence stacked against him, it would be hard for any jury to take Kurt seriously.

That must mean they found Mary's stash, she thought with satisfaction.

Even with the confidence of the attorneys, Kassidy had to squash her anxiety. Sitting in front of that man in a courtroom, relating her whole story to a bunch of strangers, responding to attorneys trying to rip her apart…It sounded like a nightmare. When she ended the call, after setting up a time and date for a more in-depth interview, she called her therapist and scheduled an appointment. She'd need a lot of support to get through this.

She wanted to call Brett. She was still annoyed with him, but she missed him all the same. She wanted him to explain how they'd found the evidence – how Kurt got involved with an organized crime group. She wanted him to calm her down about being a witness in a federal trial. But she didn't call him. He wouldn't want her to. She didn't have that right anymore.

Instead, she drove to her parents' house. Even her anxiety couldn't diminish the feeling of newly-regained freedom settling all around her.

CHAPTER 30

Kurt didn't know much, and Brett heard he rambled often, but he managed to provide a short list of locations the organization could be using in Northern California. The FBI had taken over the main investigation, but worked closely with Sac PD to investigate leads in Sacramento. Brett was assigned to other cases because of his involvement with Kassidy. The department wanted to make sure there was no conflict of interest. This was frustrating of course, because he wanted to be involved. But whenever he heard about Kurt, he had a deep desire to punch something, so he supposed it was for the better.

Sacramento seemed to be the hub for the organization's Northern California projects, so its representatives were in the city frequently. Since Kurt's captivity was already all over the news, organization members were in hiding. Detectives and agents spent countless hours making contact with informants around the city, anyone who could give them any information. They received intel about a small group of the organization's operatives living in a house in East Sacramento.

The plan was to serve them with arrest warrants on a Tuesday night, but an informant discovered the group was going to clear out late Monday night and head south. A judge signed last minute warrants for the seven men and women believed to be living in the house.

Since Brett couldn't be directly involved in arresting the operatives that night, he was one of the officers who set up the perimeter around the neighborhood. Later he'd be standing at the house's front door when Kruger, another Sac PD detective, and two FBI agents completed the search warrant process.

His adrenaline raged and his heart slammed in his chest, even as he waited at the perimeter. This was huge. Arresting any of the group's representatives before they had a chance to flee, could be considered a win for the investigation. He wanted to be the one going into that house, but was grateful to be involved in some capacity.

It wasn't a surprise to anyone when the shots started that night. Members of SWAT went in first to disarm the operatives and clear the house. The shots and yells filled the air, echoing off buildings blocks away from the scene. One of the organization's operatives was killed in the process, but the rest were brought out alive. The detectives and agents immediately took them into custody, and SWAT gave the all-clear for the house. Brett listened on his radio, ready to move.

Ambulances arrived for two of the operatives, and officers started loading the others into patrol cars.

With the house clear, the detectives and agents moved in for the search warrant. Brett took his post at the door, surveying the area around him, listening to his colleagues make their way through the building. He and Kassidy had walked this very street to see the Fab 40s lights at Christmas. Crazy how things had changed since then.

The house was well-kept with a manicured lawn and marble pillars supporting the roof, which jutted out over the raised front patio. A stylized white railing enclosed the patio. Two large, matching pots with thriving plants about to flower stood next to either pillar. The cement pathway from the sidewalk to the rounded steps leading up to the patio was perfectly smooth and lit by a row of decorative lights on either side.

The driveway was deep and currently displayed two cars, both of which cost more than Brett made in a year.

Crime shouldn't pay this well.

Two officers had loaded one of the last operatives into the back of their car and were leaving the scene. The final operative was in the back of another car. It was a dark night, and the man was a shadow to Brett from where he was standing. The house directly across the street lit up with floodlights, and Brett caught a better look at the man. He was bouncing slightly in his seat as the officer went to shut the door.

A cracking sound to his left stole his attention for a second, and he moved his hand toward his gun. Yells and the sound of a taser suddenly broke the relative silence of the street. Brett had his gun out of its holster, but the sound of running steps thumping up the stairs was on him too quick, and a force shoved him against the wall of the house.

He struggled back against the assailant, trying to push the man toward the ground. He growled an expletive as his gun fell to the cement. The man's hands were still bound by handcuffs, but he was trying to use his body weight to move toward the house. He towered over Brett and could have lifted him into the air and thrown him if his hands were free. He was screaming something, but the air around them was filled with noise, and Brett's heartbeat slamming in his ears was like thunder, so the words sounded like gibberish.

"Stop! Get on the ground!" Brett screamed back at the man, shoving him toward the porch railing. He could hear his colleagues racing up the steps and out of the house, also yelling orders at the man.

Brett had gotten the man to the ground, but flinched as the guy's teeth sunk into his left arm. The man only needed that one movement to get up, and he dodged two other officers as he again threw his entire body weight at Brett, who was kneeling by the railing. Brett and the man flew right through the wood, and Brett felt it slash his face as they sailed to the ground below. Brett closed his eyes, not remembering how far the fall was.

The man's strangled voice still tried to choke out words.

They landed on the grass, and Brett felt a shocking pain in his right arm, which had been tucked under his chest during the impact. He again felt like that seven-year-old boy in his parents' backyard, gasping for breath, trying not to panic. Then he looked over to see the man tripping a few feet from him, as if he was trying to hobble away, his hands still held behind his back. He was heading straight for Brett's colleagues, who had made it to the grass.

"What the hell? Get on the fucking ground!" Brett catapulted himself forward somehow, knocking the man to the grass once again as the other officers surrounded them, their fierce orders filling the night. He heard Kruger's voice among the group. He again heard the sound of a taser.

He had a death grip on the man's arm with his good hand, but heard several voices say, "Green, we got him. Let go. We got him."

He released his hand, managing to get to his knees and then his feet, although he swayed and his body protested with horrible pain. Two officers led the man back to the patrol car, their grips tight on his arms. The man was still yelling something, but Brett, who was trying to focus on feeling the air going in and out of his lungs, didn't understand him.

"Shit, Green." Kruger, who was steadying him with one hand, eyed him with a frown, calling for an ambulance on his radio. He asked another officer to bring a first aid kit. "It was a search warrant assignment, not an MMA fight."

"Ha ha," Brett responded, trying to ignore the throbbing in his arm, which was rapidly swelling and bleeding through his shirt. Blood was dripping down his face. He eyed the bite indentations on his other arm. "Great...Why the hell would he try to go back to the house?"

"What, you didn't hear him yelling as he was slamming you through that railing?" Kruger's attempt at overt sarcasm was comforting, as Brett's adrenaline and heart were still racing. He handed Brett a wipe and some gauze for his face. He briefly looked at Brett's arm, but it was obvious it was broken, so he didn't move it.

Brett shook his head as the sound of sirens got closer. He stood up to pace, feeling like he could jump out of his skin from the pain. He swayed again.

"Green, sit the hell down. The guy was challenging you to kill him. I'm guessing he really wanted you to. Kept yelling about it until they put him in the car. When you didn't do it, he decided to see if anyone else would." Kruger nodded toward the patrol car, which was driving away.

Suicide-by-cop, Brett thought to himself. Seeking out death rather than facing consequences. A desperate solution to a desperate situation.

The ambulance arrived. Brett tried not to look at his arm, because it felt like the limb should have been attached to someone else, and the pain was making him sick. The paramedics noted he had shards of wood in his cheek, and his right eye was now swelling shut.

His thoughts turned to Kassidy on his way to the hospital. Should he call her? Or have someone call her? He closed his eyes for a moment, thinking about the pained look on her face in the parking lot at the station. No, she wasn't his to call anymore.

***

Kassidy looked down at her ringing phone. She was working on an article that didn't want to be written. She'd shut herself off from the world in an attempt to write it, even silencing her phone in the morning, but her heart wasn't in it.

She was surprised by the name on the screen and hesitated a moment before answering.

"Elise…how are you?" She didn't know what else to say. She really liked Elise, but she hadn't expected to speak to her again.

Elise's voice was shaking when she responded, "I'm sorry, Kassie. I'm not sure if this was the right thing to do. I don't know what happened with you two, but you had to know. I thought it was wrong of him not to tell you."

A feeling of dread crawled up Kassidy's spine. "What's wrong?"

"Brett's in the hospital. They said it's U.C. Davis Medical Center downtown. He was in surgery this morning, but my mom said he's in recovery now and is doing okay. I guess he's in a lot of pain though. He was attacked on the job sometime late last night. Mom and Dad don't know many details, and he isn't very willing to fill them in. His partner, Kruger, I think, called them after Brett was taken to the hospital, which of course freaked them out. They flew up there." Her panicked voice broke, and she was silent for several moments.

The world around Kassidy froze, and she couldn't remember how to speak.

"Kassie?" Elise was saying her name, and she must have repeated it several times. "Are you still there?"

"I'm here." She had to work to make her voice louder than a whisper.

Elise hurried on, as if Kassidy would cut her off at any moment.

"I don't know how you guys ended, because of course Brett wouldn't tell any of us, but I know you loved him. And I know he loved you. He didn't want anyone to call you, but I thought you needed to know. I thought you should have the opportunity to visit him if you want to."

"I don't think he'd want that," Kassidy replied.

"I don't know about that. I know how much he loved you. That doesn't just go away."

"Our break-up involved some…unique circumstances. I've tried talking to him a couple times since. He doesn't trust me anymore. He doesn't think I handled things the right way. Love is nothing if there's no trust."

Elise was quiet for a moment. "Brett is stubborn. It's hard for him to come around sometimes. When he believes something should be a certain way, that's how it has to be. He must've told you the story of his divorce.

Immaturity was a factor back then I'm sure, but he wanted that job, and nothing was going to stand in his way. I'm glad he's grown up in the last five years, but he still has some of those same tendencies. If you could know how much he loved you, Kassie…I'm sure he was angry and hurt, but I can't see him walking away from you that easily.

"It's up to you if you want to visit him. But I thought it was important for you to know. I can't get up there right now, because Isaiah has a bad cold, and Terrance can't take the time off. So, I guess it's also me wanting to make sure he has as much support as possible. My parents don't love that he's a cop. They worry about the danger. They keep quiet about it most of the time, but I don't want them voicing their opinions while he's already in pain and annoyed about being stuck in a hospital bed. I hope they won't, but when my mom is stressed, her feelings tend to come out."

Kassidy sighed. Elise wanted her to visit Brett, but it wasn't her responsibility to solve the tension between him and his parents. A wave of guilt came over her as these thoughts entered her head.

How selfish, Kassidy. He's lying in a hospital bed, and his sister was nice enough to tell you. She's worried about him. Get over yourself. You can be mad, but don't you love him? Don't you want to help him?

"I'll look up visiting hours and go see him as soon as I can."

"Thank you so much. I know this is awkward for you, but I really appreciate it," Elise said, relief flowing through her voice. "And, Kassie, please don't give up on him. It's none of my business, but you made him so happy, and you two were so good together. Maybe you can work things out."

"I should probably go, but thank you for calling me. I hope Isaiah feels better soon," Kassidy murmured, tears forming in her eyes. Before all this mess, she'd assumed she would get to see the little boy grow up.

"Thank you," Elise answered, her voice sad. She ended the call.

Kassidy exhaled, as if she'd been holding her breath the entire conversation. Part of her wanted to run out the door right then, but part of her was dreading seeing him. She didn't want to see that distrustful look on his face again, and she didn't want to deal with the anger it made her feel.

CHAPTER 31

She heard the muffled, familiar sound of Brett's parents' voices as she stopped in front of the closed hospital door. Her stomach churned. They wouldn't be able to talk with his parents in the room, but at least she might be a distraction from any opinions they wanted to share with him.

She hesitated and couldn't make herself reach for the door handle. Her heart raced, and she tried to catch her breath. From the moment she had checked in at the desk downstairs, part of her had wanted to turn and run.

"Excuse me." A petite nurse with a quiet voice scooted past her. "He already has visitors in the room, but you can come in." She left the door ajar behind her.

"Mom, I'm fine," Brett said, his confident tone barely masking his exhaustion.

"You're not fine, Brett," Andrew Green answered in an aggravated voice.

"These are minor injuries," Brett joked, making Kassidy smile. Same old Brett.

"They are not 'minor injuries,' Mr. Green," the quiet nurse said with a firm voice, not getting the joke. "You have a very serious compound fracture in your right arm. Two of your ribs are broken. The right side of your face was cut clear to the bone. You're very lucky your eyes weren't damaged. And as Dr. Nguyen told you this morning, you will need a lot of rest and physical therapy. We also have to watch you for signs of infection."

Kassidy felt her face go white.

"See?" Jill Green's voice shook. Brett made no verbal response.

Sounds like they've already given their opinions.

"Please rest. Your lunch will be brought up in a bit," the nurse said, and the door opened in front of Kassidy's face.

"Do you…want to go in?" the nurse questioned.

"I'm sorry, I'm not quite sure." She paused and then decided to force herself to follow through. She'd driven to the hospital and walked to his room. She couldn't leave without going in. "Sorry, yes, I do."

The nurse gave her a quizzical look and shrugged as she walked away.

Kassidy pushed the door open and stepped inside. She was blocked from view by the privacy curtain, but pulled it aside enough to see him. Her heart dropped. Brett was sitting up in the hospital bed, the lower half of his body covered by a blanket. The entire right side of his face, from his cheek to his hairline, was bandaged, with small cuts covering the rest of his face, some of them stitched. His eyes were swollen and black. His right arm was bandaged and in a sling. His lower left arm was also bandaged.

"I'm not sure why she felt the need to tell me how I'm injured, like I didn't already know." He was done joking. Frustration filled his voice. He was reading through some papers, adjusting his right arm carefully.

"Because you're already asking about being discharged! She's trying to talk some sense into you, like we are!" Andrew frowned at his son.

"No, you're trying to talk me out of my job," he mumbled back, not looking up at his parents.

Uh oh. Maybe I got here just in time to stop a fight.

"Brett, have you seen yourself?" His mother was trying to sound firm, but the hand she reached toward him was shaking. "I know you're in pain. Why is this all a joke to you?"

He didn't answer.

Kassidy stepped out from behind the curtain, and Jill saw her first. Her face broke out in a huge smile, so like her son's. Kassidy smiled back, but didn't walk any farther into the room. Jill motioned to her husband, who looked equally as happy to see her.

"I'm so glad you're here!" Jill gushed.

Hearing the tone in his mother's voice, Brett looked up. When his eyes landed on her, surprise flooded his face. He didn't try to hide it.

"Kassie." He sat up straighter, flinching as something caused him pain. "How…how did you…"

"Elise called me," she answered, wondering how her own voice could sound so far away. "She thought I should know you were here."

He studied her with inquisitive eyes, and she had to look away as Jill walked toward her.

"It's so nice to see you, Kassie. I was hoping Elise would call you." Jill gave her a hug and smiled at her confused look. "She told me she wanted to call you, but wasn't sure if she should."

Then she turned back to her son. "We're going to get some lunch. Do you want us to bring you some more of that soup from the cafeteria, since you don't eat anything they bring you?"

If the air in the room wasn't so suffocating, Kassidy would have laughed at the remark.

"Sure. Thanks," Brett answered, not taking his eyes from Kassidy. She kept her eyes on his parents' faces.

Andrew squeezed his son's left shoulder and smiled at Kassidy as he walked by.

"This will give you two a chance to talk," Jill said, stating the obvious reason for their departure.

Kassidy nodded as they left the room, but didn't say anything. She wasn't sure how to start a conversation with him anymore. Brett's keen stare was making her uncomfortable. Did he expect her to start? She cleared her throat, adding some sound to the smothering air.

"I had to one-up you in the broken arm contest," he tried to joke and smile, but both fell flat.

"How are you doing?"

Stupid question, but what the hell else do I say?

"I'm fine. I know I look like a science experiment gone wrong, but it's not that bad."

"Using jokes to avoid answering questions doesn't work with me. The nurse made it sound pretty serious." She smirked back at him.

"You heard that, huh?"

She nodded. "Uh, yeah, and I can see it. What happened?"

"Did you hear from the U.S. Attorney's office?" He ignored her question.

She sighed. "Yes, they called me. Kurt's finally going to be held accountable for what he did to all those women. Racketeering charges, murder, money laundering…insane. So, my theory was right?"

He looked away from her. She hoped he felt like an ass, because he'd sure acted like one.

"You were right about everything. He was working with Mary Ronson through a criminal organization. He was a client, paying millions of dollars for a variety of requests – many of which were murders. She was some sort of project manager and orchestrated all of his requests. They answered to the California chapter's leader, who was based in Southern California. We believe Kurt and the organization were responsible for the explosion and Mary's death. The guys looking around the explosion site were connected to the same organization."

"So, she's dead? You found her?"

He nodded. "Her remains were destroyed, but we're pretty sure it's her. We also found her SUV, stripped and abandoned outside the city.

Seems like they were getting pretty sloppy toward the end. Maybe they were getting tired of Kurt. Maybe Mary was the quality factor in his previous crimes. We also found the guys who followed you…and me. They weren't part of the same organization. Kurt hired them after the organization dropped him. Paid them a substantial amount of money to follow and threaten us. They stopped working for him when they got better offers. Not guys who put a big emphasis on loyalty."

Kassidy nodded, surprised he was telling her all this. "And you found Mary's stash?"

"There was a room under the first floor of that burned-out building."

"Like a basement?"

"More like a fully-reinforced bomb shelter, and it's not reflected on any plans filed with the city. Luckily, the organization guys didn't know about it either. Kruger and two other detectives discovered an entrance the day after you came to the station. They found a bunch of documents, recordings, and photographs detailing all the crimes the organization carried out for Kurt. He'd also kept video recordings of many of his sexual crimes. Those were there, too. It does appear Mary was trying to build a case against him, so their relationship must have degraded in the years since you met her."

"He's so sick," Kassidy said as a chill went down her spine.

He nodded. "It was the evidence we needed. He had quite a few of those women on the list murdered, several in the Sacramento area, but they were all made to look like 'normal' causes of death. I think he would have kept going down that list if the organization hadn't dropped him. He couldn't get any of it done on his own."

"What about Abigail?" she asked, not sure if she really wanted to know the answer.

"We don't know about Abigail. We didn't find any evidence regarding her death, but it did take place after Mary died, so maybe someone else arranged it. We're guessing Kurt requested it."

"Why did he have them killed?" She shook her head at the sheer insanity of it all. "Were some of them threatening to come forward?"

"We didn't find any evidence of that. Maybe he figured it was a matter of time now that high-powered men aren't safe in their crimes. I don't know what happened to him, and I've never been involved in conversations with him, but I've heard he's really paranoid. Can barely string words together to make a sentence at times. Thinks someone is after him. He keeps mumbling about 'the boss,' who has to be the California leader. We think he's in Los Angeles, or was. Kurt gave us the address of his office, but it was cleared out when agents got there."

She shook her head in continued disbelief.

"And Alexis. Thanks to you, she came forward. Told us everything. She's going to be testifying at his trial. She was the one, wasn't she? The one you kept trying to call for a 'story,' but she'd never call you back?"

She nodded. At least he wasn't pissed about that partial lie. "I did meet her through my survivor series. She recognized my name and reached out to me. But she was trying to alert me to Kurt's off-brand behavior. She knew something was up with him. She wasn't comfortable being in a story. She told me I could keep in touch with her, but each time my call went to her voicemail. After I found out about Sheline and Lana's murders, I was scared he might have killed her, too."

"Her testimony is going to be important. She's the only one of Kurt's assault victims we've been able to contact so far. We hope as more victims see the news and feel safe enough, they'll contact the FBI."

"And that?" She pointed at his right arm, trying again to find out what happened.

"This," he frowned at his injury, "happened as we were taking some of the organization's operatives into custody. They were living in a fancy house in East Sacramento. One of our informants knew who they were and alerted us to their whereabouts. We got to them before they left the city."

"So, why did Mary tell Kurt she'd given me the evidence? Wouldn't that freak him out? Make him want to kill her? Is that why he killed her, because he realized she was going to turn him in at some point? Why didn't he ever have me killed?"

"We don't know why he never had you killed. All I can guess is he was worried he'd be the first suspect if there was any inclination of foul play. He'd have obvious motive with his sob story of you trying to ruin his reputation. Or…maybe in some way, he still cared about you, even though he felt threatened by you. As for Mary, maybe she thought the information would keep her alive? Or maybe she wanted to scare him before she died? She wouldn't have cared what happened to you or me after she was gone. Nice of her to pawn him off on us. The interesting thing is a couple of the operatives we arrested in East Sac told us Mary brought Kurt into the organization, so I'm not sure what happened to them along the way."

"Yeah, they used to be so close…" Kassidy responded, thinking of how close she and Brett used to be. This whole thing had destroyed more than one relationship.

"The trial will be interesting, but that might not happen for a while. His attorneys are going to stall to try to bolster their case. I think they might try to bring an insanity plea into it, ask for a change of venue, etc."

They were quiet for a few moments after that. She found herself gazing out of his hospital room window, which was masked by condensation that had seeped in between the panes of glass and dried there. It distorted the blue sky outside.

She wasn't sure what else to say. She didn't want to broach the subject of their break-up, because she didn't want to fight again. She glanced over at him and noticed his eyes looked heavy and his face was pale. Brett had suffering in silence down to an art form.

"Are you due for any pain medication?" she asked, wanting to reach for his hand.

"Not yet." He shook his head, fighting to keep his eyes open.

"I should go. You need to sleep, and your parents will be back soon." She stood up from the chair she'd settled in after his parents left.

"No, wait, Kass. We need to talk."

CHAPTER 32

"We've been talking for a while now, and you need to rest." Her face was etched with concern, but she didn't look like she was in a hurry to leave.

"I don't want to talk about the case anymore." He forced himself to sit up. He needed to stay awake. His body protested the movement with more pain, but he didn't care. They were going to have this conversation.

"I'm sorry about the way I acted that day at the mall. I was frustrated. I had no idea why you did what you did, and it was hard to deal with zero explanation when it happened. I knew there was something wrong, but you ignored me instead of confiding in me. And I missed you. I missed you so much. That made me angrier. That day at the station, I thought you were overreacting when you told us about Kurt. I had no idea why you did what he wanted instead of talking to me, because I didn't think any of his threats were valid. I didn't know why you were so scared of him. Obviously, now I know you should have been scared of him. I still wish you'd talked to me that day. I could have helped you."

Her eyes were dark as he finished and all expression of concern had been wiped from her face.

Crap.

"You wanted to talk so you could make me feel guilty again? Haven't you said these things before? I tried to explain at the station, after you said them the first time, but you wouldn't let me. So, here goes, Brett. Kurt didn't show up out of the blue at my apartment one day. He hounded me for days, calling me from different phone numbers so I would answer. He texted me. He told me to break up with you. I tried to ignore him, because I thought it was some sick joke at first. The night we fought, I was going to tell you about the calls, but I was so pissed at you by the end, that I didn't.

"A couple days later, he showed up at my place. He pointed a gun at my face and showed me pictures of you. Pictures the man following you had taken. That man was following you when I called you. He was so close to you, Brett. He was sending Kurt picture after picture of you standing in that parking lot. You had no clue! I'm sure he had a gun, like the one pointed at my face. And yes, I know you scoffed at the idea of someone killing you in broad daylight, but I'm sorry, I didn't want to take that risk, because you'd still be dead if I called his bluff and was wrong." She stopped to take a breath.

"What?" He wanted to lunge out of that fucking hospital bed, find Kurt, and beat him to a bloody pulp. "A gun? He had a gun? Why didn't you tell us that? Why didn't you tell me or Kruger that he had a gun?"

"To see you react like this in front of your colleague?" She frowned. "No. I was planning on telling you in the parking lot if you could have pulled your head out of your ass enough to listen. I was going to tell you everything. I *tried* to tell you, Brett. Why the hell do you think I stayed away from you until my stalker disappeared? Kurt was serious. I knew that from the beginning."

"You should have told me. You should have forced me to listen to you in that parking lot." His mind was spinning. She'd kept the fact that Kurt was harassing her from him. He'd threatened her with a gun, and she hadn't told him.

She laughed. "Oh, yeah, because it's possible to force you to hear something you don't want to hear. Look what happened when I suggested you take fewer hours at work? I was trying to be helpful. I thought I was doing the right thing. I thought as your girlfriend, I could make suggestions like that without you turning on me and biting my head off!"

She made to leave, but whirled back on him, raising her voice. "I know my job seems like a joke, Brett. I know I'm killing myself with stress. Do you think I don't get that? But I want to be a grown-up. I want to do what I love and be able to support myself. I already get my apartment at a discounted rate and can barely survive. How do you think that makes me feel? And, yes, I'm scared to apply to permanent jobs. I was fired from my last job for being an idiot obsessed with a monster! Even if employers don't give a shit about that, it follows me around every day. It fills me with shame and regret. It's one of the main reasons I see a therapist. So yes, I have a nice little ball of shame and fear all wrapped up inside me. But you know what? After this, I *am* going to apply to permanent jobs. I'm going to show myself and *you* that I can do it. I'm going to get a staff writer job." She stopped and stared at him for a moment, confusion on her face, as if she didn't know why she was yelling. Her cheeks turned red.

It was one of the only times in his life that he was completely speechless.

"I should go. My coming here hasn't helped, and I'm sorry. I wanted to know that you were okay." She stopped again and took a deep breath. "It's okay for you to not be the protector all the time, Brett – to let someone else protect you. It's okay to realize that someone can love *you* so much that they would do anything if it meant you might be safe. I messed everything up. I get it. But I *loved* you, and my main goal was to keep you safe."

Tell her you love her. Tell her not to leave. Open your fucking mouth!

"I hope you feel better soon," she said as she ran from his room.

He slammed his left fist down on the bed, biting his lip at the pain that followed.

***

Late Friday afternoon, Kassidy was going over changes to a story with her *Sacramento Bee* editor, but she was more than a little distracted. She'd been picturing Brett in that hospital bed since she ran out of the room. She almost expected to hear from his sister again, or maybe his parents, but she hadn't. She was proud of everything she'd said to him, but she was sure that would be the end of whatever kind of relationship they might have had.

Kurt's pending trial was constantly on her mind. Brett had been right; Kurt's attorneys were already trying to delay it. She shivered when she thought too much about the lies they might spin in court. She didn't want to face him. She didn't want to be anywhere near him. She'd started having nightmares about Kurt shoving the gun in her face, throwing down the pictures of Brett as if they were trash. It all led to more therapy. Would there ever be a time when that man would be gone from her life?

"Kassidy?"

She snapped back to reality at the sound of her editor's voice.

"I'm sorry, what were you saying?" How long had she been zoned out?

"I said, 'After those two changes in the third to last paragraph, it should be good,'" he responded. Thank God Sean was a patient man.

"Okay, I'll get those done and send it back to you in a bit." She was already making the changes.

She expected him to say goodbye, but instead he paused for a moment before speaking again, "Kassidy, when are you going to ask for a job?"

She thought she somehow misheard him. "I'm sorry, say that again?"

"When are you going to ask for a job? I figured you'd wonder why you weren't being hired as a permanent employee after all the work I've given you in the last several months. I know you said you like the freedom of freelancing, but it doesn't make sense to me that a writer as good as you wouldn't want to be a permanent staff member. Health benefits, standard hours, and a regular paycheck are usually pretty important to people."

She found herself at a complete loss for words.

"What I'm trying to say is that I have a staff position opening up, and we want you to have it. If you want it that is."

"But…I haven't applied. I didn't interview."

Why are you talking him out of it? Say yes!

He laughed. "I asked, you don't need to apply. And I'd say the mountain of work you've done for us is interview enough."

"I told you about Kurt's trial…"

Shut up! Shut up!

"Yes, and we'll give you the time you need for that, but I don't see it impacting the work you do for us. You won't be reporting on it, and it doesn't look like the trial will take place around here. This is the perfect time for you to move forward in life, and I think this job will help you do that. Again, if you would like it to."

"I'd love that!" she blurted before she could give him any other reasons not to hire her.

"Great! Come in on Monday around eight, and we'll get things set up," he said with a cheerful tone and ended the call.

She was dumbfounded. She sat on the old couch in the front room of her apartment, her laptop screen staring back at her. She turned to look out the window, and for the first time in a long time, she felt like she could catch her breath.

***

The surgery was painful, but it was necessary, and he'd done it before.

John sighed as he settled into his seat on the jet, pulling out his tablet. He looked out the window to his left, seeing Los Angeles spread out beneath him. He wouldn't be back there anytime soon. Pity, he loved that city. But they had gotten too close this time.

He checked his passport again. Seeing the picture was strange, because the face looking back at him was so different from his previous face. He'd seen it in the mirror for the first time two hours ago. Seeing a new face always gave him an out-of-body experience.

His passport also reflected his new name. He didn't like it, but all that mattered was that it was different from his previous name, so he'd have to get used to it.

He would be taking a break in Europe, specifically Italy for much of the time. His new face and name reflected an Italian heritage. He didn't know how long he would be gone this time, but he expected it to be years. He had to make sure all attention had died down. Unfortunately, he'd have to hire a new group of project managers, operatives, and support staff, as he was sure many of his current employees would be arrested in the coming days. Large numbers of them were already in custody.

This was annoying of course, but not something he couldn't move past in time. Taking care of Kurt would show his colleagues, and anyone trying to supersede him, that he still had control, even from a distance.

He had wanted to travel for some time, but hadn't thought it would happen so soon. He hadn't been prepared for another surgery, but he tried to be flexible. He sat back, closing his eyes. He was grateful that from an aggravating experience came the pleasure of new opportunity.

CHAPTER 33

Christopher leaned into his high-back chair, listening to the sound of Berlin traffic on the street below his apartment. He closed his eyes and smiled to himself.

Perfect.

This city had noise, culture, history, and amusing exploits. He'd hated to leave Manhattan, but the moment he heard about Kurt's arrest, the confirmation of Mary's death, and John fleeing Los Angeles, he knew his days with the organization were done.

He had no ties to Germany, and told no one where he was going. He'd left in the middle of the night. He'd used an alias to buy the one-way plane ticket with a credit card under the same name. He'd left many of his things behind in his Manhattan apartment. It was easy to buy what he needed when he arrived in Berlin.

He didn't have to work any time soon with the large sum in his bank account, but it wouldn't hurt to start looking around. Until then, there were plenty of things in this city to keep him entertained. He doubted he'd ever top the delicious drama of California, but he could try. He had nothing but time.

***

Kassidy let the Women's March swirl around her, enveloping her with chants, cheers, and powerful words. It was late May, and the heat was already beating down at eleven in the morning. It was a beautiful day, and she didn't even mind that hundred-degree temperatures would soon be the norm.

She stopped participants to ask what the event meant to them and got some truly fascinating personal stories. She snapped their pictures with her phone in case head shots were needed for the article. The assigned photographer was somewhere on the outskirts of the mass of people. She could see him every now and then when she turned to look around.

She gazed up at the trees near the Capitol building, closing her eyes for a moment as she walked, feeling the sunshine on her face. It felt revitalizing. The winter had been harsh in many ways, and although she loved the rain, she found herself desperately needing the sun.

And then she saw him. He was leaning against a tree, watching the crowd go by, waiting for something. His arm was still in a sling, but the bandage was gone from his face, his eyes no longer black and blue. He was wearing jeans and a green t-shirt. He'd lost some weight, but had his same confident stance.

Brett. His name blew through her mind like a breeze. She had never expected to see him again.

She must have been staring for too long, because he felt her eyes, finding them with his own. He gave her a weak smile and moved away from the tree. She felt her legs carrying her toward him. The crowd was all around them, but the noise dimmed somehow.

Her heart pounded in her chest as she stopped inside the shade of the giant tree.

"Hi," he said, adjusting his sling with his good hand.

"Hi," she responded, reminding herself to breathe.

He was close enough for her to study his eyes now. The exhaustion there was as plain as day, and she had to stop herself before she reached for him. The rest of the cuts on his face had healed, but it looked like he'd have a scar on his right cheek.

"Brett..." She wanted to ask what he was doing there, but she never wanted him to leave, so maybe if she didn't ask, he would stay.

He looked to his right, as if studying the crowd. She wasn't sure if he had heard her whisper his name. When he looked back at her, he was trying to smile.

"You have a notebook." He motioned toward the object in her hand, and she looked down at it blankly. He rolled his eyes after he said it, and she wanted to tease him like old times, but noticed he was tapping his foot.

Nervous.

"Um, yes, I'm covering the march." She motioned toward the crowd, some of which was moving around them. She tried to talk louder to be sure he could hear her.

"Big shot staff writer now, huh?" He pointed down at the press badge she was wearing around her neck, a real smile growing on his lips.

"Yeah," she responded with a laugh. "I waited so long to ask for a job that they offered me one."

"That's great. When did you start?"

"Last month. They had a staff writer position that was never filled, but they weren't being given the funds for it. My editor fought for it, because he wanted me to have it. So, here I am. He didn't even have me interview because of all of the work I'd already done for them."

"Awesome, Kassie...Kassidy."

She hated to hear him correct her name. It sounded unnatural on his lips.

"For the record," he said suddenly, "I never thought your job was a joke."

The comment surprised her, and she wasn't sure how to respond.

He looked away again, his foot still tapping.

She cleared her throat, although she could barely hear herself do it. The photographer walked past them, giving her a thumbs up. She smiled and turned back to Brett.

"Have you been okay?" She motioned toward his arm.

"Yeah," he started, but then met her eyes. "No, not really. This hasn't been going well. I've had two surgeries now, because I developed an infection after the first one, and I'm…sort of…trying my best with physical therapy." He tried to laugh at himself, but it was strained. "I can't go back to work yet."

"I'm sorry. I'm sure that's frustrating. Have you been spending your free time driving yourself crazy?" she teased.

He grinned. "I have. It sucks. My family will hardly talk about it. I think they assume it will only make me feel worse. Can you imagine my sisters being silent during whole phone conversations? And I think Isla misses her alone time."

She laughed loudly at the smirk that settled on his face. "Sisterly silence? That must be like heaven for you."

He nodded, the smile still on his face. "Truly."

"How is Isla? I've missed her," she said, knowing it might make things awkward.

"She's fine. I'm sure she's missed you," he answered, eyes on his sling.

"So, did you know I was here?"

"I went to your apartment, but you weren't there. So, I uh, called your mom. She told me you were covering the march."

"Must've been pretty important, although I'm sure my mom was happy to give out my location." She laughed again, but his eyes became serious.

"It is important. I asked to be the one to tell you, but to be honest,

I'm kind of dreading it."

It didn't sound like a profession of love, but why should it be after all this time? She felt her face go white and had to tell herself to keep breathing.

"Tell me what?"

"Kurt's dead."

The ground felt like it was tilting beneath her, and she took a moment to find the sounds of the march again.

He reached for her, but she steadied herself.

"What? How?" She fumbled to get the words out of her mouth.

Why does it feel so weird hearing that? Shouldn't I feel relieved?

He looked away again. "He was attacked. It was…prolonged. The killer sent a pretty clear message."

"The organization?"

"We assume so. We're thinking the California chapter leader, who we still haven't been able to locate. Kurt brought the group a lot of attention, which resulted in a lot of arrests. That must have pissed him off. Kurt was being held without bail, but at a safe house because of the risk of the organization retaliating. They got to him anyway, last night. It hasn't hit the news yet."

She wasn't sure what to say next. Her brain was in a fog. An extra loud group of marchers going by startled her back to reality – in time to see the concern written across Brett's face.

She wasn't going to hide anything from him again. "I don't know why it feels like this. Like a shock. Almost like a sadness."

"That doesn't surprise me. He was a huge force in your life and probably filled part of your mind most of the time. Not because you wanted him there, but because he forced himself in. His absence leaves a hole. I'm sure your feelings will run the spectrum."

His words calmed her and she nodded.

"So, there won't be a trial. The attorneys should be calling you soon. I told them I would tell you today."

It was at this point that she allowed herself to breathe a sigh of relief. "I'm glad, but I was looking forward to him serving time. Having to think about what he did every day. I'm sure this will leave a lot of people disappointed. How is Alexis?"

"I'm not sure. I'm guessing they'll call her today. I don't see any problem with you giving her a call in a couple days."

She would do that. She hoped to maintain some kind of friendship with Alexis.

She realized with a jolt that she needed to get back to work. A couple of the marchers were celebrities, and they were scheduled to make speeches on the Capitol steps.

"I should go." She motioned toward the Capitol, looking down at her notebook, which she realized she'd bent in half as they were talking. "Thank you for being the one to tell me. I...I hope you stick with the physical therapy and can get back to work soon."

She wanted to hug him, to kiss him, but she didn't. The whole thing had been one huge mess, and she wasn't sure if reconciliation was meant to be.

"Yeah...thanks," he mumbled. "Congratulations on your job. I knew you could do it."

She nodded with a small smile. Then she turned and began walking away, mixing with the crowd once again.

"Kassie!" She spun around as he called her name – the name he should call her.

"You were right. I was an asshole, and I'm sorry. I should have believed you, trusted you. I should have been grateful you were trying to protect me. My pride was hurt. I'm sorry about our fight. You had every right to suggest I work fewer hours. In the future, I plan to do that. I shouldn't have attacked you. I..."

She took his good hand in hers, interrupting him. "I was at fault, too.

I should have told you about Kurt's calls from the beginning. I should have let you shoulder the burden with me. Maybe this all could have been avoided. I'm sorry."

"I don't want to do this anymore. I don't like my life without you in it. I need you, and I love you. I never stopped." He brushed her hair back from her face, tucking it behind her ear.

"I love you, too. I've missed you so much. Can we be us again?" Tears were running down her face now. She put her arms around him and stood at his side to avoid his bad arm.

"Yes." He wiped her tears away with his thumb and kissed her long and slow, like he used to. She had missed it so much. She leaned into him and he held her tightly.

She took his good hand and they walked together toward the Capitol as the flowing crowd moved all around them. Freedom from chaos. And in that moment, they both felt safe.

EPILOGUE

It was early July. He and Kassidy were on an Orange County beach near Elise and Terrance's Costa Mesa home. A perfect moment in time.

Not far from their large beach blanket, Elise was helping the now-toddling Isaiah make his way along the beach – his little water shoes taking step after step, a concentrated look on his face. Terrance snapped some pictures on his phone, then scooped his son up and ran toward the ocean. As a small wave came up, he lowered Isaiah so the water bubbled around the little boy's feet. Elise grinned and then turned to look out over the Pacific, soaking in the sun.

Brett's parents, Lily, and Brandon were on their way for a picnic lunch on the beach. Brett looked down at Kassidy, who was laying on her back next to him. A sun hat covered her face. He smiled to himself and adjusted his Dodgers cap on his head.

He closed his eyes and turned his face to the sky. Isaiah's birthday party had been the day before, and had been a huge success. Now they had five more days before they left for home.

Brett had been at peace since they'd been in Orange County, and Kassie had asked him if he'd rather live down here. He loved his family, but she was his family now, too, so Sacramento felt more like home. And he loved his department. He had no desire to leave it. They were temporarily living in her apartment, because she didn't want to leave downtown Sacramento, so most of his stuff was in storage until they found something bigger. But he didn't care, and Isla was overjoyed to be with Kassie again.

Lily had come around to Kassie, and the two were becoming friends. She'd been livid with Kassie after the break-up, but when Brett explained everything to her, she had to see logic and couldn't stay mad.

Brett was on light duty at work, but his doctor was very hopeful that the frustrated detective could return to regular duty in September, which would mark five full months of recovery. He could have returned sooner if not for the multitude of issues with his arm, but it had taught him to slow down a little. He fully intended to keep his promise to Kassie and cut back on his hours, although she told him he'd better take the occasional patrol shift so he didn't lose his mind.

Kassidy was thriving at her job. It was the journalism experience she loved, but with scheduled hours (most of the time) and health benefits. He knew she liked having other reporters to lean on and commiserate with. He could almost see the burden of freelancing being lifted from her shoulders.

Arrests continued for the organization's members, and even if they never found the California leader, at least they were making a huge dent in the number of his employees, which would take him time to come back from.

Kassie stirred next to him, moving her hat and flashing him a smile – that smile that knocked him flat. She sat up, and he took her left hand, playing with the glittering ring that now sat there. He was never letting her go again.

"I love you, Kassie."

"Love you more," she responded and pulled him in for a kiss.

The End

ACKNOWLEDGEMENTS

First of all, thank you! If you're reading this book, you've helped make my dream a reality. I've always wanted to publish a novel, and this story has been years in the making. I'm so happy it's finally out in the world! I hope it will be the first of many, and your support as a reader means everything!

Thank you to my husband Greg and our sons for putting up with my self-imposed deadlines, and for supporting me as I venture into this new chapter. I love you! To the local experts who helped me with the research for this book, thank you for making it a more authentic story! I also want to give a huge shout-out to everyone who read the early versions of my manuscript! Your feedback helped shape it into a stronger version of itself.

Last, but definitely not least, thank you to my editor, Caroline Tolley, and my designer, Lindsay Heider Diamond, for making this book what it is today! Your ideas, encouragement, and hard work mean more than you will ever know!

ABOUT THE AUTHOR

Bridget Sheppard has been deeply in love with writing stories for as long as she can remember. Born and raised in Northern California, she enjoys reading, music, TV shows from the 1970s and 80s, and traveling to new places – and wants to write about all of it! After decades of putting words on paper for work and fun, she knew it was time to pursue her dream of becoming a published novelist. She hopes to share her stories for many years to come. Bridget lives in the Sacramento area with her husband, sons, and two dogs.

Made in the USA
Las Vegas, NV
03 December 2020

11974306R00156